Hot Water

a Sylvie Wolff novel

JJ Shelley

D1114145

ISBN: 978-1-949292-02-2

For Timothy,
who convinced me I could do this

and for

Erica and Talia,
from whom I shamelessly stole all the best lines.

Boston

www.BaneberryPress.com

Cover design by Erica Sawyer www.EricaSawyer.com

"A woman is like a tea bag –
you can't tell how strong she is
until you put her in hot water."

Eleanor Roosevelt

ACKNOWLEDGMENTS

Huge thanks to my writing group who kept me on track and never lost patience. To David Ray and Rachel Parkin, who patiently taught me about software development. To my editor, Ellen Clair Lamb. To everyone at Seascape for their advice and support. To Roberta MacPhee for her early support and insight. To Sugarbear and Stumpy for the use of their names. And to my family for listening to me read this story aloud to them over a snowy Christmas holiday.

One

The day Sylvie Wolff's life fell apart she woke, as usual, to the soothing sound of birds chattering outside her bedroom window. She leaned over and kissed her husband, letting him rise to consciousness slowly in their buttery Egyptian cotton sheets.

Mark was still pretty cute for a software nerd pushing forty. Not that he was every woman's idea of a hot ticket. His skin was too pale, and his shoulders were hunched from sitting in front of a computer all day. But Sylvie knew smart when she saw it. He was a great provider—and more fun to be with than most people would think.

In anticipation of another of his endless trips to Palo Alto, Mark's suitcase lay open on the cedar chest at the foot of the king-sized bed. *Typical of Mark to leave for a business trip, not only on a Friday, but the first day of the girls' spring vacation.* Mark was a workaholic. So, apparently, were his colleagues. Sylvie'd suggested they expand the trip to include a family ski jaunt to Mammoth but Mark had nixed the idea, saying what the girls really needed was some unstructured downtime for a change. Of course, since Mark would be in California all week, Sylvie would be supervising that unstructured downtime on her own.

Mark was always a bear when he had to travel. It was going to be a tough morning.

Sylvie took her time. She showered, shaved her legs and dressed in her new Stella McCartney tennis dress, checking the backs of her thighs in the mirror with a critical eye. It wasn't like she hadn't noticed the way Delia Grafton eyed the other ladies for signs of muffin top and back fat when they changed together in the locker room at the club. So far, Sylvie had

1

maintained her college weight despite two pregnancies, but it hadn't been easy.

On her way downstairs, she paused in the doorway of her older daughter's bedroom to observe Diana, her fourteen-year-old, bending over, head between her legs, drying the butt of her jeans with a hair dryer.

Claire, her eleven-year-old, padded sleepily past her on the way to the bathroom she shared with her sister. "Molding," Claire explained.

Sylvie glanced at her daughter, one eyebrow raised.

"Her jeans to her ass." Claire grinned and rolled her eyes, making Sylvie grateful that at least her baby hadn't yet morphed into the dreaded teenager, desperate for acceptance by her peers.

Seizing the opportunity, Sylvie opened the door to Claire's room and did a quick sweep, gathering the layers of dirty clothes and tossing them into the wicker laundry basket so the cleaners could find the floor later in the day. Claire's walls were papered with dog posters, her shelves alive with ceramic tchotchkes of puppies and dogs of every size and species. More than anything in the world, Claire wanted a dog. Despite Mark's allergy excuses, she remained optimistic that one day she would prevail. Claire also still believed in birthday wishes and shooting stars, and she never missed an opportunity to further her cause. Sylvie would have loved to grant Claire's wish for a real live dog, but they all knew that Mark would never accept the disorder a pet would introduce into the perfect Wolff household.

Downstairs in the great room, Sylvie ground fresh coffee beans and inhaled their rich aroma—her first caffeine hit of the day. As the Keurig gurgled and burped, filling the house with its morning promise of caffeine, Sylvie unloaded the dishwasher and set the kitchen table with juice, milk and cereal, though she doubted anyone would bother eating.

She opened a new can of coconut milk, poured it into the metal bowl she'd left in the freezer overnight, frothed it with a beater so it would linger over the coffee in her oversized mug, and took that first luxurious sip of sheer perfection as she admired the effect of the new low-backed dining room chairs that allowed a sweeping, uninterrupted view of her garden.

The house was almost done. Each *objet d'art* on the shelves surrounding the stone fireplace had been chosen carefully for form and texture, each object relating to the next, yet adding interest to the whole—a piece of rough coral, an Inuit mask, a ceramic vase. Sylvie sighed. For these few precious moments, it was all hers to enjoy in solitary bliss.

Mug in hand, she grabbed a handful of almonds and stepped out the French doors into her own private sanctuary. April in New England was always a crap shoot, but full of promise for the coming months. She surveyed the beds of herbs, lavender and perennials for signs of new life, admiring the blend of tranquility and utility. The morning doves that roosted on the roof trilled a greeting as she stepped around the formal beds to her secret spot behind the bursting forsythia, where she allowed the dandelions and other creature-friendly flora to run amok. She'd never been allowed to have pets—not as a child living with her parents, or with Mark. But here in her garden, Sylvie had doves and robins and bunnies that chose her sanctuary as their home, without locked doors or cages.

She sank into a shining green Adirondack chair that commanded a perfect view of her botanical masterpiece. Stumpy, the three-legged squirrel named by Diana, poked her head out from the underbrush and took a tentative step closer to collect the almond Sylvie tossed, then disappeared under the bush, only to reappear a minute later.

When her pocket was empty, Sylvie finished her last sip of coffee and reluctantly headed back inside, where Mark's footsteps on the stairs signaled the start of the usual morning stresscapade.

Two

Mark Wolff dropped his suitcase near the door and set his briefcase down on the kitchen counter. His face was drawn, and he looked tired. Sylvie handed him a fresh cup of coffee just the way he liked it—warm hemp milk, no sugar—in his favorite mug, the one with a handle big enough to fit his fingers.

He took a long sip but didn't look at her. Instead, he removed a sheaf of papers from his briefcase, laid them on the kitchen table, and retrieved a pen. "I need you to sign these before I leave," he said.

Sylvie had long ago surrendered the household finances to Mark for the sake of peace in their marriage. She did as she was told, signing the papers he handed her without question as he pointed to the signature line on each page.

When he handed her the final document, she glanced up at his face. Something about the stress around his eyes made her pick up the paper. It was a Purchase and Sale Agreement for her old student apartment on Green Street in Cambridge.

"Our tenant moved out last week and the guy on the first floor wants to buy," Mark explained impatiently. "He's bought up all the other units and he wants to renovate the building. Ramsdale's willing to pay top dollar but he wants the unit delivered empty, so this is the perfect opportunity. You know how impossible it is to evict a tenant in the People's Republic of Cambridge. And frankly, we need the money." Mark held out the pen. "Sign. I don't have time to discuss it. I have a plane to catch and I need your signature so I can get this done before I leave."

Sylvie's parents had bought the one-bedroom, fourth floor walk-up in

4

Central Square when her father was a graduate student at the nearby Massachusetts Institute of Technology. When they moved to the Queen Anne in North Cambridge, where Sylvie had grown up, they'd rented Green Street out to other students. When Sylvie was accepted at Boston University, among other schools, they'd given it to her as a bribe to stay in the area.

She and Mark had lived there together until he finished his PhD from MIT and was earning enough to marry her, buy "The Manse" in Weston, and start a family. Periodically, over the years, Mark had suggested they sell Green Street. But she'd always resisted, preferring to rent it out instead, like her parents. The income, deposited directly into her old bank account at Cambridge Trust, was the only income she had of her very own. She hated the idea of giving it up. She kept the keys on their old macramé keychain among the other treasures in her jewelry box.

So whenever Mark broached the subject of selling Green Street, she'd go to great lengths to avoid the discussion. After a while, Sylvie got the impression that whenever Mark wanted certain sexual favors, he'd bring up the idea of selling Green Street, knowing she'd go along with pretty much anything to avoid that particular discussion.

But today Mark wasn't trying to score. He was dead serious.

Just then the girls came crashing through, backpacks flying, grabbing jackets, phones and earphones. Claire filled a bowl with cereal and milk to eat in the car and started out the door. When she saw the suitcase, she turned back and threw her arms around her father, hugging him enthusiastically. "How long will you be gone this time?" she asked.

Mark managed a mid-arm squeeze, without letting go of either the mug or the pen. "A week."

"But that's our whole vacation. We won't even see you."

"We can FaceTime if you need me," Mark said and placed his coffee cup on the table.

Diana paused mid-flight to kiss her father's cheek. "Have a good trip, Dad. Coming?" she yelled over her shoulder to her mother, as the door slammed behind them.

Mark placed the pen in Sylvie's hand.

"Is this about starting your own company?" Sylvie asked. "Because honestly, Mark, I don't think this is the time to take that kind of financial risk."

"This is about Diana's high school tuition being almost twice middle school and your constant home renovations. So unless you're willing to send the girls to public school, we need the cash."

Sylvie glanced at the new dining room chairs and felt a pang of guilt as Mark's Lyft ride pulled up in front of the house. His phone beeped an alert.

Mark frowned. "*Now*, Sylvie. I've got to go."

She leaned over the table, the pen poised above the highlighted x, awaiting her signature. She wanted to make Mark happy, but something inside her didn't want to lose the last vestige of her younger self—the Sylvie she was before she became a wife and mother.

Mark gave her shoulder a gentle squeeze.

She sighed. "Isn't there anything else we can do?"

He tapped the document with his finger. "This is for our family. So the girls can have the things you want them to have. Isn't that more important than a rundown apartment we've barely set foot in for years?" He lifted her chin, looked directly into her eyes and caressed her cheek with his thumb. When he leaned over to kiss her lips, he lingered unexpectedly and she kissed him back.

"Do you think I'd ask you to do this if it wasn't necessary?' he asked. "Trust me," he said.

And she did. She signed the paper and handed it to him.

He placed it inside his briefcase, but before he could shut it, the door flew open and Claire rushed in. She tripped over the new Oriental prayer rug and slammed into Mark, knocking the briefcase and its contents to the floor. The half-eaten bowl of cereal in her hand fell, splattering soggy cornflakes onto Mark's Italian leather loafers.

"Sorry, Dad," Claire said. She gathered the scattered papers and handed them to Sylvie, who straightened them before sliding them carefully back into the briefcase.

Without a word, Mark wiped the cornflakes from his shoes, slammed the briefcase shut, latched it, then grabbed his suitcase and sprinted out the door.

"Don't worry about it," Sylvie said, giving Claire's drooping shoulder a pat. "You know how Dad is when he has to catch a plane."

Three

Sylvie eased her SUV onto the campus of the Meadowlark School and took her place behind a long line of other BMWs, Mercedes and the occasional Volvo and Prius. Diana scrambled out without a word and headed toward the upper school building while Claire sat in the back seat, waiting until the last possible second to disembark.

As they inched forward, an officious middle-aged woman in running shoes and a three-piece suit the color of overripe eggplant approached the car and tapped on the window.

Sylvie obligingly powered it down and the woman thrust a clipboard at her. "We'd like your signature, please. It's a petition opposing the new bike path from Boston. We feel it will bring the wrong sort of people through the village."

Sylvie noted the perfectly matched pearls adorning the neck of the clipboard lady, signed the petition and handed it back. The woman moved on to the next car.

"What's wrong with a bike path?" Claire asked.

"We don't want everyone with a bicycle coming through our town," Sylvie responded. "It would get crowded and it wouldn't be safe."

"Really? You think a bunch of people on bikes are going to pedal out of town with our flat screen TVs strapped to their backs?"

Sylvie came to a stop outside the middle school building.

Claire didn't budge.

"Out," Sylvie said. "It's the last day before spring break. You'll survive."

Claire coughed. "I think I have a sore throat coming on. Maybe strep. Probably contagious."

"Out. I have a game."

"We could have a girls' day out together. Get our nails done."

"Now."

"I hate this place. The girls are stupid."

"It's going to get better. Give it a chance."

"You want me to turn into Diana, obsessed with how my ass looks in my jeans?"

The soccer mom in the Mercedes behind them honked her horn. Finally, with the speed of a tortoise on Valium, Claire eased open the door and slid out.

Sylvie pulled forward and watched in her rearview mirror. Claire hung back as long as she could before reluctantly joining the throng of students heading for the entrance.

***

Sylvie pulled into the curved driveway of the Oak Crest Swim and Tennis Club and scored a parking spot just to the right of the entrance. She grabbed her Dolce & Gabbana gym bag from the back seat, gave her tennis skirt a tug, slammed the door and touched her finger to the handle to lock it.

It took her entire body weight to open the massive oak door and enter the building. She always thought of it as the first test of worthiness for membership—are you fit enough to enter? She punched in her code at the front desk and stepped into the turnstile. When she tried to step through to the inner sanctum, the metal bar smacked against her thigh and refused to budge.

The perky young thing at the front desk furrowed her brow and glanced over.

Sylvie smiled and tried to suppress her annoyance. The man waiting behind her shifted from foot to foot like a little boy who needed to pee.

"Shall I punch it in again?" Sylvie asked.

"Actually, would you mind stepping into the office? I'll call the manager," Perky Girl said.

Sylvie's patience began to ebb. "If there's an administrative error, I'll have to take care of it later. I'm going to be late for my game."

The Keeper of the Turnstile took a deep breath. "I'm sorry, Mrs. Wolff. I can't let you enter the club until you've sorted out your account with the manager. Your membership has been flagged."

"Flagged?"

"Sylvie? Is there a problem?" Fran Forsythe, Sylvie's doubles partner, had appeared, her trademark designer scarf artfully arranged to keep her blonde bob in place.

"Some sort of administrative mix-up." Sylvie smiled at Fran as Delia Grafton and Monica Jen-Wilcox entered the building. The four women, all within spitting distance of their fortieth birthdays, had been playing together regularly for years, long before Delia had begun sporting the rigid upper lip that signaled regular Botox treatments.

Sylvie stepped aside while the impatient man received his welcoming buzz without incident.

Fran paused before entering her code and addressed the girl at the desk. "Will this take long?"

Without glancing at Sylvie, the girl smiled ingratiatingly at Fran. "I'm sure we'll be able to find you a fourth this morning."

She opened the gate to the administrative offices and waited for Sylvie to step through.

***

"Are you absolutely sure? Three months?"

"Yes, Mrs. Wolff." Tom Hagen, the club's general manager, was firm. He leaned back in his massive leather chair and laced his fingers decisively on the glass desktop.

"Are you sure Mark received the notifications? There must be a glitch in the billing program. Mark is very efficient in these matters."

"I've had several phone conversations with Mr. Wolff in the past couple of months."

"And he explained that it was a mistake, right?"

"He said you were having temporary financial difficulties, but promised the payment would be in the mail by the end of the week. He's said this for the last three months."

Sylvie was flummoxed. "He never mentioned any of this to me."

"I'm sure he meant to handle it. Why don't you bring in a certified check for the full amount, and we can restore your membership immediately. No problem."

Sylvie glared at the young man, just out of business school, probably Bentley. She was being mansplained by a child, a *pisher*, as Grandma Esther would say. "Are you saying I can't even play this morning? We've been members of this club for ten years."

"I'm so sorry, Mrs. Wolff. But we do have strict rules about this sort of thing. I'm afraid you can't enter the club until your dues are paid in full."

Her head held high, Sylvie stepped through the gate into the lobby.

Fran intercepted her before she could slip, unnoticed, out the front door. "All set? Can we play?"

Sylvie wished she'd thought to ask if there was a secret escape route for indigent members. She forced an amused smile. "Nope. The tennis Nazi won't let me play until my mad-genius, memory-challenged husband sends them a check."

"Oh, dear." Fran looked genuinely concerned. "Is everything all right?"

"Absolutely. Mark gets distracted when he's working on a big project. I'll sort it out as soon as I can reach him. Have a great game."

Four

As Sylvie backed out of her primo parking spot, it occurred to her that Mark must have stopped paying the club dues as a way of getting back at her for redecorating the dining room.

"All right, Mark, point taken," she muttered as she glanced down at the gas tank icon, which had started to flash ominously. *Great.* Just what she needed.

She pulled into the nearest gas station and slid her credit card into the slot. She typically used the full service station near the house to avoid the risk of gas dripping on her clothes, but that flashing icon meant she was running on fumes. She tried to pull the nozzle out of its cradle, but it refused to budge.

She waved to get the attention of the attendant in the booth, but he ignored her so she walked over, uncomfortably aware that she was wearing a tennis dress that barely covered the tops of her thighs. "I can't get the stupid nozzle to work and it's been a really bad day, so can you come over and help me?" she asked.

The young man's pale complexion contrasted with an angry case of acne. He looked up at her. "The nozzle's fine. Your card's been confiscated."

"Nonsense. Give me my card back and I'll go somewhere else." But even as she said it, Sylvie had a bad feeling. *Damn you, Mark. I get it.*

"Sorry, ma'am."

"Try this one," Sylvie said digging in her purse for her back-up card, the one she was only supposed to use if the first was compromised. Mark was very strict about these things. He said the fewer open credit cards the better, in these days of hackers and security breeches. And since Mark was the one paying the bills and keeping track of things, who was she to argue?

She dropped the card into the slot.

The pimply young man tried the second card, then frowned and placed the offending plastic in the slot. He pushed it back to her.

Sylvie retrieved it and slid her bank debit card, her last resort, over to him. Mark would be furious. She was breaking one of his cardinal rules. *Never pay for things with a debit card. Once cash has left the account, the customer has no recourse if the purchased item is defective.* Well, what choice did she have? And how likely was she to return a tank of gas, anyway?

Mark would just have to suck it up, since this ridiculous clusterfuck was his doing.

An older man in overalls approached and stood behind the youngster as he obligingly tried the third card, shook his head, returned the card and shrugged.

Shaken, Sylvie reached for her wallet, which yesterday had contained at least six twenties. "Look, I need to get home. It's only a couple of miles from here. I'll pay cash." The wallet was empty. Even the change purse was dry.

Desperate to get home and sort out the whole fiasco, Sylvie returned to her car and turned the key. Nothing. Just as she'd feared, the flashing light had meant business. She leaned her forehead on the steering wheel and breathed deeply. Apparently it was going to be one of those days.

Someone tapped on the window and she looked up.

A small man with weathered olive skin and a mustache smiled down at her. "Vinny told me to offer you a ride home." His oil-stained finger pointed toward the clerk's booth. "So you could get some cash. I'm Tony." He indicated a filthy tow truck.

Sylvie glanced over at the older man in overalls, who nodded at her reassuringly, then back at Tony. His kind eyes told her she'd be safe with him, though she feared her Stella McCartney whites might not survive the trip.

Sylvie steered while the older man helped Tony push her car to the side. Then she climbed gingerly into the passenger seat of the tow truck, trying to avoid letting either her skin or her tennis dress come in contact with the sticky vinyl seat any more than absolutely necessary.

When Tony pulled into her driveway, she reached into her purse for a tip, then stopped and blushed with humiliation. "I'm so sorry."

"That's okay. I can wait if you want to grab some cash and go back for your car."

Sylvie considered. She might be able to find enough cash for a tank of gas stowed in purses and jacket pockets, but that would take time and right now she desperately wanted to figure out what the hell was going on. "I appreciate it, but I'll need a while. I'll take a Lyft back to the station."

"Okay, lady." Tony looked her in the eye and said, "You don't need to feel ashamed. Hard times happen to lots of folks."

Sylvie looked up at her beautiful house, with its acre of carefully landscaped gardens, and wondered what this gas station attendant could possibly be thinking. *Hard times? For me?* "It's not what you think. It's a mix-up. I'll be back for the car in an hour," she said.

Five

The first place Sylvie checked as soon as she entered the house was the dining room table. That was where she'd left the envelope full of cash for the cleaners. But the envelope was gone, and the house was clean. *Damn.*

Next she checked Mark's private study, dominated by an impressive mahogany desk that had once belonged to his grandfather, the investment banker. Sylvie seldom came in here. It was Mark's exclusive territory, and he hated any of his things to be moved. The cleaners were allowed to wipe off the immaculate surfaces, but nothing more.

The flashing light on the landline in Mark's office announced that he had new messages. Normally, she would never go near his private line for fear she'd screw up something important. Mark would never try to reach her on this line, even if he were calling from the airport to tell her that someone had stolen his identity and he'd had to cancel their credit cards, which he'd forgotten to mention in his pre-boarding anxiety. He would have called her on her cell.

But what if someone from Mark's office was trying to reach her with news about Mark? She punched the button to hear the messages.

"Hello, this is John MacElvain, at Meadowlark. This is the fifth message I've left. I hope everything's okay. I'm afraid we've waited as long as we can for the tuition. The headmaster has informed me that unless we receive a check from you before the end of the day, the girls will not be allowed back after spring break. I wish you'd called back earlier. We might have been able to allocate some scholarship money."

Sylvie sank, disbelieving, into Mark's ergonomic chair. *The girls' tuition money?* This was no longer a sulky Mark teaching her a lesson. Something serious had happened. She reached for the phone and dialed Mark's cell. It rang, then went to voice mail. Mark's cool voice invited her to leave a message.

She checked her watch. The plane should have taken off, which meant the phone should have been switched off. Shouldn't it have gone directly to voice mail without ringing? Maybe the flight had been delayed and she could still reach him.

"Mark, it's Sylvie. I need you to call me back the second you get this message. There's some kind of financial mess happening here, and I need you to deal with it." Just to make sure, she texted the same message, in case his ringer was off.

There. Done. Mark would handle it from here. Now she could concentrate on finding the gas money she needed to bail out her car.

In the master suite walk-in closet she caught a glimpse of the back of her skirt, which sported a brown stain from the tow truck. *Damn.* She'd be lucky to get it out. Best to get it right into the sink to soak, just as soon as she'd systematically checked every pocket in every item of clothing and each crevice in every handbag for cash. She scored seventy-five dollars in bills and another six dollars in change, and threw it all into the python leather Brunello Cucinelli bag slung over her shoulder.

Next, Sylvie attacked Mark's closet. She'd only uncovered a couple of dollar bills when she came across an expensive cashmere jacket she'd never seen before.

A thorough search of the inside pockets revealed an elongated flat key with a little round tag attached. The tag had a number etched on it, suggesting it was a safety deposit key, although there was no bank name and Sylvie didn't remember Mark ever mentioning a safety deposit box. He usually kept their important papers locked in the bottom drawer of his desk.

She slipped the key into her bag and started to call for a Lyft when she remembered that none of her credit cards was functioning. In the garage she unearthed Claire's old Hello Kitty bicycle from a heap of rejected toys. The tires were low and it was filthy and hard to pedal, but Sylvie mounted it gamely. Halfway to the gas station, after the fourth appreciative whistle from passing trucks, Sylvie realized she'd forgotten to change out of her tennis dress.

Back at Vinny's Gas Station, Sylvie handed over twenty dollars for a third of a tank of gas. At fourteen miles per gallon, eight gallons of gas should give her one hundred and twelve miles, more or less. She hoped it was enough to last until she could reach Mark and sort out this mess. For the first time, Sylvie wished she'd asked Mark for something a bit more gas-efficient, maybe even a Prius, instead of a Beemer just because everyone else at the club drove one.

When she hoisted the bicycle into the back of the SUV, her skirt caught in the chain. Now, in addition to the brown stain on her rear, her white tennis dress sported a splatter of black grease, which bled onto her thigh when she tried to wipe it off. She must look like a tennis playing grease monkey.

The day was definitely going from bad to worse.

She pulled her phone from her bag. No missed calls, and, yes, the ringer was on.

Why hadn't Mark called her back?

She fought back a wave of panic, climbed behind the wheel of the Beemer and floored it for the ten-minute drive to the town center, where she swerved to the curb in front of the Bank of Weston. Abandoning her car with its tail protruding into oncoming traffic, she marched herself inside to the office of Eleanor Babcock, vice president of customer relations.

"I need a printout of transactions from my checking account," she said. "Mark and Sylvia Wolff."

***

Sylvie couldn't take her eyes off the bleak balance printed at the bottom of the page. She gripped the arms of the faux leather chair so hard that the brass studs dug into her hand, but she barely noticed. "I don't understand," was all she could manage.

Eleanor Babcock pointed to the itemized debits on the sheet that had caused the final balance to drain to virtually nothing. "It seems the account was used to pay down a Visa card from Bank of America."

Sylvie scrutinized the listings. "We don't have a credit card from Bank of America. We have a Citi card and one from Chase."

Ms. Babcock folded her hands on the burgundy blotter covering her desk. "Then you might want to check your husband's credit report to make sure it's a legitimate card and not identity theft. All you need is his date of birth and social security number."

Identity theft. Sylvie nearly fainted with relief. *Of course.* That would explain everything. Someone had drained their bank account to pay off a fake credit card. It would be a pain to sort out, but Mark was good at this kind of thing. Or rather Gertrude was good at it—his grandmotherly secretary at Templeton & Brewer, Ltd where Mark had worked for the past ten years.

Ms. Babcock frowned at her computer, then typed some more. She looked up at Sylvie as if considering what to do, clicked some buttons and excused herself.

When she returned, she placed a document in front of Sylvie. "I'm afraid there's more."

Sylvie blinked. The letters swam in front of her, refusing to come together to form words. She blinked again and one word finally came into focus. "Foreclosure?"

"It appears your husband took out a second mortgage on your house six months ago. There have been no payments made on either that or your home equity line of credit."

"What home equity line of credit?"

Ms. Babcock pointed to a signature on the last page. "Isn't that your signature?"

Sylvie's hand flew to her forehead, afraid that if she took her hand away her brains would fly all over the room. Was that her signature? Right there on the page next to Mark's?

It might be. She couldn't be sure. Would she have signed a document without even looking at it? Maybe. If she had been in a rush, and Mark had shoved it at her and told her it was something routine and to "trust him."

That was when the raw food energy bar Sylvie had scarfed down on her way to the tennis club made a surprise reappearance all over Ms. Babcock's burgundy blotter.

To be fair, Ms. Babcock was very nice about the whole thing. When she returned from the ladies' room with paper towels and found Sylvie with her head buried in her arms on the desk, she truly seemed like she wanted to help. "Can I bring you a glass of water?" she asked.

Sylvie nodded, grateful for this small act of kindness. She hadn't noticed how dry her mouth was, even her tongue, and imagined her entire body shriveling.

When Ms. Babcock returned with a tiny plastic cup of water, Sylvie slugged it back, longing for more. She reached inside her Cucinelli, retrieved the safety deposit key, and placed it on the desk. "Is this from your bank?" she asked.

"I'll be back in a minute."

When Ms. Babcock returned, she said, "It was rented a year ago in both your husband's and your names, though there is no signature card for you on file. Which means all you need to do is fill out some forms and show me some ID. Then, you can go downstairs and access the box."

Ten minutes later, Sylvie was sitting in a private booth in the basement of the bank with a long metal box in her hands.

She took a deep breath and opened the box, hoping for a stack of thousand dollar bills. Instead, she found only a few pieces of Mark's grandmother's jewelry, the original mortgage document for the house, a set of gold cufflinks from Mark's grandfather, and a thick legal document folded in thirds, which she glanced at briefly but couldn't make head or tail of. Nor did she recognize the name of the business on the document, *TechnoData*, or the address in Arlington.

Puzzled, she dumped the entire contents into her handbag and closed the empty box. The attendant returned it to its place in the wall and handed her back the key.

She left the bank, thinking that any moment she'd wake up next to Mark in bed and shake off this nightmare.

Six

Sylvie sat in her car and insisted to herself that everything would soon be back to normal. Gertrude, who referred to herself as Mark's executive assistant, would know where he was and how to track him down. She always did.

But how should Sylvie word the question? *Sorry to bother you, but my husband has disappeared and left us destitute. Can you make him come home and deal with this mess, please?*

Something had happened to Mark. He must have dug himself deeper and deeper into a financial black hole. The poor guy was probably too devastated to tell her he'd screwed up.

Sylvie would have to find him and convince him that no matter how bad things had gotten, they would figure it out together. In the end, they would be fine. Stronger than ever. Sylvie was not one to desert a sinking ship. With her unwavering support and a little financial planning, her husband-the-genius would rise from the ashes and be back on top in no time.

So why did her heart refuse to slow down? Why was her breathing becoming shallower no matter how many times she repeated this mantra to herself?

Why hadn't Mark answered her texts? What if his body was lying unconscious or, God forbid, dead, in some cheesy hotel room, an empty bottle of pills open beside him? And all because Sylvie had to have barkcloth on her dining room walls.

She called Gertrude.

A recording came on: "Sorry, that number is no longer activated. Please choose zero for assistance."

Sylvie clicked off and headed to the Pike for the half-hour drive to Boston's waterfront.

***

With only two hours before she needed to pick up her daughters from school, Sylvie entered the shipping warehouse-turned-office building where Templeton & Brewer occupied the top floor, overlooking the harbor.

Thankfully Mitchell, the security guard, recognized her, though it had been at least a year since she'd last visited. "Mrs. Wolff, how nice to see you," he said.

"It's nice to see you, too, Mitchell. How's the family?" Was it her, or was Mitchell looking at her strangely?

"We're all well, thanks. And how's Mr. Wolff?"

"He's fine. Headed off to the airport early. You know how stressful it is to travel these days."

"Yes, ma'am. What can I do for you?"

"I wanted to have a word with Gertrude, Mr. Wolff's secretary."

Mitchell stared at her as if she were an alien from Mars. "I'm afraid Gertrude doesn't work here anymore. She left with Mark several months ago."

Mark had been fired from Templeton & Brewer? How could she not have known? And Gertrude had left after putting in nearly twenty years, and so close to retirement? Gertrude had always been the one Sylvie could count on to remind Mark about school concerts and dance recitals he would otherwise have forgotten. What the hell had happened? Had Mark's entire department been eliminated? Poor Mark. Why hadn't he told her?

Sylvie smiled weakly, hoping to cover her shock.

Mitchell turned toward his desk phone, a concerned look on his face. "You know Florence Whittaker. She's office manager now. Let me see if she can help you."

"Wasn't she Mr. Templeton's assistant?"

"You go on up. I'll let her know you're coming." He buzzed her into the inner sanctum.

Templeton & Brewer's reception area was a generous space lined with comfortable couches. It opened onto a communal workspace containing enormous printers and copiers along with a kitchen area and workstations for the support staff. Surrounding the communal area were doors that led to private offices, the most prestigious of which were on the left, with windows overlooking the harbor. Richard Templeton, co-founder of Templeton & Brewer, had an airy office in the left corner. Sylvie had been introduced to him when she'd first come here as the respected spouse of a T & B star player.

While she waited at the reception desk, Sylvie waved hello to several familiar faces as they rushed past in their usual workday scramble. Most were friendly, but clearly surprised to see her. Or maybe it was the tennis outfit. If only she'd remembered to change. To be fair, she'd had quite a lot on her mind.

The lovely Lisa Chang, Mark's brilliant boss, head of research and development, rushed down the hall toward her. Sylvie tried to catch Lisa's eye but Lisa charged past her toward the ladies' room, as if she were having some sort of bathroom emergency.

She still hadn't emerged when Florence Whittaker arrived to collect Sylvie.

Florence, a statuesque woman in her early fifties, hadn't changed much since the last time Sylvie had seen her, though her clothes were considerably more expensive, probably tailored, and her hair had better highlights. Sylvie remembered rumors of a divorce. And was there something about an office affair between Florence and Mr. Templeton? For a moment, Sylvie regretted that she hadn't paid more attention to office politics, though Mark was never one to gossip—not because of a high standard of ethics, but because he wasn't really interested.

Florence shook Sylvie's hand formally, then escorted her through the common area, past the copy machines and printers, to a small but tidy office in the back corner. Floor to ceiling windows overlooking the yachts bobbing in Boston harbor meant Florence's star had definitely risen. Sylvie sank gratefully into a chair, feeling oddly seasick.

"I'm so glad you've come," Florence began. "We've all been so concerned about Mark. No one was here when he cleared out his office that night and left."

Sylvie felt more confused than ever. "You mean he wasn't fired?"

"Fired? Why would you think that?"

Sylvie blinked. "I had no idea until a few minutes ago that Mark didn't work here anymore. I assumed he didn't tell me that because he was ashamed he'd been laid off."

"Hardly. Mark leaving so suddenly left us in quite a mess."

"Then why *did* he leave?"

Florence regarded Sylvie carefully. "I assumed *you* would know."

Sylvie blinked and shook her head slowly. "I'm sorry. I have no idea."

"Mrs. Wolff, Mark left six months ago. Why are you here now?"

Sylvie blinked again, because if she stopped blinking the tears would start and she knew that once they started, they would never stop. "I don't know where Mark is. He left on a business trip this morning and I have an emergency. I need to find him."

"An emergency? Are the children all right?"

Sylvie managed a weak smile. "The girls are fine. Thank you."

"Well, that's the important thing."

Sylvie nodded. "You're right. That is the important thing." She paused. "Do you know where Mark went when he left here?"

"The rumor mill has it that he started his own company."

His own company? "And his secretary went with him?"

Florence spoke in measured tones. "I'm afraid I can't discuss the whereabouts of either present or former employees with you." Something about Florence's tone gave Sylvie the feeling she knew more than she was saying.

"But she's no longer here?"

"No, she's no longer here."

"Is there anyone here who might know where to find my husband?" Sylvie's eyes brimmed with tears that threatened to spill down her cheeks.

Florence hit the intercom button on her desk. "Jane, could you ask Lisa Chang to step in here, please."

Jane's voice crackled over the intercom, "Sorry, Ms. Whittaker. Lisa left. Said she was having a stomach problem."

"I'll just bet she is," Florence murmured under her breath. She turned to Sylvie. "I'm so sorry, Mrs. Wolff, I really am. But I don't know what I can do to help."

Sylvie stood. She started to leave, then turned back. "Do you know if Mark kept his health insurance when he left?"

Florence tapped some keys on her computer. "He signed onto COBRA. You and the girls are covered for another two months. That is, if he's paid up."

Great. That was just great. Mark had neglected to pay any bills for months. Why would he bother to make sure she and the girls had health insurance?

"Thank you for your time," Sylvie managed.

Florence stood. "I'll check into the insurance."

Sylvie resisted the urge to throw her arms around Florence's neck and weep with gratitude. Instead she kept her head high, tugged the back of her tennis skirt down as far as she could, and exited the offices of Templeton & Brewer, praying that whatever was left of Mark's health insurance would at least cover a large bottle of Xanax. It was only after she reached her car that she remembered the brown stain on the back of her skirt and cringed.

Seven

Back at the Meadowlark School, Claire and Diana climbed into the backseat of the Beemer, each weighted down with an overflowing shopping bag.

"Dean Harris asked us to empty our lockers," Claire announced. "How come? No one else cleaned out their lockers. It's only spring break."

"Just drive," Diana hissed as she sank down as far as she could into the back seat. "Dad didn't pay the tuition bill, moron. We got kicked out of school."

"Really?" Claire sounded jubilant. "Does that mean I never have to go back there again as long as I live?"

"Where did you hear that, Diana?" Sylvie asked, horrified.

"I overheard the principal tell my teacher. They thought I'd left, but I hid outside the door and listened. Why didn't Dad pay the bill?"

"I'm sure it's a snafu," Sylvie said. "Dad will sort it all out when he gets back."

"Really?" Claire asked hopefully. "Because if we can't afford that snotty school anymore, it's fine with me. I can go to public school. Honest. I don't mind."

"I've got a great idea," Sylvie said, mentally calculating her remaining cash. "What say we break all the rules and have hot fudge sundaes for dinner?"

***

Later that night, while the girls were watching TV, Sylvie sat on her bed

24

in the master bedroom, staring at her wedding portrait in its pride of place on her dressing table. She couldn't make herself look away. As she stared, Mark's image seemed to fade in and out of focus, and her heart beat faster and faster until her whole body was rocking to its rhythm. No one could blame her if she succumbed to a panic attack or a nervous breakdown or whatever was happening to her. But then, who would see the girls through this crisis? Who would be there to put Mark back on track?

She willed herself to slow her breathing, then went down to the kitchen and popped the cork on a bottle of Mark's most prized Côtes du Rhône.

She drained her glass and tried Mark's phone one more time. Again, it went to voice mail. She tried to keep the panic out of her voice when she left her message. "Mark, it's okay. I know things are bad, but you have to call me so we can fix this together. We can do this, Mark, but you have to call me. I love you."

Then Sylvie walked into Mark's study, sat in the chair behind his enormous desk, and started opening drawers.

The bottom drawer was locked, as usual.

She rifled through the other drawers looking for the key. She doubted Mark took it with him on business trips. It had to be around here somewhere.

She pulled out each drawer, dumped the contents onto the desktop, and rummaged through papers and office supplies. Nothing. She turned each drawer over in case he'd taped the key somewhere. No luck.

Next she got down onto her knees and used her iPhone flashlight to check underneath the desk. *Nada*.

Nor was anything taped to the bottom or back of the chair.

Now she was pissed. Something could have happened to Mark on any of his many business trips. How would she have accessed those vital papers?

She went back to the kitchen, poured herself another glass of wine, and searched through the kitchen drawers until she found a hammer with one end shaped like a claw. She carried it back to the study, inserted the sharp edge of the claw into the top of the drawer just above the lock, and pushed on the handle with all her might until she heard a satisfying crack. But when she examined her handiwork, she realized she'd managed to pull the molding from around the drawer. The lock held.

Mark would be furious when he saw what she'd done to his beloved heirloom. What had she been thinking? The antique would never be the same.

Then again, neither would their marriage.

He should have bloody well called her back. It was entirely his fault.

She returned to the kitchen and when she opened the knife drawer, her eye fell on Grandma Esther's meat cleaver. It wasn't something Sylvie used very often. She wasn't one to hack away at a piece of raw anything. They had butchers at Whole Foods to do that for her.

She lifted the cleaver out of the drawer. It had a nice heft to it.

Back in Mark's study, she raised the cleaver over her head and was poised to bring it down on the front of the drawer when Claire's voice from the doorway stopped her. "Mom, what the heck are you doing?"

"Trying to open Dad's bottom drawer."

"Why don't you use the key?" Claire asked. She stepped into the room, removed the lid from a china pot on the windowsill, and extracted a small bronze key. She handed it to her mother, then turned and left.

Sylvie swiped her arm across the top of the desk, sweeping the contents of all the other drawers to the floor. She opened the broken drawer, pulled it out and dumped a stack of file folders on top of the desk. She took a deep breath and opened the top folder.

Inside was a letter from Herb Chambers BMW, threatening to repossess Sylvie's car. The next folder held papers pertaining to Mark's new home equity line of credit. The third contained a stack of notices from the Bank of Weston regarding their mortgage. The oldest, dated three months age, was titled "Notice of Right to Cure." It politely urged Mark to pay all back payments, fees and interest to avoid foreclosure. It had been followed up by a Notice of Acceleration, then an Order of Notice. Each successive letter threatened action in increasingly dire language.

Words on the most recent notice leapt from the page: *"You are hereby notified that the undersigned intends to foreclose…"*

The Wolffs had been given until Monday, April twenty-third, to settle their account before their home was auctioned off in a public auction, which, according to the letter, would already have been advertised for three successive weeks in their local paper. Sylvie felt utterly humiliated. How could she not have known? Had everyone in Weston seen the ads except her?

It had to be some massive error on the part of the bank. Surely Mark had responded to the first letter months ago and explained the bank's accounting error. Mark would never have allowed additional fees and interest to accumulate. It went against every fiber in his being. But why hadn't Mark mentioned the problem in all this time? Or had he mentioned it and she hadn't paid attention, assuming he would handle it as he always did?

Today was Friday, the twentieth. If the letter was legitimate, the bank would be holding a public auction here, in front of her home, on Thursday. She would never survive the humiliation. She had to reach Mark.

She texted, "Call me. Emergency" to his mobile.

Eight

The minute Sylvie opened her eyes Saturday morning, she checked her phone. Nothing. No missed calls. No message from Mark explaining the mix-up and assuring her that it was all a big mistake.

Again she called his number and left a message, not bothering to keep the panic out of her voice. She followed up with another text, in case his hotel was located in the only place without a cellular connection in Palo Alto, tech capital of the world.

What if she couldn't reach him in time? Would she and the girls really have to pack up their home and move?

And even if she did manage to face the Herculean task of sorting and packing the detritus of seventeen years of marriage, where was she supposed to put it all? She had nowhere to go.

Well, not quite. Two people in the world would always be there for her, no matter what.

She picked up the phone and made the call she dreaded most in the world.

Her mother picked up on the third ring. "Hi, sweetie, everything okay with you and the girls?"

"Yes, Mom, the girls are fine."

"And Mark?"

Sylvie sighed. It hadn't taken her mother long to get to the point. "Not so good. I'm really sorry, but I have a huge favor to ask of you."

"Honey, you know we'd do anything for you but if you're asking for extra time to pay off the loan, I'm afraid we can't help. We explained to Mark when we loaned you the money that we absolutely needed it back by last week."

"You loaned Mark money? When?"

"Six months ago. We assumed you knew. He told us it was your idea."

"How much did you give him?"

"Thirty thousand. We tapped out our liquid assets. Is there a problem?"

"Mom, Mark's gone, along with all our money. I can't find him, and our house is being foreclosed. The girls and I have nowhere to go. I was hoping you could lend me a few thousand so I could get an apartment until I can find Mark and sort this all out."

"Oh, Sylvie…wait. I'm going to sit." After a pause, she said, "I had a bad feeling. I kept telling your dad, but you know how he admires Mark. My poor baby girl. Of course you're welcome to stay here. Only…"

"Only what?"

"Only strangely enough, I was getting ready to call *you*."

"Is something wrong?" Sylvie felt an awful hardening in the pit of her stomach. She really didn't want to hear that something was wrong in the lives of her parents. They were her rock, her safety net. They needed to be okay, especially right now.

"Well, to be frank, things have been a little tight lately. Financially, I mean. When we didn't hear from you about the loan, we had to use a cash advance from our credit card to pay our taxes. And then your dad got offered a part-time emeritus position in the 'Center for Ocean Engineering' back at MIT. He was hoping to stay with you."

"You mean you're moving back up here?"

"Not me. At least not right away. Until we see how things go. But that's not until the fall, and I'm sure you'll have sorted things out with Mark by then. Meanwhile, come down. We'll have a nice visit."

Sylvie pictured herself and her daughters sleeping in the living room of her parents' one-bedroom apartment on the sixth floor of the high-rise overlooking Miami Beach. It wasn't an encouraging image, but she had no other options. "I'll make this up to you, Mom. I swear, if it's the last thing I do. Right after I kill Mark."

"We can sort it all out when you get here. Will you be driving down?"

"No. They're going to repossess my car. Do you have enough mileage for us to fly?"

*** *

29

Diana sat at the kitchen table in her pajamas, picking apart a piece of whole wheat toast. "Dad would never do that. Call him. He'll explain."

Sylvie stood gazing out the bay window at the purple and yellow mass of spring bulbs bursting into bloom. "I've left so many messages that his mailbox is full."

"Where will we go?" Claire asked from the doorway. In her Scooby Doo pajamas, hugging her stuffed beagle, she looked so much younger than her eleven years.

"Florida. We're going to stay with Grandma and Grandpa. Fun, right? So pack a suitcase. We'll put everything else in storage."

Diana threw the remainder of her toast onto the plate in disgust. "I don't want to go to Florida. There's nothing but old people there and nothing to do. Where's Dad? Why doesn't he fix this?"

Where the hell *was* Mark? Sylvie smacked herself on the forehead. It must have been the shock of all the disastrous revelations yesterday that made her forget. Mark always left a copy of his travel itinerary in a file in the kitchen in case of an emergency. He was compulsively organized about these things. She used to tease him about being OCD. Mark would argue that he was simply practical, and that establishing efficient patterns of behavior made things easier for everyone.

Sylvie raced into the kitchen and pulled the travel folder from its home between the refrigerator and the microwave.

It was empty.

No itinerary. No flights. No hotel. Nothing.

Did that mean Mark hadn't traveled anywhere after all? Or had he forgotten to leave his itinerary—for the first time in all the years they'd been married. It was all too much to think about.

That was when she remembered her Cambridge Trust bank account, where the rent checks for Green Street had been automatically deposited all these years. The expenses—taxes, insurance and maintenance costs—had been automatically withdrawn, but the remainder had been enough to allow for other "luxury" items that Sylvie had insisted on, like the expensive phone plans for the girls that Mark had refused to sponsor.

It was Saturday, but the bank would be open for a few more minutes.

She punched in the number. Nancy McGee had been a teller at the Central Square branch of Cambridge Trust when Sylvie opened her first account there as a student. They had often chatted when Sylvie stopped in.

30

To her enormous relief, Nancy was indeed working today and was now the branch manager.

"Are you calling to confirm your signature?" Nancy said after the usual pleasantries had been exchanged. "I hope I didn't cause a problem when I wouldn't let Mr. Wolff close out your account."

"Mark tried to close out my account?"

"I said I'd need your signature. I gave him the form and he mailed it in, but the signature didn't quite match the one on the card we had on file. I offered to call you to confirm, but Mr. Wolff said he'd get back to me."

"Is there any money left in the account?"

"Give me a sec." There was a pause, then, "Two thousand, nine hundred and seventy-eight dollars and fifty-six cents."

Sylvie pumped her fist into the air. It was enough to buy groceries, rent a storage unit and maybe get them to Florida—by Greyhound, if necessary.

***

By the light of a full moon, and the flashlights on their iPhones, Sylvie, Diana and Claire picked through the boxes behind the local liquor store. Diana had flatly refused to help before the store closed, though Sylvie assured her that no one would mind if they helped themselves to some empties.

"That's not the point," Diana had fumed. "We've been kicked out of school because we can't afford to pay the tuition. If any of my friends see me stealing boxes, they'll think we're homeless and we're going to live in them."

Sylvie had laughed at the idea.

"She's right, you know," Claire had chimed in, cheerfully.

With a start, Sylvie realized how close they were to living in those boxes.

***

Now, back at home, Sylvie stared hopelessly at the sheer volume of stuff that had suddenly transformed from treasured possessions to a lot of crap to be sorted, packed, moved and stored God only knew where and for God only knew how long at enormous expense. To add insult to injury, she had to decide what to do with Mark's things. If something bad had happened to him—if he'd been kidnapped or was the unwilling victim of some sort of extortion scheme, and she got rid of all his belongings out of spite, she'd have a lot of explaining to do when he got home. On the other hand, if she

31

carefully stored his stuff, and it turned out he'd deliberately deserted his family—a scenario that was becoming more and more difficult to reject—she would feel like a complete fool for wasting the little money and energy she had left taking care of his stuff. Best to hedge her bets.

He hadn't taken much with him—only the one suitcase. His best clothes remained neatly hung in his closet. Sylvie packed his suits, shirts and trousers, hangers and all, into a large garbage bag, then dumped his shoes into another.

When she lifted a pair of custom-made black boots, one felt heavier than the other. She turned them upside down and a silk jewelry bag fell out. Inside, she found Mark's grandfather's antique gold pocket watch. Would he really have left it behind if he'd meant to leave forever? She opened the back of the watch and read the inscription: *Julius Harold Wolff, 1905.* What would Mark's *Zayde* have thought about this whole mess? She placed the watch carefully back into its cloth bag and slipped it into her pocket as she walked down the hall to check in on her oldest daughter.

Diana lay on her bed, eyes closed, earphones blotting out the chaos around her. Sylvie sat down on the bed next to her and waited until Diana reluctantly removed the earphones to say, "Honey, I am truly sorry this is happening. We all are. But don't you think you'd better pack your stuff?"

"Claire's not sorry. She's thrilled. Best thing that could have happened to her."

"I'm sure she'd rather have her old life back."

"She doesn't have a life. But I do. I finally look good in Blue Lab jeans and all my friends say Bobby Wise wants to ask me out. And now I have to go to some new school where I don't know anyone."

Claire stuck her head in the door. "Jeez, Diana, you have such white girl problems."

"What kind of problems am I *supposed* to have, loser?"

Sylvie stood. "Whatever you don't pack is going to Goodwill," she said and squeezed past Claire through the doorway.

In the living room, Sylvie surveyed her elegant furniture. How much could she stuff into a storage unit that she could afford?

Claire stepped up behind her. "You know, we could sell it all on Craigslist."

"Great idea. But how do we advertise with such short notice?"

"Facebook shout out, neighborhood list serve. I've got this."

Nine

Sylvie opened her front door on Sunday morning to find neighbors they'd never met lining up outside the Wolff home. As the house filled with bargain hunters, Sylvie walked through the rooms negotiating prices and convincing customers they simply had to have the lamp or side table or knick-knack that went so beautifully with the item they were contemplating. Claire sat on a stool at the foot of the stairs taking cash and giving change while Diana stayed upstairs locked in her room.

"Seventy-five," Sylvie pronounced, trying not to think about the fifteen hundred the antique occasional table had cost as she negotiated with an older fellow in overalls.

The man studied the table, lifted it, and searched the underside. "I'll give you twenty."

Resisting the urge to smack him, she held out her hand. He reached into his pocket and meticulously counted out twenty singles, then tucked the table under his arm and disappeared out the door.

When a young mother holding a toddler offered twenty-five dollars for Mark's beloved heirloom desk, Sylvie threw in the chair for free. She spotted a middle-aged woman who looked vaguely familiar eying one of Sylvie's favorite upholstered chairs. "Great color, right?" Sylvie ventured.

The woman smiled. "I was wondering if it would fit in the back of my van."

"For a hundred bucks, I'll help you load it."

The woman handed over the cash. Sylvie tossed the cushions to the floor and lifted one arm of the chair while the woman struggled to lift the other.

Sylvie silently thanked her private Pilates instructor for her strong back. She'd have to write Myra a nice thank-you note and explain that she could no longer afford the one-on-one sessions she'd hated but faithfully attended for the last four years.

Together, the two women maneuvered the oversized piece through the front door, tipping it in various directions until it fit through, then loaded it into a blue van parked in the driveway.

When Sylvie returned for the cushions, a document was lying on the floor where the chair had been. She retrieved it then stared in disbelief at the title: *Massachusetts Limited Power of Attorney Form.* At the bottom was her signature.

It was the form Sylvie had signed, authorizing Mark to sell her old apartment on Green Street. It must have dropped out of Mark's briefcase and slid out of sight under the chair on Friday when Claire had bumped into him.

Without this paper, Mark couldn't sell the apartment. That meant Sylvie was still the proud owner of a tiny one-bedroom condo in the heart of Central Square. Not much space for a mother and two daughters who were used to the expanse of life in Weston, but it was something. And it was hers. She had a home. She wouldn't have to crowd her parents out of theirs while she figured out how her money had disappeared.

It was nothing short of a miracle. Sylvie lifted her eyes to the ceiling and whispered, "Thanks, Grandma Esther," picturing her beloved grandmother watching over her from an enormous Mahjong table in the sky.

The woman who'd bought the chair returned for her cushions. She stared as Sylvie stepped into the kitchen area, struck a match and lit the paper on fire as she held it over the sink. It smelled good, like toasting marshmallows.

Sylvie waited while flames consumed the pages, holding onto them as long as she could, then dropped the dusty ashes into the stainless steel sink. She turned on the water, aimed the stream toward the drain, and ran the garbage grinder until the last vestiges of ash disappeared.

Without Sylvie's power of attorney, Mark couldn't legally sell the apartment. But what if he tried anyway? She could fight it, but she had no money to hire an attorney.

First thing in the morning, she would go over to Green Street and stake her claim.

The key. Where had she packed the jewelry box that held the original keys on her macramé keychain?

After a frantic search, which involved scrabbling through half the boxes she had packed so carefully the night before, she finally found it.

"Mom, why are you crying?" Claire's voice beside her sounded frightened.

Sylvie hadn't noticed that while she was searching, the house had emptied of shoppers along with most of her furniture. Now her daughters hovered on either side of her with worried expressions on their faces. They had never seen her cry before, and didn't seem to know whether they should be scared or embarrassed.

"We have a place to go," Sylvie whispered. "My old apartment in Cambridge."

"Cambridge?" Diana said, as if the word tasted sour in her mouth. "Ew."

Claire grabbed her mother, forcing her to jump up and down like two middle-schoolers on a hormonal high, while Diana looked on with I'd-rather-be-dead-than-in-this-family disdain.

Ten

Early Monday morning, construction vehicles filled every parking spot that wasn't already blocked off due to ongoing projects on the narrow side streets off Central Square.

With great trepidation, Sylvie pulled into a seedy public garage on Green Street, nervous lest someone break into her beloved Beemer. As she headed down the familiar litter-strewn street toward the four-story building she hadn't laid eyes on in years, she remembered that her Beemer was about to be repossessed. *Fuck it,* she thought.

The neighborhood looked pretty much the same as she remembered: tiny ethnic restaurants that doubled as music venues; crowded, treeless streets; and front stoops occupied by homeless wanderers and mutterers. Homeless, as she'd been only yesterday, before she found the Power of Attorney form under the chair. Only a random gift of luck separated her from the folks pushing shopping carts heaped with all their worldly belongings through the streets.

Different faces sat on the old stoops from the ones she remembered from her student days—or had they simply aged, like her? She'd never really looked at their faces, so she couldn't be sure.

They sat, watching in silence, smoking cigarettes or whatever. Sylvie was pretty sure there was a lot more of whatever than when she'd lived here, at least out in the open since Massachusetts had recently decriminalized weed. From the smell, the good citizens of Central Square seemed to be up to date on the news.

Her old apartment occupied the top floor of a narrow four-family building. Sylvie turned the key in the front door, relieved to find it still worked. As soon as she entered the building, she heard hammering overhead.

She glanced up at the endless stairs leading to her old digs. No elevators in these ancient working class buildings. No wonder she'd had thighs of steel in the old days. The three long flights had not gotten any shorter over the years and, yes, the hammering was getting louder as she climbed. A feeling of dread worsened with each step.

When she reached the top, she found she had no need for her key. The door to number four was propped wide open. Sylvie stepped inside and followed the sound of banging through the tiny foyer, and down the dark hallway to the kitchen, where a pair of long legs clad in jeans and ending in Timberland boots stretched out from under the sink.

Sylvie paused in the doorway. "Hello?"

The head that went with the legs smashed itself on the inside of the cabinet with a loud clunk.

"Shit." The male face that appeared might have been attractive if it hadn't been scowling in pain.

"Sorry," Sylvie said. "I didn't mean to scare you."

A large man struggled to his feet, his hand rubbing the top of his skull. "That's okay." He smiled apologetically. "I didn't know I'd left the downstairs door open."

"You didn't. I used my key."

His brow furrowed. "Do I know you?"

"Sylvie Wolff. I own this apartment. Who are *you*?"

He grinned and held out his hand. "Jack Ramsdale. I bought this place from you. Or rather, Mr. Wolff showed up on Friday to sign the Purchase and Sale but was short a couple of docs so we're rescheduling for today. He said it was fine to go ahead and get some work done. Since the utilities are still in your name, I'll reimburse you as soon as the sale goes through. Hope that's okay."

Sylvie straightened her spine, making herself as tall as possible. "My husband doesn't own this apartment."

"Yes, I know. He said you signed a Power of Attorney, but it wasn't in his briefcase when he got to the lawyer's office." The smile on Ramsdale's face faded. "Is there a problem?"

"There's been a change of plans. I'm not selling. I'm moving in."

Ramsdale scratched his head. "I'm afraid I don't understand."

"Neither do I, Mr. Ramsdale. But there you have it."

Ramsdale's fists rested on his hips as he surveyed the apartment. "I've been working nonstop since yesterday, based on your husband's word."

"I'm afraid Mark's word isn't worth much these days. But don't take it personally. Mark's been lying to a lot of people about a lot of things lately."

"We had a verbal agreement. I'll sue."

"You can stand in line right behind me." Sylvie marched to the door and waited pointedly for him to leave.

She heard the familiar ding of a text and dug for her phone before she realized that it was Ramsdale's phone. He took it from his pocket and frowned at the screen. "That's odd."

"What's that?"

He stepped toward her, towering over her and she instinctively took a step back, not sure it was smart to have come here alone.

He turned the phone toward her to show her the screen: *Mark Wolff: "All set. 1 hour, my atty's"*

Mark was alive and well enough to send texts?

But not to her.

Sylvie's vision spiraled in as everything went black except for a pinhole of light. In that pinhole, Ramsdale was staring at her, his brows furrowed. His lips were moving, as if he was talking, but Sylvie couldn't hear a sound.

Her world was folding in on itself.

Mark wasn't in Palo Alto. He was here in town. Instead of fixing things, he was planning to sell her apartment out from under her. In exactly one hour.

Sylvie's vision continued to narrow until all she could see was the top button of Jack's flannel shirt, while her mind struggled to make sense of what had just happened.

It was several minutes before her vision began to widen and she could hear Ramsdale's voice from a long distance away: "Guess I'd better get going."

Ramsdale squeezed past her through the door and headed down the stairs.

"Hey," she yelled after him, "What attorney? Where?"

"Forget it," Ramsdale called back. "I'm not getting in the middle of some domestic dispute."

All set? How could Mark be *all set?* Did he intend to bluff his way through the sale? He probably didn't realize he'd lost the Power of Attorney in the house where she could find it. And where she could annihilate its crispy corpse down the garbage disposal.

Eleven

Sylvie tore down three flights of stairs and ran the two blocks to the Green Street garage. With shaking hands, she climbed inside and started the car. She navigated around the concrete pillars to the ground floor where she paid in cash and drove around the block on one-way streets, then back to her building in time to see Ramsdale emerge and head for his pickup truck, dressed in khakis and a black polo shirt. He cleaned up nicely.

She waited while he maneuvered his truck from the tight parking spot, then followed him down Mass Ave to Prospect Street and across town to East Cambridge, where he parked a few blocks from the courthouse. Sylvie scored an illegal spot for residents just around the corner, then dashed back just in time to see Ramsdale disappear into an old brick townhouse.

Sylvie stepped inside the building and scanned the list of occupants. *Julio DeSouza, Esquire, Real Estate Law* occupied the second floor.

Knowing Mark and his compulsion to be exactly on time, she went back outside and crouched behind a parked van, heart pounding. Sure enough, five minutes before the scheduled appointment, she spotted his red Jaguar trolling down the street, then claiming a spot at the far end of the block. Mark climbed out, no cast encasing any of his limbs and no bandage around his head. No signs of injury at all. Sylvie had an overwhelming desire to rectify that.

But the sight of him walking toward her with all the confidence in the world filled Sylvie with the desire to run to him, tell him everything that had happened and beg him to tell her what to do. It took a few seconds for her body to remember that he was no longer the husband who would fix everything for her.

She didn't realize that she had stood up and stepped away from the van until she saw him freeze and stare at her, only fifty feet away. Shock, then guilt passed across her husband's face. Before she could move or speak, he turned, sprinted back to his car, and jumped in.

He started the engine and lurched out of the parking space, burning rubber as he attempted a U turn that became a frenzied six-pointed star. After nearly taking out three bicyclists, he took the corner on two wheels while Sylvie ran down the street after him, screaming his name. She tripped over a tree root growing through the sidewalk and fell to her hands and knees on the pavement as the Jag disappeared from sight.

Jack Ramsdale stood in the doorway of the brownstone, a witness to her humiliation. But that was the least of her problems. She had blown her one chance to confront her husband.

The bastard had bolted like a coward when he saw her. She would never forget that sight.

She pushed herself to her feet. Her pants were torn at the knees, and her right knee was bleeding.

Ramsdale approached, followed by a stocky man in his mid-fifties who wore a tragically ill-fitting suit.

"You okay?" Ramsdale asked.

"Define okay."

"Nothing broken?"

She shook her head. "Nothing physical, anyway."

Ramsdale and the man she assumed was Julio DeSouza, Esquire, escorted her into the building and up the elevator to the second floor.

***

Sylvie sat in a chair in DeSouza's office, feeling like a third grader who was waiting for her parents to pick her up after a fall on the playground. Her knee was bandaged and her face burned.

Standing over her, Julio DeSouza was doing his best to bully her into signing the Purchase and Sales agreement on the table in front of her. "You have to understand. Your husband made a legally binding verbal agreement with my client, who had every reason to believe your husband was acting on your behalf."

Sylvie found herself fascinated by the contrast between the man's full head of black hair and the stark white of his eyebrows.

DeSouza's stubby finger tapped the signature line at the bottom of the page. "As his attorney, I have advised Mr. Ramsdale that he has every right to take you to court to enforce this agreement."

A few days ago, such threats would have struck fear in her heart. Now, all Sylvie could think of was the expression on Mark's face when he spotted her. She glanced up at Ramsdale across the table from her. He stared at the paper between them, avoiding her eyes.

DeSouza leaned forward. She smelled tuna fish on his breath. "The offer my client made was exceptionally generous. No one else will offer anything close, especially while the three units he already owns undergo extensive renovations."

So, there was going to be noise—a lot of noise. So what? If she could hold her ground, come tomorrow, she and the girls would have a roof over their heads.

She bit her lips tightly together to keep herself from saying anything that could make her situation worse.

Finally, his argument spent, DeSouza raised his arms in an I-can't-get-this-bitch-to-listen-to-reason gesture and left the room.

Summoning every ounce of dignity she could muster, Sylvie stood and limped toward the door. It wasn't until she was outside the building, heading to her car, that a new resolve filled her. Now that she knew Mark was unhurt, she would track him down and make him pay. A man didn't walk out on his kids. Not in Sylvie's world.

Twelve

On the way home, Sylvie stopped at Pill Hardware where she perused the community bulletin board. With her phone she photographed a flyer, advertising a "man with a truck" available for moves. Another flyer advertised a locksmith who was on call twenty-four/seven. He agreed to meet her at Green Street in fifteen minutes. She made copies of the key to the building for the girls, then hurried to meet the locksmith to change the lock to number four.

Alexis the locksmith introduced himself in a thick Slavic accent. Straight out of central casting for the Russian Mafia, the back of his thick neck bore a tattoo of a double-headed eagle. Sylvie wondered if locksmiths in Massachusetts were licensed or had security clearances. What was to stop a locksmith from returning to his client's home in the middle of the night? Sylvie quickly pushed the thought aside. She had enough problems without succumbing to paranoia.

While she waited for Alexis to change the front and rear locks to number four, she tried calling the mover. The voice that answered was actually a *boy*-with-a-truck named Connor Gallagher, but he was available tomorrow after school because it was school vacation. And he was willing to work cheap.

By the time Alexis had provided extra keys for the new lock and she'd locked up and followed him out, traffic on the Mass Pike heading west was brutal. When she finally got home to Weston, it was dark. She entered the front door and flipped on the light switch in the foyer. Nothing happened.

Claire's disembodied voice came from nearby. "Don't bother, Mom. The electricity's been turned off. Gas, too. But don't worry. I found candles and flashlights in the pantry." Claire stepped aside to reveal an assortment of candles flickering on the windowsills in the great room. The effect was quite lovely.

Sylvie sank onto one of the two chairs in the living room that hadn't sold because the upholstery was faded and one had a loose spring.

"I called," Claire said with obvious pride in her voice. "They said they'd turn it on again if we go down to their office and pay with cash. They're open 'til seven."

"Forget it," Sylvie responded. "Waste of money. We move tomorrow anyway."

Carrying a flashlight to conserve the charge on her phone, Sylvie opened the door to Diana's room where she lay motionless on her bed in the dark, plugged into her iPhone. She wore the same clothes she'd worn the day before, and smelled a little ripe. Sylvie swept the room with her flashlight. Nothing had changed. The boxes remained empty.

Sylvie stood in the doorway, exasperated. "I know this sucks, but we're moving to Cambridge tomorrow afternoon. If you're going to want a toothbrush or a change of clothes, you'd better start packing."

Diana gave no indication that she'd heard.

Sylvie felt drained of energy. But she had to keep things together until she could find a job or a pot of gold somewhere near a rainbow. Diana would have to suck it up and pull her weight or suffer the consequences. Sylvie could imagine Diana's reaction when she discovered that no electricity meant she couldn't recharge her precious phone.

She closed Diana's door, leaving her to her chosen fate, and opened Claire's door. Everything here was packed and ready to go. The boxes were clearly labeled and cheerfully decorated with doggie stickers and smiley faces.

***

That night Sylvie starred vacantly at the closed refrigerator, trying to remember what was inside so she wouldn't have to open the door and have their food spoil any faster than necessary.

Claire entered the kitchen. "What's for supper? I'm starving."

"Anything you want, as long as we can eat it raw." Sylvie opened the door to her pantry. "I've got tuna and garbanzo beans."

"Why don't we cook in the fire pit? It'll be fun." Claire was a dedicated fan of the TV show "Survivor."

"I don't know. Your dad always—" But before Sylvie could finish her thought, Claire had opened the fridge, found the chicken sausages and was heading out the door.

Together, they scavenged sticks and newspaper and lit their first real kindling and wood fire. They roasted organic chicken sausages on sticks over the copper fire pit and toasted frozen hot dog buns. Everything in the veggie drawer was chopped up for salad.

Diana never ventured outside to join them, but Claire took a plate up to her sister. As the embers faded, then died, Sylvie recounted her father's stories of ships lost at sea, or found in Arctic waters with molding bodies frozen in time. In the moonlight, Sylvie saw a shadowy figure open the window above them and linger for a while.

When the fire had been doused and Sylvie went to check on Diana, she was back on her bed, refusing to acknowledge her mother's presence.

When Sylvie turned to leave, Diana asked, "Is this what it's like to be poor?"

Sylvie paused in the doorway. "I really never thought about it before."

"This sucks."

Sylvie realized she'd never before been afraid of basic stuff like how she was going to feed her kids tomorrow and the next day, and the day after that. This kind of food insecurity wasn't supposed to happen to people like her. "Yeah, it does," she said.

***

That night, by the light of a flashlight reflected off her ceiling, Sylvie faced her own packing nightmare—everything she'd left to the last minute, because she couldn't bear to make the decisions she needed to make.

How could she possibly fit the clothes from her expansive walk-in closet, organized first by season, then by color palette, into the tiny hall closet she would have at Green Street? It was impossible to know what she'd need in her new life, because she had no idea what her new life would be.

Clearly, the outfits she wore for tennis and Pilates were out, at least for now. Nor was there much need for the gowns she'd worn to the art openings and galas that supported her favorite charities. For the foreseeable future anyway, she would have to be her own favorite charity.

She selected a classic suit with matching shoes so she could look for a job, along with some casual clothes to wear at home. Her Coach tote bag would serve as an everyday purse. She packed the rest of her impressive collection of designer bags into a large box, marking it carefully so that if things became truly desperate she could find it easily. Designer handbags would fetch a handsome price on the used clothing market, though Sylvie herself thought it was creepy to use other people's cast-off things.

Weary to the bone, with the tape dispenser still clutched in her hand, Sylvie fell onto her bed and closed her eyes, losing herself in the sweet oblivion of sleep.

Thirteen

At the break of dawn on Tuesday, Sylvie answered the door to admit Connor Gallagher, who couldn't have been much older than Diana. Connor explained that he used his father's truck to make money doing small moving jobs on weekends and school vacations. He had offered to bring along one of his buddies for an additional fee, but Sylvie had declined. With funds as scarce as they were, she had to spend every penny wisely. She and the girls would help. They'd think of it as a free workout.

Claire stood back and said "hello" shyly. Her uncharacteristic reticence caused Sylvie to take another look at Connor, a good-looking kid with longish dark hair and huge biceps set off by a white tank shirt. *Wait 'til Diana sees this,* she thought.

Connor suggested they walk through the house first so he could strategize the day's work. When Sylvie explained they were moving to a fourth floor walk-up and she and the girls would be his only help, he looked skeptical.

When they came to Diana's bedroom, Sylvie knocked on the door, but got no answer. She knocked a second time, glanced apologetically at Connor and called, "Diana, I'm coming in and I have someone with me so you'd better have clothes on."

No answer.

Sylvie turned the knob and walked in.

Diana lay on the bed surrounded by all her belongings. She glanced up at the two of them and when her eyes landed on Connor, they grew huge. She bolted upright.

"Diana, this is Connor," Sylvie said. "He's going to help us move." She turned to Connor. "I've explained to Diana that whatever isn't packed and labeled when it's time to load the truck will be left here."

47

Diana stared at Connor with a horrified expression on her face.

Sylvie ushered him out of the room and closed the door behind them.

As they walked down the hall, Sylvie heard the bathroom door slam and the shower turn on, then a shriek. Diana must have discovered that when there was no electricity, there was no hot water.

Connor looked alarmed, but Sylvie simply smiled and kept walking.

By the time they finished touring the house, Connor had convinced Sylvie that the small fee she would pay his buddy, Kevin, to help out would probably save her three times the amount in his own hourly rate. He texted his friend, who texted back that he could be there in less than an hour if someone could pick him up at the Woodland Hills T stop in Newton.

While they waited for Kevin to phone, Sylvie and Connor returned to Diana's room to retrieve her mattress. They found Diana dressed in tight jeans and a T-shirt casually draped off one shoulder and skillfully tied at her waist to reveal several inches of bare stomach, her hair wet and limp for lack of a hair dryer. But her makeup had been expertly applied, and she smelled like a Bath and Body Works store. Grinning to herself, Sylvie left Connor with Diana to disassemble her bed while she went to pick up Kevin, who, Connor assured her, would be easy to recognize by his long blond hair and Falcons sweatshirt.

When Sylvie returned with Kevin, whose physique looked blessedly capable of moving large pieces of furniture up three flights of stairs, she found everything in Diana's room packed into boxes with each box clearly labeled in black Sharpie. *Thank God for hormones,* she sighed to herself.

For the next several hours, Kevin and Connor carried the few pieces of large furniture left from the sale out to the truck while Diana and Claire helped with the smaller items. Sylvie retreated to the kitchen to find food for everyone and to clean out the fridge.

When they finally finished loading the truck, they packed the computer and a few kitchen items into the back of Sylvie's SUV. She and the girls climbed in and led the boys and their truck onto the Mass Pike toward Central Square.

When Sylvie spotted Kester's, the used clothing store where Harvard students, including John F. Kennedy, had purchased their tuxedoes and sold their slightly worn clothing for over a hundred years, she slammed on the brakes and stuck her arm out the window, motioning for the truck to pull over and park.

Fourteen

Under Sylvie's direction, Connor unlocked the back of the truck, then stood back and watched, puzzled, as Sylvie clambered inside and rifled through the garbage bags. She threw one to the ground, jumped down after it, hoisted the bag over her shoulder and entered Kester's.

Inside, it smelled like Grandma Esther's house. Unopened boxes crammed the aisles and water stains dappled the ceiling. The fluorescent lights flickered ominously, as a short man with a wild-looking fringe of sandy hair and several days of stubble approached. "May I help you?"

Sylvie hoisted the bag onto the counter and opened it. She extracted a few choice items—a silk Armani shirt, a Kiton cashmere jacket and a Stefano Ricci dress shirt. "My husband passed on. I can't bear to look at his things any longer," she said.

The man reached for the jacket and checked the label. He rubbed the fabric between his fingers, then sniffed it. "What else you got in there?" he asked, adding as an afterthought, "Sorry for your loss," as he reached into the bag. With great deference, he removed item after expensive item. "I'd be willing to take it all off your hands," he said.

"There's more in the truck."

Kevin and Connor unloaded all nine bags labeled "Mark."

Sylvie stuffed a wad of cash into her bag as she climbed back into the SUV, feeling a little bit better, though she really wished she could take a shower.

*****

Parking was permitted on only one side of Green Street, and all the legal spaces were taken. The only way to unload the truck was to park it on the sidewalk, up against the wall of the building next door, directly under a "No Parking" sign. Just in case things weren't challenging enough, today was garbage day. Overflowing garbage barrels and recycling bins crammed what little sidewalk was left.

Sylvie and the girls carried small appliances and boxes up the stairs and took turns watching over the truck so none of their belongings ended up in the grocery carts pushed by Central Square's ubiquitous homeless population.

On the third trip up the stairs, Kevin and Connor ditched their shirts, much to the delight of Diana and Claire, who mugged silent over-the-top expressions of jaw-dropping lust whenever the boys' backs were turned.

For the first time, Sylvie was thankful the apartment was small and required only a manageable number of trips. One couch, two living room chairs, beds, dressers, a computer desk and a kitchen set filled it to capacity. But even those few pieces proved challenging, especially maneuvering the larger items around the tight corners on the staircase-from-hell. The boys sweated and strategized while the girls shouted encouragement.

The apartment wasn't in bad shape, mostly thanks to Jack Ramsdale's involuntary contribution. It had a light-filled living room, a combination dining room and kitchen, one bedroom and a small study leading to a sun porch that Ramsdale had started to enclose. Sylvie assigned the girls to share the bedroom. She would take the tiny study and use the closet in the hall. Yes, they would be cramped and the girls had never shared a room before, but it sure beat living in a cardboard box under a bridge.

When the truck had been emptied, Sylvie walked to Hi-Fi Pizza around the corner to pick up dinner. The old neighborhood wasn't exactly pristine. Cambridge's once-a-month street cleaning schedule couldn't keep up with the litter in this crowded working-class neighborhood, which stretched along Massachusetts Avenue between Harvard and MIT. Buildings hugged the narrow sidewalk, leaving little room for such suburban luxuries as trees and grass. Everything looked gray, dim and soiled. It smelled of restaurant garbage and bus exhaust. Too many people were vying for too little space, and too many cars competed for parking. Sylvie ached for her lush garden and private driveway.

Now they were lucky to have a tiny apartment on a dirty, crowded street. Two days earlier, she hadn't known she could provide this much. She knew she should be grateful, but how would they ever manage to make the adjustment?

And where was Mark living? Where was he parking his beloved Jaguar?

When she'd seen him yesterday, he'd looked great—clean, shaved, well dressed. Sylvie spotted a beer can on the sidewalk. She visualized Mark's face on the surface as she stomped and crumpled it.

When she returned with the pizza, the sun had nearly set. Sylvie found all four kids perched on the front stoop, exhausted. Diana was making an effort to hide her general displeasure with the world in front of these tanned, pectorally-blessed boys. She giggled and shrieked obligingly with her sister whenever Connor and Kevin splashed their water bottles over everyone.

As Sylvie was enjoying these rare moments free of adolescent drama, the front door opened and Jack Ramsdale, the last person Sylvie wanted to see, emerged. Unfortunately, they now shared a building, a front door and a front stoop. Sylvie scooted to the side, hoping he would pass and be on his way.

Instead he said, "I left some tools in your apartment yesterday. When I went to get them, my key didn't work. I need them."

Sylvie sighed, left her half-eaten pizza and struggled up the stairs for the umpteenth time. Jack followed and retrieved his toolbox from the kitchen. Before leaving, he paused in the doorway.

"I thought it was only right to let you know—" He hesitated. "I mean, I actually considered not saying anything, but—"

Sylvie's eyebrows shot up. "What is it?"

"I got a call from your husband."

Fifteen

Claire charged into the kitchen carrying four water bottles. Ignoring the two adults, she proceeded to fill the bottles from the tap. Sylvie caught Jack's eye and shook her head, signaling not to discuss Mark in front of Claire.

Jack nodded. "I'll be in later tonight if you want to stop by," he said and left.

Sylvie desperately wanted to follow him, bang on his door and demand to know exactly where Mark was holed up so she could find him and kill him. Well, maybe not kill him literally, although perhaps it would be best not to have any sharp knives within reach.

Claire bounded off, leaving Sylvie alone to contemplate the disaster that was their new home. How would she ever turn this tiny urban tree house into a home for her girls? At a time when stability was so important to their emotional development, she'd had to uproot them from the only world they'd ever known. While she'd waited for her highlights to set at the salon, she'd read plenty of articles in psych magazines about the mental health of adolescents. With all this displacement and trauma, how could she possibly keep them from turning into juvenile delinquents?

With whatever it takes, she vowed to herself, and followed Claire back down the stairs to the front stoop, where the kids were finishing their pizza. Sylvie managed to rescue her unfinished slice and watched in amazement as Diana, without being asked, stood up, folded the empty pizza box, and carried it to one of the blue recycling bins crowding the sidewalk.

She opened the lid, then jumped away shrieking, "It's moving." She knocked the bin onto its side, spilling cardboard and plastic containers everywhere.

Something small and furry squealed and skittered past, disappearing into a pyramid of garbage bags.

"A rat," Diana wailed, retreating to the highest step of the stoop.

Connor stood up. "Never seen a rat with curly fur before," he said. Using the beam on his phone to illuminate the dark spaces between the bags, he approached the pile with Kevin and Claire right behind. The beam landed on a grey fur ball in the shape of a puppy, shivering behind a garbage bag, its tail wagging hopefully. A pair of soulful eyes peered from beneath a fringe of matted fur.

"Oh, my god!" Claire squealed and plopped herself straight down onto the filthy sidewalk. She reached into her pocket for one of the dog treats she always carried with her, in case she ran into a dog willing to be bribed into friendship, and opened her hand to display the offering.

The little dog considered, then approached with caution, tempted beyond its better judgment.

Claire let the little vagabond devour the treat, then sat perfectly still while it climbed onto her lap and settled in. "Oh, Mom, it's only a baby!" She scooped up the puppy and hugged it to her chest. It looked to be no more than a couple of months old, barely old enough to be separated from its mother. "Someone threw it away like a piece of garbage. Please, can we keep him?" Claire turned the puppy over briefly. "I mean *her*."

"No, Claire. We can take it to a shelter, but Dad would never—"

"Dad's not around, in case you haven't noticed," Diana said, plunking herself down beside her sister to stroke the matted fur. The two boys squatted beside them.

Sylvie cringed at the thought of the germs and God only knew what else crawling all over the little dog. "It's filthy. It's been living in the garbage—"

"On it." Kevin jumped to his feet. "CVS is just around the corner. They'll have some kind of dog shampoo." He was gone before Sylvie could protest.

Sylvie sighed. "You're going to fall in love, and then it's going to be even harder to give her up when Dad—"

"When Dad *what*?" Diana demanded.

Sylvie looked at the two girls, side by side, pleading for the little tramp. Her heart melted.

Screw Mark, she thought.

***

While Sylvie busied herself slicing open the boxes she'd marked "FIRST NIGHT" and locating bed linens, pajamas, toothbrushes and towels, the sound of giggling, splashing and yipping from the bathroom made her smile despite her misgivings. Definitely an improvement over the emotional breakdown she'd anticipated for the first night of their back-to-basics adventure.

The door flew open. Claire popped out, snatched the towel Sylvie was holding and disappeared again into the bathroom, slamming the door behind her.

Moments later, the four kids emerged, damp and tousled, with a squirming ball of fluff wrapped in one of Sylvie's best guest towels in Claire's arms. The little dog, now white and fluffy, bore no resemblance to the dingy creature they'd found only an hour earlier.

Exhausted and longing for her bed, Sylvie left the girls with their new pup and accompanied the boys to Cambridge Self Storage on Concord Avenue, across from the Armory. She supervised as they unloaded, stacked and organized the overflow boxes into her newly rented storage cubicle, grateful for the endless energy of teenage boys. When she gave them an extra twenty-dollar bill to split as a tip, their faces fell in disappointment. She felt badly that after all their hard work it couldn't be more, but even a few dollars was more than she could afford, especially with a new member of the household to feed and vet. She added another five to cover the dog shampoo, murmured an apology and said goodbye.

Back at Green Street, the girls were sound asleep, both curled around the puppy on Claire's bed.

When Sylvie entered the room, the little dog opened her eyes and sat up.

Sylvie lifted her gently from her nest and carried her down to the tiny patch of crab grass that separated their building from the next. The puppy squatted and peed without encouragement. Sylvie praised her enthusiastically, then carried her back up the stairs. She replaced the puppy between the girls.

In the bathroom, Sylvie tiptoed around the puddles of water, ignored the soap foam congealing on every surface, and headed down the stairs to Jack Ramsdale's apartment.

Sixteen

Ramsdale's door opened to reveal an inviting, masculine space, scattered with comfortable, mismatched furniture. Instead of a sofa in the living room, a variety of overstuffed chairs and a faux leather recliner stood in a semicircle around the fireplace.

Jack gestured for Sylvie to sit as he poured two glasses of red wine. She accepted hers gratefully, sank into a dark brown wing-backed chair and lifted her aching feet onto the ottoman.

Jack chose the wooden rocking chair opposite her. "Long day?"

"You could say that." She took a sip of wine. It felt smooth and rich sliding down her throat. She placed her glass on the coffee table so she wouldn't be tempted to down the entire contents in one gulp. "So, Mr. Ramsdale, what did my husband have to say?"

"He wants to move ahead with the sale."

Sylvie sat up straight. "Did you tell him the girls and I are living here?"

"No, I thought I'd leave that to you."

"What the hell did he think I was doing at the attorney's office?"

"Obviously you were there to put the kibosh on the sale. But if you want my opinion—"

Sylvie retrieved her glass and downed the rest of the wine.

"I think your husband is a desperate man."

"Desperate? How do you mean desperate?"

Jack stood and retrieved the wine bottle. "He claims he can provide your signed Power of Attorney."

"He's lying." She paused as realization dawned. "He's going to forge my signature?"

Jack shrugged. "You tell me. You know him better than I do." He refilled both their glasses.

"Mark outright offered to commit a crime?" She gulped half the second glass. "Did you agree to go along with him?"

"No. I don't like to throw good money after bad. But Mark knows he has me over a barrel. I refinanced based on owning the entire building. He thinks that makes me as desperate as he is."

"Are you? Desperate?" Sylvie grasped her glass firmly in both her hands and finished the second glass.

"I'm pretty stretched financially. But that doesn't make me stupid."

"Mark's not stupid either. He's one of the smartest people I know. That's why I don't understand any of this." She leaned forward. "Do you know where Mark is staying?"

"No. He uses his attorney's address on all the documents."

Sylvie reached for the bottle, but it was empty.

Jack opened a second bottle and filled her glass. "Come to think of it, he's been acting squirrelly since we started negotiating. Do you think Mark's in trouble with the law?"

"I don't know what to think. I know I must sound naïve after everything that's happened, but that's not the Mark I've known all these years."

"Or the Mark you've known all these years isn't the real Mark."

Sylvie started her third glass of wine. "Do you really think a straitlaced guy like Mark is capable of criminal behavior?"

"Do you know how many bankers end up in jail? Besides, under the right circumstances anyone is capable of anything. You know the saying, 'we're all three meals away from a life of crime.'"

Sylvie sat back. Her face was hot and the room spun. She was never much of a drinker and now, too late, she remembered why. Alcohol made her emotional and nauseated. She needed to go upstairs and crawl under her covers. But if she stood up now, she doubted she'd make it to the door, never mind locate the doorknob.

"It's me," she sobbed. "I've been a terrible wife. I've broken our home." Tears spilled down her cheeks, her nose dripped. Her entire face was a snotfest. All she had to stem the flow was a flimsy cocktail napkin that was saturated, no longer capable of mopping anything. She hiccupped. The room spun as a tsunami of grief and regret washed over her.

She knew she should shut up, but she was helpless to stop the words from gushing out. "I'm an awful person. I tried to do the right thing. I wanted to send my kids to good schools and give them all the advantages they needed to be successful in life. And all I did was screw everything up."

She struggled to focus her eyes and saw Jack Ramsdale staring at her.

Her hand flew to her chest. "Oh, my god, I'm sorry. I hardly know you and here I am—" She stood up, swayed, then belched.

Jack was on his feet. "Are you going to throw up?"

She shook her head, assessing whether to aim for the glass coffee table or the wood floor, endangering the rug. She forced air into her lungs to tamp down the nausea, and tried to be still. Could she possibly embarrass herself any more?

Now he was studying the floor under his feet in that helpless way men do when they're desperate to make it better but don't have a clue how to go about it. *Why can't they simply let you cry and tell you how strong and brave you are, like girlfriends do? Honestly.*

He took a tentative step toward her, but she recoiled. He was going to pat her on the back. She just knew it. And she couldn't bear it if he patted her on the back. She would simply dissolve in a liquid puddle of humiliation.

After what seemed like an eternity, he shrugged and raised his arms helplessly in the air. "Do you want to have sex?"

She blinked. Had she heard him correctly? Behind him, in the mirror over the fireplace, she spied the reflection of a white face, red eyes and smeared black eye liner that resembled a drunken raccoon. When she realized it was her own reflection, she gasped.

She looked back at him, and this time she spotted the twinkle in his eye.

"Kidding. If you are," he ventured.

She dissolved in laughter.

She laughed so hard she was afraid she'd need mouth-to-mouth resuscitation. No matter how hard she tried, she couldn't stop long enough to get air into her lungs. Tears still flowed from her red, puffy eyes, but now they were tears of laughter. She gasped for air and doubled over. When she finally managed to suck a little air into her lungs, she straightened up. He was laughing, too, either because she looked so ridiculous or because that kind of hysteria was so contagious.

She dissolved again and her stomach cramped painfully.

He left the room and returned with a wad of toilet paper and a glass of water. She mopped her face, drank the water, and focused on her breathing.

He grinned. "Feeling better?"

She smiled back at him. When her breathing was close to normal she said, "I think I'd better get some air."

Seventeen

Sylvie concentrated on placing one foot directly in front of the other as she stepped out of Jack's apartment into the foyer.

She opened the outside door. A blast of cool night air nearly knocked her off her feet. She wiped her nose and eyes with the wad of toilet paper in her hand and walked out onto the front stoop.

The street wasn't dark and deserted at night, like in Weston. People were at the bus stop, chatting loudly as they waited for their ride home. She descended the four steps to the sidewalk and walked to the end of the block and back. A lively beat drifted from the Middle East Restaurant down the street, where a double-parked touring bus for "The Leftovers" forced the stream of cars to mount the sidewalk to get around it. The streetlights illuminating the corners made her feel better. Life continued. The world hadn't ended, though her small corner of the universe might have shut down.

Sylvie walked up and down the block, willing her mind to clear.

As she passed the parked bus for the third time, she heard a voice coming from a darkened stoop. "Hey, girlie, you okay?"

The voice was so hoarse that Sylvie couldn't tell if it came from a man or a woman. She peered through the shadows and discovered a small figure puffing enthusiastically on the minuscule butt of a cigarette that glowed brighter the harder she sucked. The woman smiled, which made her look like a brown elf with bad teeth, and patted the seat beside her.

Sylvie hesitated, but the little gnome brushed the debris from the stoop and patted it again. She reminded Sylvie of the imps that fairy tale characters inevitably encountered whenever they were sent out into the world to seek their fortunes.

Sylvie sat down on the stoop.

"Bad day?" asked the gravelly voice.

Sylvie nodded.

"Man trouble?"

Sylvie nodded again, afraid to speak, lest the emotional floodgates open once again.

"You can tell LaVonda. I got no place to go."

Sylvie rested her chin on her knees. "I think I screwed up." Somehow, it felt perfectly normal to be sitting on a dirty stoop, talking to a gnome in a raggedy turban.

"What are you going to do about it?" asked the gnome.

Sylvie shrugged. She had never before been tempted to smoke. But as she watched the woman inhale, she longed for a quick hit of anything that brought even momentary relief.

"You'll figure it out," LaVonda said. "I got faith in you."

Sylvie smiled, wiped her eyes, then stood and headed back inside to check on her girls.

***

Standing in the doorway, Sylvie surveyed her new bedroom. The narrow micro suede convertible chair that had once occupied an extra guest bedroom in their old house was supposed to serve as her bed. It was the only mattress that fit the tiny room. She grabbed the handle at the foot with both hands, lifted and pulled with all her might, transforming it into a cot-sized bed that stretched the entire length of the room. Forget brushing her teeth or making up the bed with fresh sheets. She collapsed onto the bare mattress and pulled a blanket over her, then realized she'd forgotten to call her mother to tell her they weren't coming to Florida after all. She reached into her pocket and found her phone but when she tried to call, there was no reception. She couldn't imagine maneuvering herself out of bed again and searching the condo for enough reception to make the call. It would have to wait 'til morning.

Also, in the morning, when her brain wasn't fogged from too much wine drunk too fast, Sylvie would try to figure out what would make Mark this desperate. Right now, she couldn't bear to consider the possibility that everything that had happened to her in the past couple of days was her own fault.

Eighteen

Sylvie stared up at the blackboard in the front of the classroom. On it, "Physics 101, Final Exam" was scrawled in stark white chalk. An old, familiar panic somersaulted inside her gut.

She remembered signing up for the class, the science requirement she needed in order to graduate next week, but she couldn't remember attending any of the classes or completing any of the assignments.

The teaching assistant, a bleary-eyed youth with a scraggly beard, was handing out exams and blue books to each student.

Sylvie opened her exam and tried to make sense of the formulas that swam on the page. *How could I have let this happen?*

She looked around at the other students, busy scribbling into their notebooks, then down at herself and realized, to her horror, that she was naked, sitting on a toilet in the middle of the classroom.

The panic rose from her gut to her throat, constricting her breathing.

She gasped for air and woke with a start.

She was not where she should have been—enveloped in her soft cotton sheets, with bird songs wafting through the window from her garden.

Instead, a nappy woolen blanket scratched her skin. Trucks beeped back-up warnings again and again and again from the street below, while sirens screamed in the distance.

The alarm jangled. Sylvie sat up, stretched her aching back and stared at the chaos around her. Then, eyes still half-closed, her head pounding, she found the bathroom and parted the yellowed shower curtain that hung at awkward angles inside the old claw foot tub she had once found so charming. She glanced down and saw she was still dressed in the same clothes she'd worn the day before. When she was stripped down and soaking wet, she realized she'd neglected to unpack the shampoo or soap. So she stood under the streaming water trying to avoid the mold on the bottom of the brittle curtain that clung to her when she moved, and made a mental list of her chores for the day. First on her list was finding a vet to make sure their new roommate didn't expose them to a host of unwelcome parasites.

In the girls' bedroom, Claire and Diana were still sound asleep but a pink puppy nose peeked out from under Claire's arm, looking relieved to see her. Sylvie gave Claire a gentle shake.

Without a word of protest, Claire forced her eyes open, gathered the puppy and left, still in her pajamas. She was halfway down the stairs when Sylvie remembered to toss her a plastic bag, calling, "Don't throw away the poop, we need to take a sample to a vet."

Claire gave a thumbs-up and skipped down the stairs.

Back in her tiny cell, Sylvie rummaged through boxes until she located a casual pair of khakis and a tunic length sweater. She dressed and fluffed her dripping hair, then opened her computer to find a vet within walking distance.

That was when she remembered she had no cable or internet yet. She picked up her phone to use her cellular connection, but it had decided she was in a dead zone. Holding the phone up in front of her, she moved to the front of the apartment, then headed down the stairs. No luck.

On the first floor, Jack Ramsdale's door was ajar. She knocked and the door opened slightly, but there was no response.

She peered inside. His computer was lit up, a lightshow screensaver dancing around the screen. She called his name, but no one answered. She argued with herself briefly, but in the end expediency won out and she stepped inside without an invitation. *What kind of idiot leaves his apartment empty with the door open and his computer on? Probably someone who's used to being the sole occupant of the building.*

She approached the computer, touched a key and it came to life. *This guy didn't even bother with a password.* He must be the only person in Cambridge less computer savvy than she was. She double clicked on the browser, looked up the nearest vet and entered the contact information into her phone. She quit the browser and was about to leave when an email alert popped up in the corner of the screen announcing a new email from Mark

Wolff, with "Green Street Condo" in the subject line.

Without hesitation, Sylvie clicked it open. *We need to talk. Flour Bakery, Fort Point Channel, 10 AM. Do not inform my wife.*

Her hand gripped the mouse, the pointer hovering over the delete button.

Outside on the street, she heard Ramsdale greet Claire and footsteps approach. She clicked and Mark's email vanished from Ramsdale's inbox.

Sylvie slipped out to the foyer at the bottom of the staircase seconds before Ramsdale entered the building. "Hey," she said, holding up her phone. "I can't get service. Who should I call?"

He held up one finger and disappeared inside his door, reappearing with a small black plastic box, which he handed to her. "It's a service extender. You can use my wi-fi 'til the cable company hooks you up. ID and password are on the bottom."

***

Back upstairs, she quieted her guilty conscience long enough to call Happy Tails Veterinary Associates to determine the cost of owning a healthy, legal pet in Cambridge. It wasn't cheap, but they had an appointment available in an hour.

"Go wake up your sister," she instructed Claire. "If you want to keep the puppy—"

"Sugarbear," Claire announced.

Sugarbear?

"If you want to keep Sugarbear, you both need to get dressed and take her to this address in one hour." She texted it to Claire's phone. "It's just down Mass Ave. They'll scan for a implant in case Sugarbear already has a home."

Claire's face fell.

"It's what you'd want someone else to do if she got separated from you. If there's no implant and no one is looking for her, they'll give her an exam, shots, tests for parasites and an implant."

Claire looked skeptical.

"It's tiny—the size of a kernel of rice, and it doesn't hurt. If you lose Sugarbear and someone else finds her, they can take her to a shelter or a vet who will scan for the implant and return her to you."

She handed Claire $250 in cash from her precious stash. Only a few days ago she would have thought nothing of spending three times that amount. Now, counting out that much cash made her neck stiff. But when she remembered that Mark's precious clothes were paying for Claire's new pet, the stiffness disappeared.

"Give them my number for the microchip in case Sugarbear gets lost when you're in school. Oh, and I might not be here when you get back." She handed Claire two set of keys. "Give one set to your sister. One's for the front door and the other's for number four. And when I get back, I expect you to have organized your room. I have some errands to run. Will you two be okay alone?"

"We're not alone. We'll never be alone again. We have Sugarbear." With that, Claire ran in to wake her sister.

Nineteen

Sylvie headed up the street to where she'd left her car, relieved to find that here on the street her phone had a strong signal with good reception. She dialed her mother's cell. When her mother failed to pick up, she left a message explaining that they'd moved to Green Street and she would call again soon.

She clicked off and looked around for her car. Surely, she had parked it right here, only a few houses from her building. She remembered the triumph she had felt when she'd scored a spot so close to home. But her SUV was nowhere to be seen. In fact, strangely enough, no cars were parked on the street at all. She approached the closest street sign with trepidation.

Sure enough, today was the dreaded once-a-month street cleaning that traumatized Cambridge drivers between April and December. There were no cars on the street because the ones owned by responsible drivers had been moved elsewhere. The rest, owned by morons like her, had been towed by the city. When she'd last lived in Cambridge, her car had been towed at least once each season.

The costs to retrieve her car were bound to be prohibitive. To add insult to injury, not only did the city kidnap your car, but they made the victim pay for the tow, a hefty parking fine and storage fees. And that was only after you managed to discover where the car had been taken and make your way over there with proof of ownership, which you had probably left in your glove compartment.

Sylvie had no time to track down her car, nor could she spare the money to pay the fines. It was only a matter of time before the repo men found it, anyway. Let Herb Chambers track his own car down, she thought as she made her way to the corner taxi stand. Once she would have summoned a Lyft, but without a functioning credit card, that was no longer an option.

Behind the wheel of the first cab in line sat a woman close to her own age with mocha colored skin, big hair and the determined expression of someone capable of running a small nation. Sylvie climbed inside. "Flour Bakery, Fort Point Channel, please."

As the cab pulled out into Mass Avenue traffic, Sylvie glanced at the ID card attached to the back of the front seat. It showed a Desiree Jefferson wearing an expression so fierce that no sane customer would dare consider skipping out on the fare.

"Great choice. But you do know there's one right down Mass Ave, right?" Desiree asked without turning around.

"I didn't, but good to know," Sylvie said. "I'm new to the neighborhood. Sort of. But I'm meeting someone down there. Sort of."

"Got it. Sort of." Desiree winked into the rearview mirror.

Sylvie immediately liked this woman. She looked so fierce in the photo, but her smile made Sylvie want to lay her head on her ample bosom and tell her all her troubles. "I was wondering if you'd be willing to wait outside the bakery? I won't be long," Sylvie said.

Desiree glanced again into her mirror. "Sure. But I'd have to leave the meter running. You coming back to Cambridge?"

"I'm not sure. It depends."

"No problem. I'll wait."

"And would you mind terribly if I waited with you and we stayed someplace where we can watch the bakery without being seen?"

Desiree's eyes darted once more into the mirror, then quickly back to the crawling traffic. "Honey, we can do whatever you want, so long as you pay the tab."

Sylvie couldn't even think about the money she was spending. It made her want to puke.

"You want to tell me what we're doing? Are there guns involved?" Desiree's tone was surprisingly nonchalant.

"Guns? No. Not yet, anyway. My husband took off with all of our savings. I'm trying to track him down and I found out he's got a meeting there."

"I've always wanted to do this stuff. How long you think this meeting's gonna take?"

"Not long. The other guy isn't going to show."

They found a spot in a small parking lot across the street from the bakery.

Desiree turned off the motor. "You want to tell me what this jerk looks like so I can help watch?"

"He's white, late thirties, around six feet, fit, brown hair and glasses. And he drives a red Jaguar."

"A Jag? Whoa. Midlife crisis?"

"Ya think?"

"So, how long 'til the meeting?"

Sylvie glanced at her watch. "Ten minutes."

"Think there's time for me to step inside for a cup of coffee and a pee? You could wait here and text me if you spot him."

"Mark's always very punctual. He arrives exactly on time. Not late, not early. And he'll wait exactly fifteen minutes before he leaves in a huff. He calls it the 'fifteen minute rule,' and there are no exceptions."

"Sounds like a real laid-back dude. You want anything?"

Sylvie yearned for a grande soy cappuccino with cinnamon. "Just coffee. Black." She dug in her purse for change.

"That's okay. This is on me." Desiree handed Sylvie a card with her cell phone number, hauled herself out of the car and slammed the door.

Sylvie scrunched down in her seat, trying to watch all directions while keeping her head low and out of sight.

A few minutes later, the door of the bakery swung open. Desiree emerged just as Mark turned the corner and approached on foot. Desiree held the door open for him, then headed toward Sylvie in the cab.

"That our boy?" Desiree asked as she handed Sylvie a bear claw and a large covered cup.

"That's him." Sylvie peeled off the lid and discovered a cloud of whipped cream sprinkled with cinnamon. She mentally calculated the calories but weighed them against appearing ungrateful for the generous gesture, along with her own longing for the sugar and caffeine. Those feelings grew exponentially as she watched Mark through the window of the café. He chose a table next to a window and consulted his watch every two minutes.

The hot coffee warmed her, and she sighed with pleasure as she bit into the bear claw. It tasted even better than it looked.

"Good, huh?" Desiree mumbled through a mouthful of pastry. "Best in town."

"Sounds like you've done your research," Sylvie said.

"I'd better. My sister and I are planning to open a bakery. I gotta know the competition."

"So, the cab thing isn't—"

"A career choice? Hardly. But it pays the bills for now."

"You're not scared of being held up?"

"These days people mostly use credit cards, so there's not much cash. I'm more worried about some drunk jerk throwing up and having to pay to get it cleaned. That's why I only drive during the day. I'm taking business classes at night at Harvard extension."

"Business?"

"My sister's a genius in the kitchen. But she couldn't add a column of numbers if her life depended on it."

Through the window, exactly on schedule, they watched Mark stand and storm out the door, a vein throbbing furiously in his forehead.

"Should I follow him?" Desiree asked.

"Yes, please. I need to know where he's staying."

"Hang on." Desiree eased out of the lot.

Mark turned the corner, walked another block and climbed into his parked car.

Good. It would have been much harder to follow him if he'd taken the T.

Desiree stayed just the right distance behind, blending into downtown traffic. The Jag turned onto Congress Street, then onto Seaport Boulevard, and entered the gated underground parking beneath the Harborview, a new luxury condominium building situated directly on the water.

They watched as Mark leaned out of the window and entered a code into a keypad. The gate lifted and Mark's Jag disappeared inside.

"What next, Sherlock? You want me to follow him on foot?" Desiree asked.

"You'd do that?"

"Why not? I'm on the clock."

Five minutes later, Desiree returned to the cab and settled into the driver's seat. "I couldn't get past the concierge. But I watched his elevator go up and stop on the fifth floor. Place has some serious security. You wanna hang here and see if he comes back out?"

"I can't. I've got to get back to my girls, and I can't afford any more of your time. You should probably let me out at South Station. I'll take the T back from there."

Desiree switched off the meter. "Don't worry about it. I'm heading back to Cambridge anyway."

When they pulled up in front of her building, Sylvie pulled her wad of cash from her pocket and peeled off the bills, adding a tip to the meter reading. "Thank you. I couldn't possibly repay you for what you did today."

"You got my card with my cell. You need me, give me a call."

Twenty

Sylvie could hear the yelling long before she reached the fourth floor. A major battle was raging.

"Leave my stuff alone, you little shit." It was Diana. "What the hell do you have that needs to be hung up? You don't own any decent clothes."

"I'm warning you," screamed Claire as Sylvie unlocked the apartment door, "move your crap or you'll be sorry."

The building dated from the early 1920s, when working class families had few clothes and little need for storage. Apparently, Diana had claimed the entire meager closet for herself.

Claire was trying to snatch Diana's clothes out of the closet and Diana was energetically guarding her turf, while Sugarbear barked excitedly from the safety of Claire's bed.

Sylvie poked her head in the bedroom door.

"Mom, this isn't going to work. I can't live like this," Diana wailed. "You can't possibly expect me to fit all my stuff into this pathetic excuse for a closet."

"You only get half this pathetic excuse for a closet," Claire said as she sent an armful of her sister's clothing flying across the room.

The girls had drawn a chalk line down the middle of their new bedroom. Boxes had been ripped apart, and their contents seemed to have exploded all over the room.

Sylvie had hoped for a calming cup of tea. Her head throbbed, and all she wanted in the world was peace and quiet so she could think about how

Mark could have managed to land in a luxury apartment on the waterfront. "Both of you. Stop. Diana, you get half the closet. Work it out."

She stepped aside as Diana stormed past her and slammed the door to the bathroom. Sylvie escaped into the kitchen and was just heating the water in the kettle when Claire called out that she was taking Sugarbear for a walk.

A few minutes later, Sylvie heard the bathroom door open, then the girls' bedroom door close. She crept toward the bedroom and listened outside the closed door. Something about the silence was eerie. No yelling, no barking, no music playing. Nothing. She knocked. No answer. She turned the knob and opened the door. There sat Diana, looking like someone in a state of shock. No earphones plugged into her ears. She sat, staring into space, tears silently streaming down her face.

Sylvie approached warily. "Sweetie, are you okay?"

Diana's eyes met hers. "I hate you," she whispered. "I hate Dad and Claire and you and I wish I was dead."

Sylvie sat down on the bed. "What happened?"

"My life is over and it's all your fault."

Sylvie steeled herself for the worst. "Tell me."

Diana took a ragged breath. "I texted Bobby Wise and he hasn't texted me back."

Sylvie reeled with relief. "Maybe he's busy and he'll text you later."

"No. It's over. He's never ignored me before."

"Why don't you give him a little time?"

"Madison Reynolds texted that Bobby Wise's mother said I live too far away for her to drive him to see me."

"Bobby's mom can drop him at the T in Newton and he can take the train in. You can hang out in Harvard Square."

"Bobby's mom said there are drug dealers in Cambridge. Bobby told Jared who's dating Madison that I'm not worth the hassle."

Sylvie stood up. "Then screw Bobby Wise. Come on. Let's make dinner."

Diana flopped back on the bed. "You don't get it," she sobbed.

As Sylvie closed the door softly behind her, she murmured, "May this be the worst thing that ever happens to you." It hadn't been all that long since Sylvie herself had thought her entire future happiness depended on some random boy whose name she'd long since forgotten.

While Sylvie was taking stock of her options for dinner in the kitchen, the door to number four banged open. Claire, Sugarbear and Kevin, the kid from moving day, tumbled in.

"Diana, come look who I found." Claire yelled and threw open the bedroom door, exposing Diana, mid-meltdown, sprawled on the bed.

Claire froze in the doorway. "What's your problem?"

Diana lifted her head, glimpsed Kevin starring at her and hissed, "Shut the fucking door."

Sylvie took Kevin's elbow and steered him firmly toward the kitchen. "How about a snack or something to drink?" Sylvie asked loudly in an effort to distract him from the angry voices coming from the bedroom.

Finally Claire emerged. "Mom, can me, Kevin and Diana listen to music at the Pit? Connor's band is playing."

Sylvie hesitated. While Kevin and Connor were slightly older than her girls, she had watched them carefully during the move. They both treated the girls as they would younger sisters. Her maternal instincts were usually pretty good, and she felt the girls were safe with these boys. But the Pit in Harvard Square, at the entrance to the T Station, was a popular gathering place for young people as well as an infamous shopping mall for drugs.

"We'll all stay together, and we'll walk the girls home," Kevin said. "The Pit's cool whenever there's a band playing because there are cops everywhere. And Connor's sister, Maddie, will be there. She's Diana's age. She's cool."

"Please, Mom? Even Sugarbear can come, because it's outside." Claire batted her eyelids at her mother, a move designed to dissolve any parental objections.

"Did Diana agree to go?"

"She's spackling makeup over her zits now."

Sylvie weighed the choice between having Diana weeping in the next room or making friends in her new community. "Okay," she said.

A few minutes later, Diana emerged from the bedroom, remarkably recovered from her suicidal depression, wearing a little too much make-up and blush.

Sylvie let it go. She reached for her purse and extracted a precious ten-dollar bill. "Ice cream is on me," she said as she handed the money to Claire.

"What about dinner?" asked Claire.

Sylvie had forgotten about feeding her kids. What was wrong with her?

"Tacos on us," Kevin said.

Sylvie glanced at the girls, who nodded enthusiastically. "Home by ten or I come find you. Wearing the purple hat."

The hideous purple hat decorated with enormous red poppies was Sylvie's secret parenting weapon. She had bought the abomination at a garage sale years ago and used it to threaten the girls with total humiliation whenever she needed to establish her ultimate authority. Claire couldn't have cared less, but it worked like a charm on Diana.

Sylvie watched the three of them hustle out the door with Sugarbear. Then she pulled Desiree's card from her jeans pocket and mentally calculated how far she could stretch her remaining assets.

Desiree answered on the first ring.

"Do you know anyone who might be interested in doing some surveillance work?" Sylvie asked.

"You want to find out if your old man is living in that fancy condo building?"

"Yes," said Sylvie. "Can you help me?"

Twenty One

Sylvie waited on the sidewalk in front of her building as a dark green minivan with tinted windows pulled up. Desiree stuck her head out the passenger-side window and waved. Sylvie slid open the side door and climbed into the back seat, then shoved the door closed behind her. The minivan took off, heading toward Memorial Drive.

The driver looked to be Hispanic, in his twenties, but it was hard to tell because he wore a baseball cap pulled low over his eyes.

Desiree twisted to face Sylvie. "This is my friend, Raul. He works for a private detective."

Without turning, Raul raised his hand in greeting.

Desiree continued, "Raul charges twenty-five an hour plus travel time and gas. Cash only. He's not licensed yet, so he's not supposed to be doing this, and he says if you get him in trouble he'll come and find you. I *think* he's kidding. I'm along for the hell of it."

Sylvie looked at the rearview mirror and caught Raul glancing at her. He said nothing. She smiled nervously, but Raul's face remained blank.

When they arrived at the Harborview, Raul asked in a soft voice, "What's your husband's name?"

"Mark Wolff," Sylvie said, suddenly not sure she wanted to confirm what she suspected—that her husband was living in this swanky building and he wasn't living here alone.

"Hand me that package," Raul said, nodding toward a small box on the floor of the van. Sylvie handed it to him. He wrote Mark's name on the package, then left, slamming the door behind him. As he walked away, Sylvie saw he wore a ubiquitous Boston Red Sox tee shirt that he filled out nicely. Several other tee shirts and baseball caps were stacked on the seat beside her.

When he was gone, Sylvie asked, "So, how do you know Raul?"

Desiree shifted in her seat. "He's a friend of my baby brother. I've known him since we were kids."

"And he's okay? I mean, he's not dangerous? He seems a little dangerous."

"Mostly he's fine," said Desiree. "But you need to be careful with him. His dad was some kind of crazy hit man for Whitey Bulger's Winter Hill Gang. They called him 'the Whacker.'"

"His father's a hit man?"

"He's been in jail forever. Raul hasn't seen him since he was little. I get the feeling he hates the guy. Not that he talks about him."

"I thought the Winter Hill Gang were all Irish."

"Long story."

Raul climbed back into the van, minus the package. He took a small notebook out of his pocket, ripped off the page and handed it to Sylvie. It read: *Apt 502.*

"How did you learn that?" Desiree asked.

Raul settled himself into the driver's seat and buckled his seat belt. "I watched the concierge write the number on the package."

"What was in the package?" Sylvie asked.

"A lovely free bank calendar. He's gonna love it," Raul said. "What do you want to do now?"

Sylvie checked her watch. It was only six-thirty. She had plenty of time before the girls got home. "Can we wait for an hour and see if he shows up?"

Raul shrugged. "I got the time if you got the cash. But if you're thinking about confronting him, you might be better off going home and sleeping on it first."

Sylvie shook her head. "If I think about it, I'll chicken out."

Raul pulled the van across the street where they had a view of the underground garage entrance. He reached into the glove compartment, retrieved a small electronic device and attached it to his phone just as Desiree yelped, "Sweet Jesus, here he comes."

The red Jag turned the corner and stopped at the security gate, giving Raul time to snap a photo of the license plate. The gate went up and the Jag disappeared into the garage.

Sylvie shoved open the sliding door and jumped out. Behind her, she heard Raul ask Desiree, "Does she have a weapon?"

Sylvie ducked under the security gate and caught up to Mark as he climbed out of the Jag.

He didn't see her until he turned and they collided. Mark looked like he was going to wet himself.

Though it had only been a few days since they'd last spoken, it felt to Sylvie like a lifetime. She crossed her arms in front of her chest and asked, "Is there anything you forgot to tell me the other morning when you left for Palo Alto?"

His eyes darted from one end of the garage to the other, landing on everything but her. "There's nothing to say."

"What about 'goodbye?'"

A Mini Cooper entered the garage and pulled into a numbered space twenty feet away. Two impeccably dressed women in their forties climbed out.

Sylvie felt her voice go up an octave. "What about 'I'm not coming back and by the way, I've taken all our money and the house is about to be foreclosed so you and our kids might want to look for a place to live?'"

The two women from the Mini Cooper paused to stare at them.

Sylvie swung around to confront them. "Do you mind? This is private."

They hastened toward the elevator, glancing back over their shoulders.

"What's going on, Mark?" Sylvie could hear the pleading in her voice. "Please, talk to me." She didn't care if she sounded pathetic. She needed answers.

Mark stared down at his shoes. "I want a divorce."

"Just like that?" She touched his arm and he shrank back. Who was this stranger? What had happened to the man she'd shared her life with all these years?

He turned his back on her and walked toward the elevator, where the two women waited nervously.

Sylvie blinked. When had her husband come to hate her? She called after him, "Where's our money, Mark?"

"It's gone," he spat over his shoulder.

She chased after him. "Gone where?"

He jabbed the elevator button though it was already red. "Invested. I can't get my hands on it right now. If you'd only had a little faith—"

The two women stepped to the side and focused hard on the numbers that showed the elevator descending excruciatingly slowly.

"Faith in what?" Sylvie demanded.

Mark jabbed the button again. "In me."

With a glance at each other, the two women opened the door to the stairwell and disappeared inside.

Sylvie waited for the door to close behind them. "I don't understand."

"That's my point."

She felt strangely removed, as if she was watching herself on a television screen. "What am I supposed to do?" she asked but even as she said it, she wondered at herself. Why did she always ask Mark what to do?

He spoke as if the answer was obvious. "I'm selling the apartment."

"You can't. It's mine, and we have nowhere else to go."

For the first time, he turned and faced her. "It's a done deal. You already signed over your power of attorney to me. Remember?"

She raised her chin. "Quit bluffing, Mark. You don't have the papers, so you can't sell it."

The elevator doors opened and he stepped inside. "We'll see about that." The doors closed behind him.

Sylvie stared after him. When she finally turned away, she was surprised to see Raul's minivan inside the garage, waiting only a few feet away. She climbed in and sank into the back seat. "How did you get inside?"

Raul held up his phone with the electronic device attached. "Thermal imaging. It read the heat from the keypad where Mark touched it."

"You have the code? What is it?" Sylvie asked.

Raul guided the van out of the garage and onto the Mass Pike. "Sorry, can't risk it."

Sylvie was about to say something rude, but a sharp look from Desiree stopped her. She swallowed her response and hugged herself.

Raul glanced at her over his shoulder. "Did that little convo tell you what you needed to know?"

Sylvie didn't answer, offended by the fact that Raul assumed she would do something stupid with Mark's key code—though, were she completely honest with herself, she could see his point.

Besides, she was frantically sifting through years of conversations in her mind. What exactly had Mark said about starting his own business? Sure, he had complained a lot about his bosses not being as smart and forward-thinking as he was. The big bad corporate executives had refused to listen to reason. They said there were holes in Mark's logic. That Mark's ideas for breaking new ground in cyber security and global hacking weren't developed enough to be worth the risk for their company. No imagination, Mark had complained.

And he had threatened to go off on his own and show everyone that he was the Bill Gates of cyber security.

When he'd approached Sylvie with his plan, she'd asked whether it made sense for Mark to risk all their savings and their home if an up-and-coming company like Templeton & Brewer didn't feel comfortable investing their considerable resources in Mark's ideas. Mark usually went on to something else pretty quickly, and the argument never seemed terribly serious.

Maybe she should have paid closer attention.

Desiree touched Sylvie's arm. "Are you okay?"

Sylvie jerked to attention. "What? Fine. I'm fine."

"Raul asked if you found out what you needed to know."

"I know my husband hates me. And he deserted us to start his own business."

Raul glanced into the rearview mirror. "What kind of business?"

Sylvie sighed. "Who knows? His passion is cyber security. He was always coming up with some groundbreaking new software that would accomplish something remarkable if only the powers that be would give him enough money to develop it. He never talked about it much with me. Whenever he'd try to explain, my eyes would glaze over. I guess he sort of gave up. I should have taken a class or something."

The van pulled up in front of Sylvie's building and she leaned forward to open the sliding door.

"What's next?" Desiree asked.

Sylvie sank back into the seat. "I don't know. Somehow I have to find a job and raise my kids without their father. And figure out where our money went and get it back. But at the moment, I can't afford a lawyer. And I don't think Mark has the money, anyway."

"So, how can he afford to live on the waterfront," Desiree asked, "in the most expensive real estate in town?"

Sylvie pressed her fingers against her temples. "He's not living there alone, is he?"

Raul and Desiree looked at each other, then at Sylvie, who fished some twenties out of her wallet and handed them to Raul. "Does this cover it?"

Raul nodded, and took the bills.

"I really appreciate everything you did," she said. "Maybe if I can get my hands on some cash, we could figure out the rest."

Raul tipped up the brim of his cap and regarded her from head to toe. "How about a quid pro quo?"

Sylvie's hand flew to her chest. "I'm not quite that desperate."

He pulled the brim back down and suppressed a smile. "Me either. I meant I need a MILF your age on a surveillance case. Let me know if you're interested."

He handed her a business card and waited for her to climb out before heading down Green Street. Sylvie stood on the curb, unsure whether she'd been propositioned, insulted or offered employment.

Twenty Two

Early Saturday morning, Sylvie emerged from the Blue Line T stop at the Aquarium Station, dressed in a maroon Escada suit and black Manolo Blahnik pumps. She'd left the girls to sleep in with a note to call her when they got up. They'd earned a sleep-in.

The night before, when they returned jubilant from the concert, both girls had surprised Sylvie by pitching in to the task of unpacking boxes and arranging their shared space without complaint. They'd fallen in love with Sugarbear. Despite her own feelings toward Mark, Sylvie found it somewhat disconcerting that given the choice between returning to their old life in Weston with Mark and staying in Cambridge with Sugarbear, their preference for Cambridge seemed clear.

Sylvie could imagine the pain on his face if he knew his kids preferred their new puppy over their father. Then she wondered if he'd even care.

Outside the Aquarium, Sylvie paused to watch the sea lions frolicking in their outdoor exhibit. When the girls were young, this had been their favorite spot in the city. The whole family would take the train into town, an adventure in itself, and watch the young sea lions slide off the rocks and splash into their pool. Lunch was clam chowder from Legal Seafood, devoured on benches overlooking Boston Harbor. For dessert they'd eat ice cream cones drowning in chocolate sprinkles in a messy, melting race against the beating sun.

But that was before Diana was old enough for winter trips to Aspen and summers on Nantucket to become minimum requirements for social acceptance among her peers.

Sylvie lingered as long as she could, then tore herself away from the sea lions and the laughing children to make her way along the waterfront. Was it her mood, or had the sky suddenly become darker? She looked up and saw purple clouds gathering, threatening to block the sun.

She hurried a little faster, hoping to get inside before the deluge. The day had started out so beautifully. She had neglected to bring a jacket, never mind an umbrella.

The air smelled briny, a combination of the seaweed, fish and salt water of Boston Harbor. It was a good smell, one she could get used to. Then again, there was little chance she could ever afford to live around here.

She stepped into the Harborview lobby with her most sophisticated smile and approached the concierge with all the fake confidence she could muster.

"I'm here to see Mark Wolff. He's expecting me," she lied, wishing she'd been able to coax Mark's key code from Raul so she could really surprise him.

The concierge was a small man in his mid-forties with a fringe of salt and pepper hair and an optimistic comb-over. "Your name, please?" he asked.

"Mrs. Wolff," she said. "I'm his wife."

The man's eyes opened wide. He pressed a button on the intercom.

A female voice answered, "Yes?"

"Mrs. Wolff is here to see Mr. Wolff," he said. *Was that a hint of glee in his voice?*

There was a pause. Then the voice said, "He isn't here." Something was familiar about that voice.

The concierge raised his eyebrows inquiringly at Sylvie, who announced loudly, "I can wait."

The voice asked, "Is she alone?"

Before he could answer, Sylvie leaned in close to the intercom and said, "I'm alone and I'm unarmed."

"Send her up."

Sylvie stepped inside the elevator and the concierge pushed a button. The doors slid shut. Sylvie watched the numbers overhead light up one at a time as the elevator climbed.

On the fifth floor, the doors opened. Sylvie stepped out of the elevator, directly into a magnificent white room encased in floor to ceiling windows that provided an expansive view of Boston Harbor. Her feet sank into the plush carpet, and she noted a spicy vanilla scent emanating from three pure white orchid stems.

Lisa Chang, who had developed a bathroom emergency when Sylvie last saw her, stepped forward, holding out her hand. Dressed in a midnight-blue caftan, the only color among all that white, she looked like a China doll. Her silken hair, usually pinned up, hung down her back like raining ebony.

Sylvie's arm remained glued to her side.

Lisa Chang, the brilliant chair of the Research and Development Department at Templeton & Brewer, of whom Mark had always spoken in the most glowing terms.

So Mark and Lisa were shacked up in Lisa's fancy waterfront apartment. Perfect.

Lisa dropped her hand. "Mark isn't here."

"So I heard."

"Is there something you want?"

Sylvie almost laughed. Damn straight there was something she wanted. She wanted her old life back, and she wanted Lisa Chang lying in a pool of blood at her feet.

"I want to speak to my husband," Sylvie said. "We have things to work out."

"I'll tell him you stopped by."

Sylvie stepped to the window. The view was indeed breathtaking. Through the scrimmed blinds, she could see the yachts in the harbor and the Channel Islands beyond. "Mark seems to have landed on his feet," she said. "It's too bad his children and I haven't been as lucky. But then, we didn't see this coming, and apparently he did."

"It's your own fault, you know."

Sylvie resisted the urge to smack Lisa's porcelain face. "I had no idea any of this was going on."

"My point exactly. Mark is a genius. You're his wife and you have no idea what he's capable of."

"You're right. I had no idea he was capable of being a thief and a coward."

"Standing up for himself and his dream is not cowardly," Lisa said, with a toss of her shimmering hair.

Sylvie could only imagine what that hair toss would do to a red-blooded heterosexual male.

"And he had the right to invest in himself with the money *he* earned," Lisa said. She stepped closer to Sylvie. Sylvie had the urge to step back, but held her ground.

Lisa crossed her arms. "He's never coming back to you."

"Why would you think I'd take him? I simply want my money."

"Good luck with that." Lisa pushed the elevator button, and the doors opened.

Sylvie didn't move.

Lisa pressed the intercom button. "Ms. Wolff is coming down now." She lifted her finger from the button and let it hover in the air as she turned back to Sylvie. "Or should I call security?"

Sylvie stepped into the elevator.

***

Walking the block between the Central Square T and home beneath black billowing clouds and the sound of distant thunder, Sylvie tried to absorb it all. Mark was living in luxury while she struggled to keep his children fed and a roof over their heads. Fury and righteous indignation started a low, simmering roil in her gut.

As she neared her home, she heard loud voices coming from her building.

She couldn't make out the words, but the voices were so familiar that the hackles went up on the back of her neck. She picked up her pace as much as she could in her high heels and passed LaVonda squatting on her usual stoop sheltered by an overhang, just as the sky opened and sheets of rain poured down.

"Hey, girlie," LaVonda rasped through a soggy haze of smoke and rain. "I think you'd better hurry on home." Her finger jabbed toward the top floor of Sylvie's building in a get-yourself-up-there-now gesture.

Sylvie entered her building dripping wet and hurried past Jack Ramsdale's partially open door. She took the stairs two at a time all the way to the top where the door to her apartment stood wide open. Inside, she heard Claire sob, "I'm not leaving her."

Just inside the door to number four, Mark stood blocking the entry, a suitcase in each hand. "Put that damn dog down and get downstairs," he stormed.

A hysterical Claire, clutching a frightened, squealing Sugarbear to her chest, pushed past her father into Sylvie's arms. "He won't let me keep Sugarbear," she sobbed.

"How did you get in here?" Sylvie demanded, her arms around a shaking Claire.

Diana stepped out of the shadows behind Mark. "I let him in. He says we have to go with him." Tears streamed down her face. "And I have to start school in Boston because you can't afford to take care of us. And just when we'd made friends with some really cool kids from Cambridge."

Sylvie snorted. "Wow, Mark. Guess I underestimated you again."

"So you didn't tell him to come get us?" Claire asked, her eyes wide with confusion.

"Of course not. You're not going anywhere." Sylvie gently pushed Claire behind her and rounded on Mark. "You bloody, bold-faced liar. How fucking dare you?"

"They can't stay here." Mark put down the suitcases. "I'm selling this apartment."

"You can't sell this apartment because it's not yours," Sylvie said.

Diana grabbed both suitcases, ran back to the bedroom and slammed the door.

"Does Lisa know about this? Does she really want two teenagers in her ridiculously white apartment?" Sylvie asked.

Claire's tremulous voice came from behind Sylvie. "Who's Lisa?"

"The woman your father deserted us for. His boss."

"She's not my boss anymore. She's my partner," Mark said, trying to pry Sugarbear from Claire's grip.

Sugarbear's upper lip curled upward into a snarl.

"What the hell is wrong with you, Mark?" asked Sylvie.

Sugarbear gave a low, warning growl.

"What's wrong with me? You're the one who can't face reality," Mark said, ignoring the warning.

Sugarbear's puppy teeth sank into the soft flesh of Mark's hand.

He yelped and let go.

Still clutching Sugarbear, Claire squeezed past her distracted father and scurried to the bedroom where she banged on the door, yelling, "Let us in."

Her sister opened the door, snatched Claire and Sugarbear inside, and slammed the door again. Sylvie heard the lock click into place.

"Oh, I may be a little behind, but I'm catching up fast," Sylvie said.

"That mutt better not have rabies. Get me a clean towel," Mark demanded in that imperious tone Sylvie was now realizing she despised.

Sylvie stepped forward, forcing him backwards toward the door. "Get your own damn towel. And if I were you, I'd get some shots. Lots of them. The painful kind. Posthaste. Sugarbear's a stray. Probably rabid."

Mark stepped back across the threshold. "I'm going to sue for custody. And I'm going to have that mongrel put down."

"Fuck you." Sylvie slammed the door and shoved the deadbolt home. She listened by the door until she heard his footsteps recede down the stairs, then she ran to the front window, opened it wide and leaned out to where she could see Mark emerge from the building onto the street below. He paused to speak to Jack Ramsdale, who stood on the street, glancing up at her window. Sylvie couldn't hear what they were saying but she could imagine them plotting the best way to extricate her from number four.

Ramsdale had probably only been nice to her so he could get his hands on her unit. And it had been such a long time since an attractive man had flirted with her that she had almost fallen for his act.

Well, reality was a bitch, but she had kids to protect. She knocked on the girls' door.

Claire's voice came from inside. "Is he gone?"

"He's gone."

The doorknob turned. Claire, her face wet with tears, opened the door and stepped aside to let her mother in. Sugarbear trembled in the corner and a Diana-sized lump lay on the bed, hidden under the covers. Sylvie sat down next to it.

A remorseful Sugarbear tunneled her way behind Sylvie's legs to wedge herself between Sylvie and the bed. Sylvie scooped her up and kissed the pink nose. "Good job," she said. "You are a fierce and feisty little bitch."

Diana's muffled voice asked, "What's wrong with Dad?"

"He's being an idiot." Sylvie patted the lump that was Diana. "He must be in love."

"With his boss lady?" Claire asked. She reached for Sugarbear, depositing the dog onto her lap, where the puppy turned a few times and collapsed, exhausted.

"It appears so."

"Aren't we even going to get the 'I'm not divorcing you, I'm divorcing your mother' speech?" Diana asked.

Claire reached for a tissue and blew her nose. "At least that's what he's supposed to say at first. Then when he gets married again and has more kids, he'll ignore us more and more. But it's not supposed to happen so fast."

Sylvie couldn't suppress a smile. "How do you guys know so much about it?"

Diana's head emerged from under the blanket, her eyes red from crying. "Happens all the time. The Webbers, the Kirkpatricks. First there's a big fight over custody. Then the dad remarries and has a new family and either the older kids have to babysit all the time or they get ignored."

"Honest, I never saw this coming," Sylvie said.

Claire lifted her chin and looked at her mother. "Mom?"

"What is it, Claire?"

"Dad told us to go to our room and pack a suitcase."

"I know, honey."

"And then he closed our door."

Sylvie looked at Diana, who shrugged.

Claire looked guilty, and her voice halted. "He went in your room and it sounded like he was going through your stuff, looking for something."

Twenty Three

Sylvie's tiny bedroom looked like a burglar had ransacked it. Most of the boxes hung open, their contents spilled everywhere. The blanket and pillow from the foldout chair had been tossed to the corner.

That sneaky bastard. He must have been looking for the Power of Attorney document.

Thank goodness she had destroyed it. *Take that, Mark. Score one for the home team.*

She straightened her room, brushing off each item with her fingers, erasing Mark's presence as she restored her space to its normal level of chaos.

It had only been a week since Sylvie's life had turned into one long clusterfuck, but it felt so much longer. Her life had changed in ways she could never have anticipated.

She started a mental list of problems she needed to tackle immediately: one, research a health care alternative. Two: raise some cash. Three: get a job.

It was all so overwhelming.

Raul's business card lay on the side table where she'd left it.

She picked it up, considered, then called the number.

It rang several times, then, "*Hola. Digame.*"

"Raul?"

"*Si*, Senora Wolff. So, you want the job?"

"What *is* the job?"

"Nothing illegal. Not even immoral—really."

"What exactly does that mean?" Sylvie asked.

"Don't worry about it. We swap. Two hours of your time for one hour of mine."

"How about one for one? Even swap?"

"How about take it or leave it?"

She paused, puzzled at the little butterfly of a thrill fluttering around in her stomach. She mentally calculated her remaining cash along with the jewelry and designer clothing she could sell versus her family's immediate financial needs. Would her time be better spent finding out what had happened to their considerable savings or working in a low-paying job?

"I'll take it," she said.

She could afford a couple of weeks to track down her money. If she failed, she would have to find a way to earn some kind of living.

"Fine. I'll pick you up at eight fifteen. Dress sophisticated. You know, rich but classy."

Sylvie hung up the phone and evaluated the reduced wardrobe she'd brought to her new life until the yelling startled her out of her reverie. She took her time getting to her feet, figuring if both girls were making that much noise, neither was seriously injured. She padded down the hall and opened their bedroom door.

"Get your disgusting clothes off my side." Claire grabbed an armload of clothes from the closet and hurled them across the room where they landed on Sylvie's head.

She batted them off in time to see Diana yank Claire's hair. Claire twisted around, fists raised while Sugarbear barked from the safety of the bed.

Sylvie shoved each girl down onto a bed, opposite each other, with slightly more force than she intended. "No touching. Sit. Talk. Work it out. I mean it." She made herself very large. "Or you'll both be sorry."

She slipped out of the room before she was forced to be any more specific.

After a period of relative calm when no sounds of violence had come from the girls' bedroom, Sylvie silently congratulated herself on her parenting.

She sat down at her computer.

A few minutes later, Diana passed her in the living room, headed for the door. "Connor's sister, Maddie, called. I'm meeting her and some of her friends down by the river."

Sylvie returned to her job search.

Half an hour later, when Claire called out, "I'm taking Sugarbear for a walk," Sylvie never even looked up. The door slammed and she continued filling out an online application form for a temp agency, racking her brain for a list of useful skills she must surely possess.

She barely noticed when Claire came in with Sugarbear an hour later.

She was finishing the last application when Diana returned and headed straight for the bedroom.

She finally looked up when Diana flew at her, shrieking, "The little shit sold my clothes. *Mom, do* something!"

Claire peeked out from the hallway, looking sheepish yet defiant. "You told us to work it out. She had too many clothes, so I got rid of some of them."

Diana had murder in her eyes. "You little skid mark!"

Claire cautiously held out a wad of bills. "You can have the money. I only wanted half the closet."

Diana smacked Claire's hand away and the money went flying.

Claire held her ground. "I did you a favor. You dress like mall rat Barbie."

Diana fled to the bedroom and slammed the door.

Claire hung her head. "She acts like I don't even count."

"You'd better steer clear until the storm passes," Sylvie said.

Claire gathered up the money and handed it to Sylvie, who stared at the pile of cash in her hand. There must have been nearly two hundred dollars.

"Where did you sell the clothes?" Sylvie asked.

"That consignment shop on Franklin Street. 'Second Chances.'"

Sylvie thought about knocking on Diana's door, then decided to give her time to cool off. After all, she'd told them to work it out on their own.

***

Sylvie was chopping vegetables for soup when Diana emerged from her room carrying a suitcase. "I'm leaving," she said.

89

Sylvie looked up. "Where are you going?"

"To stay with Dad."

Sylvie put down the knife. "You talked to your father?"

"He's on his way. You can't stop me. Dad said so."

Sylvie leaned against the sink. "Are you sure? He's living with a woman. You might not like her." To say nothing of the fact that Lisa Chang didn't seem like the kind of woman who wanted a teenager messing up her relentlessly white home.

"He's my father."

A horn blared under the window and before Sylvie could think of a way to stop her, Diana stomped out the door. From the window, Sylvie watched helplessly as Diana climbed into Mark's Jag and disappeared, leaving Sylvie reeling from whiplash.

***

Later, Claire sat across from Sylvie, holding Sugarbear on her lap and looking miserable. "Aren't you going to make her come back?" she asked.

"No. She's too old for me to hold prisoner."

"Are you sad, Mom?"

"Of course. I'm sad every time one of you walks out that door. Sometimes I wish I could wrap both of you in bubble wrap to keep you safe. But that's not very practical."

"What if I wanted to live with Dad, too?"

Sylvie looked up. "Is that what you want?"

"Would you stop me?"

"No."

"Would you be sad?"

"Yes," Sylvie said.

"I don't want to live with him. I'm too mad at him. And he doesn't want Sugarbear."

They sat quietly for a while. Then Claire asked, "Did you meet the lady he's staying with?"

"I did."

"Was she nice?"

"Not to me."

"Do you think she'd be nice to me?"

"You'll need to find that out for yourself," Sylvie said.

"Do you think Dad loves her more than us?"

"I think that's something you should discuss with your father."

"He left us and moved in with her."

"Yes, he did," Sylvie said.

"So, he must love her more."

"It would appear so."

"If he changed his mind, could he come back?"

Sylvie started to answer, then stopped. When she thought about it, she didn't know how she felt. A part of her still longed for everything to go back to the way it had been. But she didn't know if that was possible any more. "He could come back to visit you girls," she said.

"Do you still love him?"

"I don't know," Sylvie said quietly. "Trust is a very big part of love between married people.

"Can I still love him?"

"Of course. He'll always be your father."

"Do I have to love him more than Sugarbear?"

"No. There aren't any rules about how much you have to love someone."

"I love you a lot," Claire said. She kissed her mother's cheek, then stuffed her earphones into her ears.

**

An hour later, dressed in a grey Chanel suit over a deep V-cut mauve blouse, Sylvie paused to tell Claire she was going out. Her make-up had been carefully applied and her hair swept up and held in place with a mother of pearl clip. Raul had said "sophisticated," and that was a look Sylvie could pull off.

Claire waved her off, not even bothering to look up, deep into a "Walking Dead" binge, courtesy of Jack Ramsdale's cable connection.

As she stood on the front stoop, waiting for Raul, Sylvie remembered her younger self, waiting in this very same spot all those years ago for a much younger Mark to pick her up. Back then, her life had been spread before her like a sumptuous feast, with too many choices to contemplate—an embarrassment of riches.

And she had made her choices and filled her plate with a husband and kids and a beautiful home and volunteer work and tennis. But had she ever really known the man she had chosen to share her life with? How could she have misjudged him so completely? What had happened to her life? How had she managed to lose it all so suddenly?

As she waited, pacing nervously, Jack Ramsdale approached from the direction of the T station. He passed her, nodded, then did a double take, turning to check her out again. Sylvie smiled to herself. She still had it when she needed it.

The van pulled up. She opened the door and hoisted herself into the passenger seat. Raul gave her a long look, scanning her up and down, then nodded his approval and hit the gas.

As they merged onto Storrow Drive, Raul handed her a grainy photo of a man in his mid-fifties. It looked as if it had been taken from a considerable distance, then blown up. The man was thick and swarthy with hair way too black for a man his age, a white shirt unbuttoned by one button too many, and a thick gold chain nested in an abundance of chest hair.

"That's your mark," Raul said. "Big Eddie Abruzzi. The man you need to get close to."

"Close to? How close do I have to get?"

"He'll be at the bar. Find a way to sit next to him. Be friendly. I'll be nearby, taking photos."

"What's this for? A divorce case? Am I being used to entrap this guy?"

"You're a decoy. And it's not a divorce case, at least not yet. A friend of mine needs these photos for leverage."

"And by leverage, you mean blackmail?"

Raul glanced over at her, then focused on the road.

She twisted to face him. "This better not be illegal. Blackmail is illegal."

"Taking photos isn't illegal, unless we take sound. Then it's illegal unless you get consent."

"You're splitting hairs. This is wrong."

Raul took the Copley Square exit and was immediately confronted with stop and crawl traffic. "Mike's an old friend of mine. He's in a tight jam with Big Eddie. The only thing that scares Big Eddie is his wife. He loves spending her inheritance."

"And if the wife goes away, so does the money?"

"You got it."

"How do you know he'll be interested in me?"

"Because he's interested in anything with—"

She cut him off. "I get it. So why not take a photo of him with whomever he picks up?"

"His wife's a pragmatist. Doesn't give a crap about the whores. But a classy lady like you—that's a threat."

"I'm classy?"

"In Big Eddie's world, you're a New York Twelve."

"Thank you? So my job is to do exactly what?"

"Flirt. Act like you're interested in him. Touch his hand, his face so I can get a picture, then excuse yourself and get the hell out of there." He glanced over at her and his eyes narrowed. "Do not go anywhere with him."

"Damn! I was hoping he'd be the perfect rebound. And where will you be?"

"Nearby. But if you see me, do not acknowledge me. At exactly nine fifteen, you turn into a pumpkin. Cross the street and lose yourself in the theater crowd at the Shubert—they'll be pouring out for intermission. Make sure he's not following you, then cut down the alley next to the Abbey Lane Restaurant. I'll be waiting in the van outside the food court on Stuart. Think you can do this?"

"What? Flirting?" She tossed her hair artfully, exposing her neck, hoisted and readjusted her boobs to achieve maximum cleavage.

He raised his eyebrows, then reached into his wallet and extracted a twenty-dollar bill. "Here," he said, "you're going to need this for drinks."

Sylvie swatted his hand away. "No, I'm not."

Raul grinned at her for the first time.

"What if Big Eddie's not there?" she asked.

"He will be. Sitting in the fourth barstool from the door. Every Saturday

93

night. He's a creature of habit."

"Do you think he's dangerous?" she whispered.

"Not to you. But you do not want to be alone with him. If it starts to get weird, get the hell out of there."

Twenty Four

Sylvie stepped inside the Intermission Tavern and let her eyes adjust to the dim light. The swarthy, middle-aged guy from the photo sat at the bar, fourth stool from the door, exactly where Raul said he'd be, wearing a loud Hawaiian shirt that strained to cover a generous gut. He looked confident, like a regular. No empty stools nearby, so she sat down at the other end of the bar and positioned herself so he could see her.

The bartender, a young woman with a long blond braid, probably a student at one of the many local colleges, asked, "What can I get you?"

"Do you have a wine list?" Sylvie asked.

The waitress nodded. She placed a menu in front of Sylvie, then turned to another customer.

Sylvie surveyed the room casually. When she caught Big Eddie's eyes on her, she let her eyes drift past him without pausing. Slowly, she crossed her legs, adjusting her skirt so it draped seductively over the top of her thigh.

The waitress leaned toward Sylvie to check in and Sylvie held up one finger. "Just give me a minute."

She dropped her napkin on the floor, slid off her stool and bent over to pick it up, offering a full view of her cleavage. Coming up, she risked a glance in Big Eddie's direction. His eyes were on her. She focused on smoothing the napkin on her lap, knowing she had Big Eddie's undivided attention and feeling twenty-five again.

When a powerful wave of cheap cologne assaulted her, making her eyes water, Sylvie didn't need to look up to know that Big Eddie was standing over her. He was enormous. She looked up at him through stinging eyes and smiled encouragingly.

Big Eddie glared at the young man in the Berkley College of Music sweatshirt sitting on her left, who quickly slid off his stool and moved to a table. Big Eddie plopped himself down on the vacated stool, signaled the waitress, then pointed to Sylvie.

The waitress nodded. Sylvie wasn't sure what the signal meant, but hoped it didn't mean "drug this woman's drink." Hopefully, Raul was somewhere in the bar with his camera, but Sylvie didn't dare look around to make sure.

"What's your name, gorgeous?" Big Eddie asked.

"Monica," Sylvie replied, thinking of her tennis friend, who hadn't bothered reaching out to her since the fiasco at the club.

"Get this little lady a glass of anything she wants," he said to the waitress. He turned to Sylvie. "Anything you want, honey. Sky's the limit."

Sylvie pointed to a Merlot on the menu and the waitress nodded and left.

Big Eddie leaned in. "Monica have a last name?"

Sylvie nearly gagged, overpowered by a smell that reminded her of Black Ice air freshener. She smiled up at him. "Does it matter?" she asked.

"Not to me, gorgeous."

He probably called all his hook-ups gorgeous because he couldn't be bothered to remember their names.

"What should I call you?" she asked.

"Most people call me Big Eddie. You can call me anything you want. But don't call me late for dinner." He paused, waiting.

Too late, Sylvie realized she was supposed to laugh. She chuckled, not at the tired joke but at the man's unabashed delight in himself, which could be a charming quality in a person with less exposed chest hair. Raul had better be getting the photos he needed, because she needed to get the hell out of here before she puked.

She placed her hand over Big Eddie's and smiled.

Thrilled by her response, he chatted on and on while she patted his arm occasionally. She longed to douse her entire body with hand sanitizer and climb into a giant condom, but she did her best to appear utterly enthralled, though she didn't register much of what he said. Something about how he owned a pool and a lot of other great stuff, though he never alluded to what he did to afford his extravagant toys.

Sylvie wondered what kind of woman could be attracted to a man who smelled like air freshener and bragged incessantly about his stuff.

After what seemed like an acceptable amount of time for Raul to take the photos he needed, Sylvie glanced at her phone, relieved to see it was 9:13. She announced that she was late to meet friends at the theater.

Big Eddie's face fell and his eyes darkened. Sylvie flashed back to her dating days. She'd seen that look before—the distinctive look of the spurned alpha male. He had put in a lot of brag time and apparently felt he deserved to get something for his trouble. She made a mental note that she could never again, under any circumstances, frequent the Intermission Tavern.

Sylvie touched his cheek, which felt like a porcupine, and told him that it had been a pleasure. Perhaps she'd be lucky enough to run into him again sometime.

She stood slowly, careful not to make any sudden moves, and edged toward the door. To her relief, Big Eddie remained perched on his barstool.

She stepped outside and felt a breeze at her back. She sucked in the air. Tremont Street might be crowded and noisy, but the smell of automobile exhaust was a huge relief from the stink inside.

To her horror she smelled it again, faint but distinct behind her, and she knew that Big Eddie had followed her outside. Without looking back, she stepped off the curb and hurried across the street. The smell followed her. She moved steadily, fighting the urge to dash for the theater entrance.

Ushers were propping open the Shubert's doors in anticipation of the smokers who could barely wait for the house lights to come on, signaling intermission. Sylvie slipped inside as a stream of smokers hurried outside to light up.

She plastered herself against the wall, waiting for the lobby to fill and conceal her before edging back to the exit.

Ten feet away, she spotted Big Eddie hovering near the doorway. She scooted down, out of his line of sight, then turned and collided with Fran Forsythe, her former doubles partner.

"Sylvie," Fran yelped, seeming genuinely glad to see her.

Sylvie smiled, only too aware that Big Eddie had spotted her and was heading her way, through the thickening crowd.

Fran kissed the air vaguely in Sylvie's direction. "We've all been so worried about you. We got home from Aspen and saw a 'for sale' sign on your front lawn. No one knew where you'd gone. Are you and the girls all right?"

Not at the moment. "We're great. It's so good to see you."

"Are you here alone?" Fran asked.

"My friend stepped outside."

"Well, you look fabulous. We miss you at the club. Can we do lunch sometime?"

"Love to. How about we find each other after the show and make a date?" Sylvie said, backing away. She scooted off toward the far exit, thoroughly annoying a cranky man in a flannel jacket.

Sylvie trotted around the corner and ducked down the alley beside the Abbey Lane Restaurant, sticking to the shadows.

Raul's van was nowhere to be seen so she slipped inside the food court at City Place and leaned against the wall, where she had a clear view of the street. Outside, Big Eddie was heading toward her, pounding down the sidewalk like a hunter in search of prey. And he wasn't alone. Two large men in cheap suits followed close behind.

Shit. Her heart pounded and her mouth went dry. Big Eddie was one scary dude who did not take kindly to the word "no."

She needed to find Raul.

Twenty Five

Sylvie spotted a young woman with a body type similar to hers heading toward the ladies' room, and followed her inside.

A few minutes later, Sylvie emerged wearing skinny jeans, a brown Suffolk University windbreaker with the hood pulled down over her face and a worn pair of white Reeboks, half a size too small. Slung over her shoulder was a Northface backpack that reeked of weed.

She spotted Big Eddie and his entourage spread throughout the food court, each facing a different direction. The largest of the three, whose pink and green-checkered shirt clashed hideously with his plaid jacket, glanced her way, then continued searching.

Sylvie adopted a coed swagger and headed toward the exit. Outside, she spied the green van across the street, motor running, Raul at the wheel. She crossed the street casually and yanked the passenger door open.

Raul did a double take as Sylvie tossed the backpack to the floor and flung herself inside. She slammed the door, smashed down the lock and peered into the side mirror, holding up her hand to signal for Raul to wait. She needed to make sure she hadn't put the young woman in danger.

Big Eddie burst out of the food court and searched up and down the street.

When the Suffolk University co-ed exited the food court wearing Sylvie's Chanel suit and Manolo Blahniks, Big Eddie grabbed her shoulder roughly and spun her around. Without missing a beat, the co-ed raised her elbow to disengage his arm. In one fluid motion, she used his own momentum to smash her closed fist into his jaw, then pulled his head toward her to smash her raised knee into his groin. The last thing Sylvie saw as the van headed down Charles Street was Big Eddie crumpled on the sidewalk in a fetal position as the co-ed strode off toward the Boston Common with Sylvie's Coach bag slung jauntily over her shoulder.

Sylvie peeled off her hood. "That man is a psychopath," she choked. "You left me alone with a psychopath."

Raul grinned at her. "You did great. I got what I needed."

"Good. Because you bought yourself a Chanel suit, a pair of Manolo Blahniks and a vintage Coach bag."

"Fine." He paused. "How much are those worth?"

"About as much as your first-born son."

He raised his eyebrows. "I can think of a way to give you my first-born son for free. Say the word."

Sylvie felt herself blush. "Twenty-five hundred."

"In your dreams. For used clothes?"

"Those were classics. Their value increases with age." Sylvie pulled off the ill-fitting sneakers.

"Put it on my tab," he said.

Sylvie wiggled her toes. "Fine. You can work it off."

He gave her another smoldering Raul look.

"With your time," she stammered.

"Fine. We'll find out what your husband did with your money. Then we're even. You pay expenses. Deal?"

"Deal." She looked at him. "So, what exactly is the story with Big Eddie?"

"Need-to-know basis only."

"I need to know. If that man ever sees me again, I'm in trouble. Especially if you show him those pictures and he links me to whatever you've got going. So spill. Now."

After a moment's consideration he said, "You're right. The man's a psychopath. He's been trying to force a friend of mine to sell his store, which is next to Big Eddie's restaurant, so he can expand. My friend needs some leverage for pushback. Thanks to you, we got it."

Sylvie could tell there was more to the story, but she let it ride because they were pulling up to her building.

100

***

When Sylvie got home, Claire was sound asleep on the couch with Sugarbear on her chest. But there was a strange smell in the flat, like something had curled up and died. Sylvie hoped it wasn't a large rodent decomposing inside a wall.

She spent the next five minutes tracking the odor to a half-chewed unidentified wad of toilet paper abandoned on the bathroom floor. Sylvie lifted it gingerly with two fingers, dropped it into the trash bin, then snapped the leash on a guilty-looking Sugarbear. She carried the bin down the back stairs to the garbage cans outside with Sugarbear trailing along behind for her last pee of the night.

As they passed the back entrance to Jack's apartment, Sylvie could hear his voice through the door. "Okay, okay, I get it." He sounded seriously stressed.

A male voice with a heavy Slavic accent answered, "Then we have no problem."

"You'll have a problem collecting if I'm in the hospital," Jack responded.

Sylvie lingered, straining to hear, but the voices seemed to have moved away from the back door and Sylvie could no longer make out the words. When they stopped altogether, Sylvie went outside to deposit the garbage bag in the bin.

As she walked Sugarbear to the few patches of dirt on the street, she heard a motor start with a testosterone-laced roar. Peeking around the corner of the building she watched an incongruously long black Lincoln Continental, two wheels on the sidewalk, its lights blazing, bump down off the curb and drive away.

When she reentered the building, Sylvie noticed the original dumbwaiter—a charming feature of the building she'd forgotten. She'd loved the idea of it when she'd first moved in. As a student, she'd used it to bring kegs up to the number four for parties and to lower heavy loads of laundry to the communal washer and dryer in the basement. Its ropes were frayed, even back then, and eventually she had stopped using it because it was only be a matter of time before they would give out. The cost of fixing it had been too much for her meager budget, and no one else in the building had wanted to pitch in. Now, left unused all these years, the old ropes were covered in spider webs. Sylvie made a mental note to caution the girls to stay away from it.

"Got a minute?"

Sylvie turned to see Jack Ramsdale standing in his back doorway.

She was about to ask if it could wait but the look on his face stopped her. "Was there something you wanted?" she asked.

"I don't think you're safe here."

"Are you trying to scare me?"

"I think I'm trying to warn you."

"Now you *are* scaring me."

He looked at her. "If I didn't say anything, and something happened—"

"Oh, I *get* it," she said and trudged back up the stairs with Sugarbear in her arms.

That night Sylvie lay in bed exhausted, her eyes wide open, adrenaline from the day's adventure still percolating in her veins. She tried to convince herself to fall asleep, but her mind refused to stop churning.

She kept thinking about Jack Ramsdale—his conversation with the Russian or Ukrainian or whatever, about owing the man money and the expression on Jack's face when he told her she was in danger. He really had looked worried. But what was he worried about—her, or his own problems?

He'd overextended himself financially and she felt mildly guilty, but why would that put *her* in danger? He was probably colluding with Mark to scare her out of her home. Well, she wasn't going anywhere.

And was she really in danger from Mark? *Her* Mark? Had he changed in some fundamental way? Lately, when he'd spoken to her she'd had the feeling his words weren't his. It wasn't difficult to imagine whose words they were. Lisa Chang had him under her spell. Or was Sylvie doing exactly what Mark had accused her of—not facing reality, not accepting the fact that she no longer mattered to him?

And when exactly had everything changed? She racked her brain trying to recall the last time they'd made love (honestly, she couldn't remember) or the last time Mark had smiled at her the way he used to.

She tried turning on her back, then on her side, willing the demons in her mind to let go. Did it really matter how or when he had turned on her? Now he was her adversary, and she'd have to get used to the idea.

Time to lock and load.

Twenty Six

Sylvie woke to the sound of her phone demanding her attention. She struggled to peel one eye open, then the other and peered at the phone. She recognized Raul's number. Seven o'clock on Sunday morning. She hit the answer button.

"I'm on my way over."

"Why?" She sat up. "What's wrong?"

"Nothing's wrong. We have work to do. I'm free now, so I'm coming over."

The call ended.

Sylvie staggered out of bed, started a pot of coffee and headed for the shower.

When the buzzer rang she was dressed in jeans, a sports bra and an oversized sweater, sipping her first cup of coffee with wet hair and no makeup. She pressed the button to open the front door and heard footsteps jogging up the stairs. *Who the hell jogs up three flights of stairs at 7:20 a.m.?* That was just excessive.

Raul sat down at the kitchen counter and helped himself to an orange. Sylvie sat across from him, trying to ingest enough caffeine into her system to function. Apparently they were going to find Mark's assets on Raul's timetable, which was fine with Sylvie, if she could only get her sleep-deprived body on board.

Raul's pencil hovered over his pocket-sized notebook. "So, what do we know?"

Sylvie ticked off the points on her fingers. "Six months ago Mark left his job at Templeton & Brewer to start his own business. Gertrude, his secretary, left with him."

"Gertrude's last name?"

Sylvie thought hard, but couldn't remember.

"What town does she live in?"

Sylvie couldn't remember that either. She wasn't sure she'd ever known. This was the woman who had known more about Mark's life than she had. What exactly did that say about Sylvie?

"What about your tax returns?" he asked.

"What about them?"

"If Mark was in business last year, he probably referred to this new business venture in your joint returns."

"I never look at them. I simply sign where Mark tells me," she said.

"He must have kept a copy in his files."

"If he kept it in his home office, then it would be in the storage locker, but I don't remember seeing any tax returns when I packed up Mark's things."

"Maybe it's on his computer."

"He took that with him when he left," she said.

"Contact your accountant," Raul persisted. "He should have a copy."

"Right. His name is Bernie. I can't remember his last name."

"Does Bernie work for a firm?"

"I have no idea."

Raul sighed in exasperation. "What would have happened if Mark had dropped dead?"

That took Sylvie aback. What *would* have happened? Would she be in less pain if Mark had dropped dead of a heart attack? Would grief have been easier to deal with than all this anger? Cleaner, certainly. Mark would have died a martyr to his wife's exorbitant life style. But she probably wouldn't be facing such a climactic financial disaster. In fact, Mark probably had a generous life insurance policy in place for just such an emergency.

"I'd have called Mark's attorney," she said.

"What's his name?"

"Samuel Rosenthal. I can try calling tomorrow but since Mark's not dead, he might not be willing to talk to me without getting Mark's permission."

Raul gave her an odd look. "Is that a bad thing? That Mark's not dead?"

"I don't think I should go there right now." She spilled the remains of her coffee into the sink.

Raul tossed his orange peel into the garbage. "Let's go."

Sylvie sent Claire a text with strict instructions to call Sylvie's cell and check in if she planned to leave the apartment. Then she grabbed her purse, locked up and followed Raul down the stairs to his van.

"Mind telling me the plan?" she asked as they headed toward the waterfront.

"You're going to plant a GPS on Mark's Jag. Which is legal because since you're married, the Jag is half yours. But you can't do it in the condo garage because they're likely to have security cameras. We'll have to wait for Mark to drive somewhere else."

They waited for an hour and a half in near silence. Sylvie would have loved to ask Raul about his work and what inspired him to take up private investigation, but her attempts at conversation were met with one- or two-word responses.

When she dashed off to use the bathroom at the Starbucks across the street, she barely made it back to the van in time to see Claire arriving at the front door of the Harborview with Sugarbear.

Raul turned to Sylvie. "Were you expecting her?"

Sylvie shook her head, too surprised to speak. She watched Claire dig out her cell phone as she entered the building.

Sylvie's cell rang.

On the other end of the line, Claire said, "Hi, Mom, just checking in."

Sylvie resisted the urge to demand what the hell Claire was doing at her father's mistress's apartment. Instead, she adopted a neutral tone. "Where are you, sweetie?" she asked.

"Home. On Green Street."

Sylvie took a deep breath. She had never known Claire to be deceitful.

"Taylor invited me to spend the night at her house. Her mom said she'd pick me up and I can bring Sugarbear."

When Sylvie didn't respond, Claire asked, "Is that okay? Will you be lonely?"

"I think I can survive the night," Sylvie said softly. She hung up before her voice gave her away. After all, she couldn't exactly call out her child's dishonesty while she sat spying on their father.

Ten minutes later, Mark, Diana and Claire sans Sugarbear emerged from the building on foot. Sylvie ducked out of sight, but they never turned in her direction. Instead, they turned the corner and disappeared from sight.

Frazzled by the sight of Mark strolling along with her two girls after everything that had happened, Sylvie was about to suggest to Raul they give up and try again another day, when Lisa Chang stepped out the door with Sugarbear trailing reluctantly behind on her leash.

Wearing a determined look on her face, Lisa turned toward the water and Raul's van. Once again, Sylvie dove out of sight.

"That's one hard woman," Raul said to Sylvie, who was crouching on the floor, "Where do you think she's taking the puppy?"

"To pee." Sylvie said, climbing back onto the seat. "So she doesn't end up with yellow spots on her white carpet."

Lisa stepped onto the ramp that stretched over the water to the docks that floated beside the Harborview. Sugarbear, terrified of the movement under her feet, tried to pull back but Lisa dragged the puppy forward.

Raul's eyebrows furrowed. "If you were taking a dog out to pee, wouldn't you walk along the sidewalk where there's grass, not on the dock?"

Sylvie's chest tightened as they watched Lisa drag Sugarbear all the way out to the end of the dock and down the furthest pier, disappearing behind the *Ghost Rider*, a cabin cruiser docked at the end.

Moments later, Lisa reappeared, nearly running back up the ramp and past the van. But there was no Sugarbear in sight. Sylvie exchanged glances with Raul. The tightening in her chest turned into a death grip. Without a word, they both jumped out of the van, and ran, full tilt, toward the water.

Sylvie didn't stop running until she got to the edge of the farthest finger, behind the *Ghost Rider*. She shielded her eyes from the sun's glare and scanned the murky water until she spotted the soggy handle of a leash floating a few feet from the dock. It was still attached to a panicked Sugarbear, who sputtered and coughed, her little paws desperately paddling at the water.

Sylvie kicked off her shoes, shrugged off her sweater and dove, head first, into the harbor.

She surfaced a few short strokes from Sugarbear, struggling to gasp for air through the shocking cold constricting her lungs. She tried to grab the leash but her limbs were frozen, unconnected to her body. The terrified pup was swimming in circles. It took several seconds for Sylvie to force the connection between her brain and her limbs, then a few strokes to get close enough to slip one numb hand through the loop.

She swam back toward the dock through frigid, oily water littered with cigarette butts, seagull feathers and a used condom, pulling Sugarbear, still paddling frantically behind her. As she approached the *Ghost Rider*, she could feel her body slow, unwilling to obey her brain. She was only a few feet away, but it might as well have been miles.

On the swim platform of the *Ghost Rider*, a man with a red beard waved a boat hook at her. "Grab the gaff," he yelled, reaching it as far out toward her as he could.

She tried to grab it, but her frozen fingers refused to obey.

Twenty Seven

Sylvie felt the gaff slide along her back to the top of her jeans, where it snagged her belt loop. Then she was being reeled in like a fish with Sugarbear trailing behind her.

She lifted her face from the scummy water and saw Raul and Redbeard, both backlit by the sun, kneeling at the edge of the deck, reaching for her. Redbeard grabbed one arm and Raul grabbed the other, then scooped Sugarbear out of the water. Sylvie landed on the deck with a thud.

Raul unzipped his jacket, opened his shirt and popped the puppy inside next to his skin while Redbeard wrapped Sylvie in a warm blanket.

"You do know how crazy it is to jump into freezing cold water?" Redbeard demanded. "You could have died."

"I got this. Thanks," Raul said, helping Sylvie to her feet. "I'll get them home."

He half-carried her back to the van where a police officer, citation book in hand, stopped recording their license plate number and stared at the unlikely trio over the top of his sunglasses. Raul fumbled for his keys. "Accident," he said. "Sorry officer, our puppy jumped out of the window and we pulled over to chase her."

The officer looked at Sylvie. "You okay, lady?"

"I'm f-f-f-fine."

"I can call an ambulance," the officer said.

Raul waved him off. "No need." He opened the passenger door and helped Sylvie climb inside.

The officer pocketed his citation book. "The harbor's a lot cleaner than it used to be but with all these boats, it wouldn't hurt to have a tetanus booster," he said, returning to his motorcycle.

And a pregnancy test, Sylvie mumbled to herself.

Raul shut the passenger door then came around to the driver's side and settled himself into the seat with Sugarbear's head sticking out of the front of his jacket to better co-pilot. Raul started the engine. "Phew," he said. "You both smell like eighteen flavors of seagull shit."

"S-s-sorry," Sylvie shivered.

"Don't be," he said. "It's sort of sexy in a really perverted way."

He turned up the heat full blast and aimed the hot air straight at her, then drove through Boston and onto the Mass Pike with no regard to speed limits. He exited in Cambridge, then wound his way through Cambridgeport.

When Sylvie's eyes started to close, he barked, "Don't sleep."

Her eyes flew open.

When they got to Green Street he pulled up onto the sidewalk outside her building and rifled through Sylvie's purse for her keys. He placed Sugarbear under one arm and the other at Sylvie's back, and hustled them up the stairs and into the bathroom, where he sat her on the toilet and placed Sugarbear in her arms. He turned the hot water on all the way, creating a virtual steam bath, and pulled his shirt off over his head, revealing colorful tattoos that snaked over his body and ended midway between his elbow and bicep.

Sylvie looked away when he started to unzip his pants.

When he lifted Sugarbear from her arms, Sylvie looked up and was relieved to see he'd left his underwear on. He adjusted the water temperature on the showerhead, then climbed into the claw foot tub and under the shower stream with an unenthusiastic Sugarbear.

Despite the cold in her bones, Sylvie couldn't deny there was something adorable about a well toned, half naked man struggling to wash the remnants of Boston Harbor off a protesting puppy.

With Sugarbear rinsed and wrapped in Diana's towel, he turned to Sylvie. "You need to get into the shower." He blotted himself dry with a hand towel, grabbed his clothes and stepped outside the bathroom door. "I'm leaving it open a little so I can hear you if you need help."

Sylvie knew she needed to take off the blanket and her sodden clothes and wash herself ASAP. And she dutifully told her fingers to unbutton her pants. The problem was, it seemed there was no longer a functioning pathway between her brain and her fingers.

"Are you in the shower?" Raul's voice came from the direction of the kitchen.

"W-w- working on it," she called back. She let the blanket drop from her shoulders and stepped under the shower, letting the warm water thaw her until she could remove her clothes and wash herself. When the hot water ran out, she stepped out of the tub, wrapped herself in a towel and brushed her teeth, rinsing her mouth several times, then gargled with mouthwash.

Back in her room, all she could think about was what Lisa Chang had done. Any minute, her cell would ring. What was she going to tell Claire? If she told the truth, Sylvie would have to admit she was spying on Mark.

Sylvie pulled on a pair of old sweat pants and a sweatshirt, clothes that made her feel like an old friend's arms around her.

Her body was finally warming up, but she thought her soul would never recover from the thought of Lisa Chang tossing the helpless puppy into Boston Harbor.

When she emerged from her room, Raul had Sugarbear's leash on and was heading for the door. "Time for that tetanus shot," he said.

***

Sylvie left the Minute Clinic with a Star Wars Band-Aid over the spot where the nurse practitioner had injected the tetanus booster. She was climbing into the van, where Raul waited with Sugarbear, when her cell rang.

"Sugarbear's gone!" Claire's voice was frantic. "Mommy, do something!"

Mark's voice took over. "Claire's with me. I took the girls out to lunch and we left the dog with Lisa. When she took it for a walk, it slipped out of its collar and ran away."

"Mark, put Claire back on the phone," Sylvie said.

She heard Mark say to Claire. "I'm sure someone nice found it. They don't allow dogs in this building anyway."

Then Claire was on the phone again, begging between sobs, "Mommy, can you find Sugarbear, please."

"I have Sugarbear here. Someone found her and Animal Control checked the microchip," Sylvie lied.

Claire's voice was a whisper, barely audible. "You have Sugarbear? Really?"

"Yes. She's fine. I'm holding her right now. Hang on." Sylvie snapped a photo of the puppy, still a little damp, and texted it to Claire. Then, because she couldn't help it, Sylvie said, "I think she misses you."

"I'm coming home," Claire said and the phone went dead.

***

Claire and Diana were already sitting on the front stoop when Raul pulled the van up to let Sylvie and Sugarbear jump out.

"Later," he said, and drove away.

Claire ran to enfold Sugarbear in her arms and both girls jumped up and down with the puppy, who did her best to lick both their faces at the same time.

Seeing them together in that moment made Sylvie's heart skip. *It doesn't get any better than this*, she thought.

Watching from her stoop, LaVonda nodded at Sylvie and grinned. Sylvie nodded back.

***

When the girls had finished their grilled cheese and tomato sandwiches and were curled up in the living room drinking cocoa, Sylvie asked, "So, how was your visit with your father?"

Instead of answering, Diana headed for the bathroom.

"I don't think she wants to talk about it," Claire said.

"Did something happen that I should know about?"

"It's a really nice place. But that ice queen freaks out if you even put your drink down on the glass coffee table."

"Maybe taking a puppy over there wasn't such a good idea," Sylvie said.

"Dad swore it was okay. I didn't want to leave her when we went out for lunch, but he said she'd be fine. I didn't know Lisa was going to take her for a walk."

"It sounds like Lisa isn't used to dogs."

"I know, right?" Claire looked down. "I'm sorry I lied to you. I didn't want to hurt your feelings."

Sylvie pulled her youngest into her arms. "Next time," she said, "tell me the truth. I can handle it."

Diana came back into the room. "Sugarbear is terrified of getting lost. She never tries to get away. Mom, why do your clothes stink?"

Sylvie mentally smacked herself on the forehead. She'd left her soggy, smelly clothing and dirty towels all over the bathroom floor. "Sugarbear smelled bad when I got her back," Sylvie said, not exactly lying. "I tried to wash her and she got me soaked."

"Did the man who brought her back say where he found her?"

"He said she was down by the water."

"Lisa hates dogs," Diana said. "Almost as much as she hates us. Maddie says in China they eat dogs."

Claire stared at her mother, horrified. "Do people really eat dogs?"

"Lisa wants Dad all to herself. She's a bitch," Diana said.

Claire gazed up at her mother, her eyes wide. "Is that true?"

"Ladies," said Sylvie, "let's not visit her apartment with Sugarbear any more, okay?"

***

Sylvie lay motionless on her bed, her thoughts spinning, when she heard a light knock on the bedroom door. Diana entered and sat down beside her mother. "Mom, do you remember, when we were little, you said you could always tell when we were lying?"

Sylvie smiled at the memory. Small children were easy. It seemed difficult at the time when she had to be so vigilant all the time, but compared to now when they could take off on their own and have their hearts broken, those days seemed simple.

Diana stared at her hands, folded in her lap. "Well, I can tell you're lying and you're probably doing it to protect us but I'm not a child. I don't trust Lisa. I don't trust her to take care of Sugarbear and I don't trust her to take care of Dad."

"Honey, your dad can take care of himself."

"No. He can't. You don't see it because you're mad at him, but someone needs to do something."

"Did something happen that made you worry?" Sylvie felt that raw wound in her heart that opened when she pictured Lisa with her girls.

"Nothing I can explain."

"More like a feeling?"

Diana nodded. "Except there was something I heard." She traced the stitches on Sylvie's green bedspread. "They were whispering. I don't think they wanted me to hear."

"It's all right to tell me if you want." Sylvie's heart thumped against her chest, but she focused on remaining absolutely still.

"She told Dad that someone was watching them."

Sylvie closed her eyes. Lisa couldn't have known that she and Raul had been surveilling Mark. They had been so careful. She felt like a child caught stealing candy.

Diana left the room and returned with the blanket Sylvie had left on the bathroom floor. On the blanket, *Ghost Rider* was embroidered in bold cursive letters—white thread on a navy blue blanket.

Sylvie stared at the letters. "That's the blanket the nice man wrapped Sugarbear in."

"What's a Ghost Rider?" Diana asked.

Sylvie shrugged. "Honey, I have no idea."

"It's creepy." Diana looked stricken. "Mom, I have to tell you something."

Sylvie tried to look encouraging.

"It was all my fault Claire brought Sugarbear to Dad's place."

"It's okay if you want to spend time with your father," Sylvie lied. *Wasn't that what divorcing parents were supposed to say?*

"If Sugarbear had been lost forever, it would have been my fault."

"No, honey, you didn't mean for anything bad to happen."

"You don't understand. I wanted Claire to come over to help me spy on that Lisa person. But then we almost lost Sugarbear."

"Sugarbear is fine, she's home with us."

Diana threw her arms around her mother and held on for a long time. "I'm sorry I've been such a bitch."

"It's okay."

"I thought it was your fault Dad left. But it's not. It's hers." Diana headed for the door.

"Get some sleep," Sylvie said. "We have to register you both for school tomorrow."

Twenty Eight

Early Monday morning, Sylvie switched on the light in the girls' bedroom, but her cheerful, "Good morning, ladies," was greeted with moans and invitations to "Go away."

Sylvie finally lured them out of bed with the promise of breakfast at Dunkin' Donuts. She was desperate. She had forgotten to buy coffee, and a wicked caffeine headache was getting worse.

After an infusion of caffeine and sugar at the local cop hangout, Sylvie and the girls walked to the Family Resource Center located at the only public high school in the city, Cambridge Rindge and Latin. The building sprawled over an entire city block, just down the street from Harvard's Art Museums and the Graduate School of Design. Crossing the campus toward the main entrance, Sylvie heard at least ten different languages being spoken among the clusters of students loitering on the lawn.

Just inside the door, a friendly black gentleman in his sixties, wearing the uniform of a security guard, cheerfully directed them down the crowded corridor to the Resource Center.

As they merged into the throng, teenagers of every size, shape and color surged past them slamming lockers, jostling and yelling obscenities. Most ignored the teachers who stood sentry, calling out greetings and warnings.

The chaos was a far cry from the relative calm and pale faces of Meadowlark Academy. When a basketball flew overhead, narrowly missing Diana, she stared straight ahead, her expression frozen.

Inside the Family Resource Center, Mrs. Moran, a large, dark-skinned woman who looked like she could handle pretty much any situation that

115

came down the pike, introduced herself as the family liaison. She explained with pride that the three hundred and fifty-year-old Cambridge Public School System had originally been affiliated with Harvard College. The high school's two thousand students were divided into four learning communities—C, R, L and S—each with its own Dean of Curriculum and Dean of Students.

Mrs. Moran suggested that Diana might like to shadow one of the students for a day or two while her application was being processed. Sylvie saw the terror behind her child's frozen smile and ached for her. When she watched her oldest child walk out the door with Ms. Filo Espanoza, the tiny, powerhouse dean of School R, who barely reached Diana's shoulder, Sylvie couldn't shake the feeling that she was abandoning her daughter to a war zone.

While Claire distracted herself on her iPhone, Sylvie sat down at the table Lorraine Moran indicated. Mrs. Moran handed her a sheaf of forms to fill out. When she handed Sylvie an application for the reduced cost meal program, Sylvie quickly handed it back. "No thank you, we won't be needing charity."

"Most kids eat breakfast here with their friends. You know teenagers. They'd rather sleep five extra minutes then fix themselves a nutritious breakfast." Mrs. Moran placed a reassuring hand on Sylvie's shoulder. "Half of our students are on the plan. Nutritious breakfasts and lunches are vital to their education." She placed another form in front of Sylvie. "Each student has a prepaid account. You can use your vouchers online. No one else will know how the account is paid." She smiled at Claire, who was completely absorbed in her game. "Not even the student."

Sylvie glanced at the form and was shocked to realize that she now qualified for government help feeding her kids. Her face warm with shame, she picked up her pen and signed.

***

Luckily, the Putnam Avenue Upper School, only a few blocks from Green Street, had an opening in the sixth grade for Claire. Mrs. Moran alerted a liaison, who would be waiting for their arrival.

Together, Sylvie and Claire stepped outside onto the high school campus. Cambridge Rindge and Latin shared a campus between Cambridge Street and Broadway with the main branch of the Cambridge Public Library, an H.H. Richardson gem from 1902 that had been tripled in size by a gleaming glass-walled modern addition. Even in daylight, without the lights shining from inside, it sparkled like a jewel. Sylvie imagined it enticed even the most jaded inner city kids to explore its gleaming interior.

Across the street, a newly renovated building housed three venerated Harvard art museums: the Fogg, the Busch-Reisinger, and the Arthur M. Sackler. Meadowlark Academy, the girls' elite former prep school, couldn't hold a candle to that kind of culture, Sylvie thought smugly as she pointed out her old haunts to her daughter.

They walked through Central Square, past Green Street to Putnam Avenue, where Ms. Rodriguez swept Claire up in her enthusiastic welcome.

When Sylvie left her there, Claire waved and smiled, looking only slightly more excited than terrified. Knowing Claire, she would probably have three new besties before the end of the day.

Sylvie headed home by way of the market to buy ingredients for homemade soup. Soup was nourishing and inexpensive—a practical use of her reduced food budget, which, to be honest, she hadn't yet figured out.

For the first time since she could remember, Sylvie picked up each item and scrutinized the price. When had food gotten so expensive? For the last fifteen years, she had simply gone to Whole Foods and bought whatever appealed to her. She'd never worried about the prices, and she'd barely noticed the final total. She'd simply swiped her credit card and taken her purchases home to feed her family.

She chose a package of celery from the bin, checking the price. Several dollars? For celery? She didn't even like it and neither did Diana, yet it seemed that every soup recipe demanded it. How much could celery actually contribute to the flavor?

She replaced the celery and examined a bunch of carrots.

When had carrots turned to gold? It was all too much.

She agonized over each decision as she chose her produce, slowly filling her basket.

She had planned her life so carefully. Everything had been on track: successful husband, lovely home, two healthy children, private school, country club. She had dreamed it, set her sights on it and made it so.

Now, suddenly, without any warning, everything had gone to shit.

She placed her basket on the counter and paid with her roll of cash, then headed home where she hauled the bags up the stairs and put the perishables away. The overwhelming job of unpacking and organizing their new home loomed large. But being back in her little apartment on Green Street also brought back a flood of memories of the Sylvie she was back then—independent and confident, even cocky. She'd looked pretty damn good and felt entitled to land a husband who could provide the prosperous lifestyle she'd been raised to expect.

Sylvie blew her nose. *Man plans, God laughs,* as Grandma Esther used to say. Sylvie gazed up at the ceiling. "Must be a laugh riot up there right about now," she said out loud.

Sugarbear was curled up on Claire's bed, her head on a pair of Claire's dirty underwear. Sylvie attached the leash and urged the puppy down the stairs to relieve herself outside. When Sugarbear insisted on bringing the underwear along, Sylvie gave up the battle and resigned herself to walking the puppy down the street with a pair of yellow polka dot underpants hanging from her mouth as they searched for a patch of grass.

Along the way, Sugarbear stopped and searched every tree and signpost for pee mail while Sylvie's thoughts grew darker, turning in on herself so that she was barely aware of where the pup had urged her until she heard a familiar gravelly voice say, "Hey, girl."

LaVonda grinned up at her with a battered pipe in her mouth and a pile of cigarette stubs beside her.

Sylvie sank down beside her. Sugarbear sat down on her haunches and waited expectantly.

They sat in silence while LaVonda selected a cigarette stub from her stash, sliced it open with a grimy fingernail and emptied the tobacco carefully into the pipe.

"I don't know how I got here," Sylvie whispered,

"I hear ya," LaVonda said. She puffed harder, creating a haze of smoke between them.

"I don't know what I did to make this happen," Sylvie said. "So, how can I know how to fix things?" Sylvie sniffed. "I don't know what to do."

"You got groceries," LaVonda said. "That's a start." She sliced open another stub and slid the contents into the pipe bowl.

Sugarbear watched Sylvie wipe her nose with her sleeve. "When I married Mark I thought it was forever. We'd have a beautiful house where we'd raise our children and grow old together with plenty of room for grandchildren. But none of that is going to happen now. Because once things start to go wrong, it never stops. Every decision I've made has turned out to be wrong. I can't trust myself not to fuck everything up. I'm old and ugly and poor and I'm going to grow old alone and end up on the street."

Sylvie stopped abruptly and looked at LaVonda. "Oh, my god, I'm sorry. I didn't mean…"

"That's okay, girlie. I know I live on the street. I like it that way. I got my spot here right where I'm supposed to be. Maybe could be you're right where you're supposed to be, too."

Twenty Nine

Hours later, when Claire got home, Sylvie was curled in a fetal position on the couch. She still hadn't unpacked the dishes into newly lined cupboards. Or organized the living room. Or removed the empty boxes to the alleyway for trash pick-up.

For the first time since Claire had left that morning, Sugarbear dropped the underwear and bounded to Claire, wriggling with joy.

Claire dumped her backpack just inside the door, grabbed a plastic bag and bounded down the stairs with Sugarbear without even glancing at her mother.

Thank goodness she hadn't noticed Sylvie's red eyes and splotchy face. Sylvie would hear all the details of Claire's first day at her new school later, but she could tell there was nothing to worry about.

Diana would be a different story. Sylvie didn't have enough energy to lift her body off the couch, never mind pull herself together for that shitstorm.

"I hate that school," Diana announced as she stormed through the door and headed for the kitchen. "I'm not going back. You're going to have to homeschool me."

Sylvie sighed. Apparently, her own pity party was over.

"Everyone stared at me like I was some kind of alien. I went to the nurse with a headache and she offered me a pregnancy test and gave me free condoms. They treat us like sluts."

"Did anything good happen? Anything at all?"

Diana thought for a moment. "They play music to change classes, which is sort of cool, but then randomly, for no reason, they'll play a tape of a baby screaming and crying instead. Which is super annoying."

"Maybe that's to encourage the kids to use the free condoms."

"Mo—om."

"Sorry. Anything else?"

"Well," Diana began, trying desperately to suppress an emerging smile so as not to dilute the full impact of her angst, "I did have lunch with Maddie. The drama club is rehearsing for the spring drama competition and they need more kids on the crew. The set has to be assembled and taken down in less than five minutes. You get timed. Rindge is famous for its complicated sets, so being on the crew is a really big deal."

"That sounds like fun."

"I know. But I can't do it."

"Why not?"

"Because I don't know how to use the tools, and I'm embarrassed to ask."

"Can't you just pick it up by watching the other kids?"

"No, Mom. There's this huge circular saw and drill guns and electric sanders. Everyone wears goggles and knows what they're doing. And they look so cool." Diana threw herself onto the couch in despair.

"Why don't you ask the shop teacher for a little extra help?" Sylvie asked, even though she knew from experience that anything she said right now would be wrong.

"Are you completely out of your mind?" Diana demanded and stomped off to her room.

"Well, do it or don't," Sylvie said to the empty room.

Diana would survive. Life was going to throw boulders in her path. She'd just have to learn to climb over them, she thought, remembering Grandma Esther's advice to "prepare the child for the path, not the path for the child."

Diana and Claire were young. They had their whole lives ahead of them. Unlike Sylvie, whose life, for all practical purposes, was over.

Thirty

The next morning, after the girls had trudged off to school, Sylvie climbed into Raul's van. They were on their way to the Harborview to plant the GPS tracking device they had failed to plant when they'd leapt from the van to rescue Sugarbear. Sylvie wore oversized sunglasses in a futile attempt to hide her puffy eyes. She hadn't been able to face her usual makeup ritual.

"Rough night?" Raul asked.

Sylvie ignored the question.

"Guess so," Raul said and headed toward the waterfront.

It was the first of May and although the air was nippy, the sun was shining and the water in the harbor glistened a brilliant blue against the white yachts bobbing in their slips.

As they waited for Mark's Jaguar to exit the Harborview garage and go someplace where they could plant the device, Sylvie searched for the *Ghost Rider* at the far end of the dock. The freshly laundered blanket lay on her lap. She needed to return it and thank the red-bearded man, but neither the bridge nor the deck showed any signs of life. She had no intention of calling attention to herself by standing on the dock waving and shouting to see if anyone was aboard.

The cabin cruiser was still deserted twenty minutes later when the Jaguar emerged from the bowels of the Harborview. Raul followed it down Atlantic Avenue, then onto State Street, staying a few car lengths behind. He had to burn rubber through a yellow light to avoid losing it in traffic, and swerved into the oncoming lane to get past a slow-moving bus. Sylvie clung to the panic handle until the Jag pulled into a public parking garage on Broad Street.

Raul hung back a few seconds before following and parked a few lanes away. They watched Mark get out and head toward the elevator.

Raul handed a small plastic transponder to Sylvie as he opened his door. "When there's no one around, stick this to the bottom of the Jag."

"How do I—"

He tossed her a magnetic mounting case and headed for the elevator, calling back over his shoulder, "The steel framing under the bumper."

Sylvie slipped the transponder into the magnetic case and waited, checking the mirrors for a quiet moment to plant the box. Cars pulled in and out while a steady flow of busy Bostonians left and returned to their vehicles.

While she watched and waited, she imagined herself planting a bomb instead of a tracker. In her mind's eye, she saw Mark's beloved Jag exploding, then dissolving into red metallic rain. She conjured the expression on Mark's face when he returned to a crimson puddle in place of his sports car.

When the coast was finally clear, Sylvie jumped from the van, darted around the rows of parked cars to the Jag, dropped to the ground and rolled as far as she could under it. She moved the magnetic case holding the transponder around under the bumper until it tugged at the steel framing, then clung.

She rolled out from under the Jag and found herself staring at a pair of wing tip shoes attached to the legs of a distinguished gentleman with gray hair, who gazed down at her.

"You all right?" he asked, offering her his hand.

She brushed her hair from her face, then glanced at her hand and saw it was covered with grease.

The man was still holding out his hand so she smiled, took it and let him hoist her to her feet.

"My bracelet fell off," she said. "I thought I saw it roll underneath."

"Is it yours?"

"The car? Oh, no. Wish it was," she lied. She'd always hated the stupid thing. *Why would a married man with two kids want a car that only seated two people? Well, now she knew.*

"You're not kidding. It's a beauty. Did you find your bracelet?"

"No. But it's okay. It wasn't expensive."

The man paused.

"Really, it's no big deal," she said. "My daughter made it."

She could tell he was trying to decide what to do.

"Out of macaroni," she said. "She'll make me another."

"All righty, then," he said, looking relieved as he headed toward his car.

Sylvie returned to the van. She refused to check herself in the rearview mirror. Some things were better left unseen.

When Raul returned, he studied her face, said nothing, started the van and exited the garage.

"Did you figure out where he went?" she asked.

"Intellectual property attorneys. Buckley, Ivy and Associates. Know them?"

She shook her head.

When they reached the cashier, he held out his hand to her, palm up. She rifled through her purse and extracted one of her precious twenty-dollar bills to pay the exorbitant garage fee.

She took the receipt he offered and placed it in her wallet. "Now what?"

"We wait a few days, then retrieve it before the battery runs out. It'll record where he goes. Hopefully, at some point, he'll go to his new office. Then we can figure out what he's doing over there."

When Raul dropped Sylvie in front of her building, the shot of adrenaline from nearly getting caught under Mark's Jag was still buzzing through her veins, and she felt a little like a character in a John Le Carre novel.

***

Two days later, Raul sat next to Sylvie in his van downloading the GPS output, which had traced Mark's wanderings for the past forty-eight hours. "Any idea why Mark would be traveling to several different locations in Arlington both days?" he asked.

Sylvie shook her head.

Raul started the car, "We could check Google maps, but I think we're better off going over there."

Sylvie nodded and Raul guided the van through the crowded streets of Somerville, then out Mass. Ave to Arlington, where he turned right on Park Street and pulled into the parking lot of Gold's Gym.

"First stop," Raul said.

Sylvie nearly choked. "I can't afford to feed my kids, but he has a gym membership?"

"Dude's got to maintain his stamina." Raul grinned but Sylvie failed to see the humor. She was literally shaking with rage.

Stop number two was an office building on Mill Street. Raul waited in the van while Sylvie checked the list of businesses posted in the front hall. Among various doctors' offices, lawyers, and a physical therapy office, "TechnoData" was listed in suite 110. That name rang a bell, but Sylvie couldn't quite put her finger on where she'd heard it before.

She wound her way through the maze of linoleum-tiled corridors to suite 110. As she approached the glass entrance, Sylvie recognized the familiar face of Mark's long-time secretary. Beyond Gertrude, Sylvie could see a large room divided into six areas, each containing a desk with a computer. At the desks sat young people who looked to be in their mid-twenties, of varying genders and ethnicities, working diligently.

Gertrude glanced toward the door and their eyes locked.

Sylvie smiled and started to enter, but Gertrude shook her head and held up her hand in a "stop" gesture. She grabbed a key attached to a substantial chunk of wood with the word "Ladies" in black letters, came to the door and handed it to Sylvie. Then she pointed down the hall and raised her index finger in the universal "give me a minute" sign.

Sylvie walked in the direction Gertrude had indicated and located the ladies' room. She unlocked the door and waited inside, pacing.

When Gertrude arrived, before saying a word, she checked under both stalls. Once it was clear they were alone, she handed Sylvie a piece of paper and said, "Meet me at this address in an hour." Then she opened the door just wide enough to check the hall in both directions and peeked out.

"Can you tell me—" Sylvie started, then stopped when Gertrude abruptly stepped back inside, shoved Sylvie into a stall and slammed the door shut.

From inside the stall, Sylvie could hear the ladies' room door open.

Gertrude's voice, louder than necessary, announced, "Good morning, Ms. Chang."

"Good morning." Lisa's voice was curt, dismissive.

When the lock on the stall next to hers clicked into place, Sylvie slipped out, nodded to Gertrude, and fled to the safety of Raul's van.

***

Sylvie sat at a table in the back corner of the Bean Pot Coffee Shop, savoring a generous portion of coffee served piping hot in a soup-size ceramic mug. She'd been squatting there for more than an hour, since Raul had dropped her off and headed back to his other life. She sipped slowly so she could justify holding on to the table.

Gertrude was already fifteen minutes late. Sylvie was starting to worry when the older woman bustled through the door and paused at the counter, where she armed herself with a cup of tea and a scone before making her way over to Sylvie. "It's nice to see you," she said. "I hope you and the girls are well."

"We've been better. I assume you know that Mark has moved out of—"

"I have noticed certain changes," Gertrude interrupted.

"Like a change of address?"

Gertrude poured milk into her tea and took a sip.

"I take it you don't approve," Sylvie said.

"I can assure you it makes no difference to anyone whether I approve or not."

Sylvie leaned forward in her chair. "It makes a difference to me."

"What can I do for you, Mrs. Wolff?"

"I was hoping you could help me understand."

"Isn't this a conversation you should be having with your husband?"

Sylvie felt chastened. She had never before reached out to this woman, who had spent much of her life accommodating Sylvie's family. The two of them had shared her husband's life, yet they had no common ground. "My husband isn't interested in explaining anything to me," she said.

"I'm afraid I have no special insights into your family dynamics."

"I don't think I've ever thanked you properly for looking out for us all these years," Sylvie said and placed her hand on Gertrude's.

After a moment, Gertrude moved her hand away. "When the girls were little, your husband used to bring them to the office and they would sit next to me and draw pictures. Those pictures still hang over my desk."

Sylvie felt sick. She had failed to see the woman sitting across from her as a person, with a life. Not someone who only existed to make her own life easier. Now, she was at this woman's mercy. Unable to meet the older woman's eyes, Sylvie starred down into her cup.

When Sylvie looked up, Gertrude was waving at a tall, thin woman in the doorway. Florence Whittaker, the office manager from Templeton & Brewer, waved back.

"I hope you don't mind," Gertrude said. "I invited a friend to join us."

Moments later, Florence carried tea and biscotti to the table, where she and Gertrude exchanged a significant look.

"Well," Florence said, reaching out to shake Sylvie's hand, "we meet again. Gertrude asked me to join you because she felt that there might be matters you wanted to ask about that she's not at liberty to discuss."

Gertrude's face was unreadable, but Sylvie noticed the corner of her mouth twitch.

"But first," Florence continued, "we need your word that this conversation will remain absolutely confidential."

Sylvie nodded. "Of course." Were these women willing to stick their necks out to help her and her girls? Or was this some sort of revenge scenario? After all, it wasn't as if Sylvie deserved their help. She cleared her throat. "Can you tell me why my husband would want to leave Templeton & Brewer to start his own company?"

"I'll tell you what I know," Florence said, "but I must say, the whole thing is a bit of a mystery." She broke her biscotti into several pieces. "Mark is a rare combination of talents. He sees the big picture and can identify creative solutions to complex problems."

Sylvie wondered why Mark couldn't see the big picture when he decided to eviscerate their family.

Florence stirred sugar into her cup with a wooden stick. "And he is exceptionally good at structuring a detailed, efficient process to accomplish a herculean task."

Gertrude was nodding, and Sylvie realized that the older woman took a great deal of personal pride in Mark's abilities, as one who made a significant contribution to his work and shared in the reflection of his glory.

"So you can imagine how surprised I was," Florence continued, " to hear Mr. Templeton complain to Ms. Chang that while Mark's latest proposal was intriguing, his plan lacked the necessary logic and detail to accomplish his goal. Which didn't sound like Mark. He's a stickler for detail, as I'm sure you know."

Oh, Sylvie knew all right. Mark's attention to detail had always kept her on her toes, often walking on eggshells lest she fail to live up to his standards.

Florence continued, "In fact, the difference in his style was so sudden and so significant that Dick Templeton asked me whether I thought Mark might be using drugs."

Sylvie blinked. Drugs? Mark? A man who hesitated to order a second glass of wine with dinner, lest he feel, however briefly, slightly out of control?

"As head of the Research and Development team," Florence continued, "Ms. Chang had always championed Mark, sung his praises to Mr. Templeton whenever she got the chance. So, naturally, I would have expected her to defend Mark. But she just stood there. Like she agreed that Mark's work was no longer up to snuff. And she didn't seem particularly interested in finding out why."

Florence folded her hands in front of her and said, "Which made me think she already knew."

"I don't understand." Sylvie looked at Florence, who wore an expression of pity aimed squarely in Sylvie's direction. It was one thing for Sylvie to have a personal pity party for herself. It was another to be *seen* as pitiful by two elderly spinsters. Sylvie cleared her throat and tried to make her voice sound casual. "I know they're living together."

Florence nodded, clearly relieved. "Aaah. Well, we suspected they had become more than colleagues, but they've been discreet."

"What exactly was Mark working on at Templeton?" Sylvie asked.

"I have no background in software systems except what I've picked up over the years," Florence said. "But it involved cyber security."

Sylvie turned to Gertrude. "Is that what Mark's working on now?"

Gertrude twisted her napkin in her lap. "Even if I understood his work better, I simply couldn't say. It would be a betrayal of confidence. I wouldn't be here at all except that I want what's best for Mark."

"Does that mean you don't think Lisa Chang is best for Mark?" Sylvie asked.

Gertrude looked directly into Sylvie's eyes. "Something's not right. I can't put my finger on what it is."

Sylvie glanced down to see the napkin in shreds in Gertrude's lap.

Florence said, "We thought you should know. There's nothing more we can do."

Sylvie's mind raced. "So, Mark got frustrated and started his own company to pursue his project when Templeton wouldn't support him?"

Florence frowned. "I imagine so, though Mark's actions are a bit dodgy from a legal perspective. After all, Mark developed his ideas while he was on salary at Templeton & Brewer. And Mr. Templeton thought Mark's concept could be worth a fortune if he could really pull off what he was proposing. But apparently the proposal wasn't concrete enough to justify the kind of investment in time and resources Mark was demanding. Mr. Templeton said Mark was delusional if he thought his theories were ready for serious consideration."

None of this made sense. What had caused a change in Mark so drastic that he would not only desert his family, leaving them destitute, but cause him to compromise his professional reputation—his *raison d'être*—as well?

Could he have a brain tumor? That thought stopped her short. It was possible. She'd heard of brain tumors causing drastic changes in people's personalities. When Fran Forsyth's mother developed a brain tumor, she also developed a sudden taste for raw meat. Had Mark ordered steak tartar recently?

And did the thought of Mark with a fatal brain tumor make Sylvie feel better or worse? She wasn't exactly sure.

Or perhaps Mark *had* been producing the same high quality of work he always had and Mr. Templeton simply couldn't comprehend what Mark was trying to accomplish. Mark was always complaining that he worked for idiots. Perhaps he was right. Which meant she was a terrible wife. She hadn't believed in Mark enough, either.

So he'd found someone who did.

Thirty One

Inside the crowded Middle East Restaurant, just around the corner from her building, Sylvie sat across from Raul, his long legs manspread at awkward angles in an attempt to fit them under the tiny wooden table. Neither spoke as the waitress, nose ring dangling from her left nostril, delivered two steaming Arabic coffees to the table.

Sylvie sipped the steaming liquid. The bitter taste triggered a tidal wave of memory of her student days when the person sitting across the table was a young, eager Mark—the love of her life.

She placed the cup in its saucer and took a deep, cleansing yoga breath, just as her teacher had taught her.

Raul poured a stream of sugar into the muddy liquid and stirred the tiny spoon in the tiny cup. "I'd start with that proposal. Find out where Mark's logic went wrong. Maybe that will provide some insight into his 'personality change.'"

"I can't. Templeton & Brewer take the security on their developing projects seriously. There's no way I can get my hands on that proposal."

"Can't that old lady help?"

"Her name's Florence, and she's already stuck her neck out to help me. I can't ask her to do more."

Raul shrugged.

Sylvie looked up. "Could *you* get your hands on the proposal?"

"How would I do that?"

"Break in and steal it."

He tilted back in his chair. "I'm not breaking in anywhere."

"But PIs do it all the time."

"Yeah, on TV. And they never get caught. Which is why they don't lose their licenses."

"But you don't *have* a license," Sylvie said.

"And I'd never get one with a B & E on my record. Sorry. Not gonna happen."

"Then how am I going to find out what happened at Templeton?" Sylvie's voice sounded whiny, even to herself.

"No one said *you* couldn't break in."

"Me? I have no experience breaking into buildings."

Raul snorted. "You implying I *do*?"

"I just assumed—"

"Well, don't."

Sylvie sipped her coffee. Apparently, no one was going to do this for her. "How do I do it?"

"You could pretend to be one of the cleaners."

"Me?"

"Why do you keep saying that?" he said. "It sure as hell isn't going to be me."

"Seriously? Do I *look* like someone who cleans other people's offices for a living?"

She did not like the way one of Raul's eyebrows arched in response.

Thirty Two

Late that afternoon, Sylvie waited in the passenger seat of Raul's van, outside Templeton & Brewer, dressed in clothes she'd bought at the Goodwill Store on Mass. Ave: generic mom jeans with an elastic waistband, probably originally purchased on sale at Wal-Mart, a tank top, beat-up sneakers and a head scarf. All items had been washed in hot water and dried for an hour on the "fry" setting before she'd put them on. Surely, even the most resilient body lice eggs had succumbed.

Raul handed her a khaki tee shirt with the Corp-Clean logo and a nametag that read "Asmilla." "I made friends with one of the regular cleaners, a woman named Liliane, who 'rented' this name tag from another cleaner."

Sylvie couldn't help imagining what special skills Raul had employed to obtain the nametag for her. She was not about to ask.

"Liliane said the crew leader drinks and never looks the women in the face. Don't talk. Try to stay near her. She'll look out for you. You should be okay, but if things get weird, make an excuse and meet me in the parking lot."

Sylvie pulled the Corp-Clean shirt over her tank top and attached the nametag. "So, I'm paying $150 for the pleasure of cleaning Templeton & Brewer's offices?"

"Yep. So, keep your head down and don't talk. Act like you don't speak English."

Right on time, a minibus labeled Corp-Clean Services pulled up and five workers, four women from various ethnic backgrounds and one Latino man, hopped out. The women each carried a metal bucket of cleaning products. The older man, whose tag read "Julio," carried an industrial-sized vacuum cleaner.

Sylvie jumped out of the van and slipped in behind the group as they approached the building. A small woman with a red headscarf, whose nametag read "Liliane," hung back to join Sylvie and handed her a bucket. Neither spoke as the group made their way into the building where Mitchell, the security guard, waved them through without even glancing at their faces.

Once safely past security, Sylvie breathed a sigh of relief as they made their way to the third floor and the offices of Templeton & Brewer. She walked, head down, wearing someone else's cast-off clothing: a non-person. No one she passed looked at her or acknowledged her existence. It was as though she had donned Harry Potter's invisibility cloak. The sensation was disconcerting.

She did a quick scan of the space. It was empty except for a few secretaries and worker bees, some buzzing around printers or scanners, others gathering their belongings and preparing to leave. The cleaners had spread out and seemed to have started their routine on the right, moving toward the left like a search and rescue team. It would take them some time to make their way to the other end where Sylvie needed to be.

The women wiped down desks and chairs and emptied wastebaskets. The man, who moved slightly unsteadily, moved chairs out of the way and vacuumed the floor. Periodically, he pulled a small flask from his pocket, took a swig and put it back.

Sylvie caught Liliane's eye and jerked her head in the direction of the left rear corner. Liliane nodded. Sylvie pulled an enormous commercial-sized garbage bag from her bucket and unfurled it, causing an unexpectedly loud snap.

Sylvie glanced around nervously. A short woman with black eyes and a green bandana covering her hair was studying Sylvie. Liliane approached the short woman and whispered something Sylvie couldn't hear. Green Bandana gave Sylvie a sharp look, then turned back to her work.

It took several minutes for Sylvie's heart rate to slow down to something approaching normal.

Armed with paper towels, a spray bottle of generic cleaner, and a garbage bag, Sylvie spritzed and polished her way toward Mr. Templeton's office. She emptied wastepaper bins filled with half-eaten food, scraps of paper, plastic, and used ink cartridges into the plastic bag as she went, all the time gaining new respect for the cleaners she used to pay to clean up after her twice a week. Liliane followed her lead, staying a few feet away and glancing back at the others every few minutes.

Sylvie paused outside Mr. Templeton's closed door. What if he was inside, working late? Would he recognize her as the same woman he'd greeted on Mark's arm at Christmas parties over the years?

She spritzed, then polished a glass framed print on the wall next to his door and checked her image in the clean glass. Without makeup or hair blown dry to perfection, there wasn't much resemblance to the old Sylvie. The events of the past two weeks seemed to have permanently etched themselves into new creases around her eyes.

She summoned whatever guardian angels had been foolish enough to follow her into her life of crime and eased open the door marked "Richard Templeton" far enough to peek inside.

A woman was hunched over the computer, pushing buttons on the keypad, her movements furtive. She jumped when the door opened, and Sylvie quickly yanked the door shut again, dove behind the nearest desk and grabbed an overflowing wastebasket. She emptied the questionable contents into her plastic bag, then pretended to search for something inside and instantly regretted her decision. The contents smelled even more questionable than it looked.

A hand landed on her shoulder and Sylvie froze. *Shit. Busted. And while she languished in jail, Mark would gain custody of the girls and sell her apartment.*

Sylvie raised her head and found herself face to face with Florence Whittaker. For a split second, the two women stared at each other.

Florence's eyes scanned Sylvie from headscarf to battered sneakers. "I see you found a job," she said softly.

"I really need a copy of the proposal Mark was working on," Sylvie whispered, wiping down a desk.

"Whatever for?"

"To figure out what happened," Sylvie said.

Florence frowned. "That proposal contains proprietary information. Whoever shows it to anyone outside of this company could be charged with industrial espionage."

"That proposal had something to do with ruining my life. I need to read it. I don't need a copy of the digital file, only a printout. Something I can read. I can have it back to you tomorrow."

Florence hesitated, then stepped back inside Templeton's office, leaving the door open.

A sudden loud clank startled Sylvie. She turned to see Julio watching her.

Sylvie smiled submissively and tried to move past the man, but he blocked her path. Waves of alcohol fumes rose from his body and his eyes were slightly unfocused. "Do I know you?" he asked.

Sylvie stared down at her shoes, keeping her head bent, trying to impersonate someone who didn't speak English.

"Did you do something to make you in trouble with that lady?"

Sylvie kept her head lowered and glanced toward Templeton's office where Florence was searching along a shelf filled with blue binders, while Julio scolded her in a language she didn't understand. She shifted her feet and waited. Finally he turned away and went back to his cleaning.

Sylvie turned back toward Templeton's office and saw Florence place a blue binder in the center of the desk, knocking over a framed photograph. When she picked it up, she studied it for a moment and a strange look came over her face. Then she replaced the photo on the desk and Sylvie quickly looked away.

Florence walked passed Sylvie and said, "I'm all set. You can go ahead and clean in there."

Sylvie glanced over at Julio, who seemed to have forgotten about her. He appeared to have trouble remaining steady on his feet. She retrieved her bucket and entered Templeton's office.

The blue binder Florence had placed on the desk was labeled "Assuranz Project." The name meant nothing to her. When she was sure no one was looking, she opened the cover. Inside, she found a series of incomprehensible equations and graphs. She closed it and slipped the binder into a clean garbage bag. She placed that bag inside the other, half full bag. Then she finished cleaning Mr. Templeton's office. As she polished the rich wood of the desk, she lifted the picture Florence had held – a photograph of Richard Templeton with his blonde trophy wife and three smiling blonde daughters, each more lovely than the next.

Sylvie stepped out of Templeton's office. *Mission accomplished.* All she had to do now was get out of there without getting herself and Liliane busted.

The other cleaners were cleaning the individual offices, except for Liliane who lingered nearby. Julio was across the room on his hands and knees, concentrating on scraping something sticky from the floor.

Sylvie worked her way along the row of offices that had not yet been

135

cleaned and found herself outside a door marked *Lisa Chang, Research and Development*.

How could she possibly resist?

She ducked inside and pushed the door mostly shut behind her.

The desk was bare except for a desktop computer. A shelf held a neat row of binders like the ones in Templeton's office, but these were red. On the otherwise bare walls hung two modern landscape prints in the minimalist style. An antique lacquered Chinese desk, inlaid with pearl, dominated the room. The rest of the office was as cold and impersonal as the woman herself.

Unable to stop herself, Sylvie opened the desk drawer. All she found were pens, paper clips and other office supplies, all neatly organized—nothing to help her understand her husband's feelings toward this woman.

Outside Lisa's office, Sylvie could hear a vacuum cleaner being dragged along the floor. It stopped outside the door. Sylvie quickly shoved the drawer closed and kicked the wastebasket onto its side, spilling the contents under the desk. She dropped to her knees and began to gather the spilled trash. From under the desk, she saw the door open and Julio's sneakers enter, then pause in the doorway. She ignored him and continued to gather up the trash. Finally, he stepped back outside and the sound of the vacuum resumed.

She started to her feet when her eye caught a glint of metal. A small object was taped to the inside of the chair leg. The sight of it gave Sylvie a strange little thrill like she'd discovered buried treasure. She scraped at the tape with her nail, pulled it back and uncovered a flash drive just as he heard footsteps outside the door. With no time to think, Sylvie slipped the flash drive into her jeans pocket and stood up. *Jesus, what the hell am I doing,* she thought. She tied the top of the trashcan liner inside Lisa's wastebasket and placed it inside her large garbage bag, then grabbed her bucket and joined the other cleaners.

For the next hour Sylvie cleaned conscientiously, head down, heart pounding as the minutes dragged on. She was sure that any second Green Bandana would rat her out to Julio, or Julio would sober up and realize she was an interloper. But whatever Liliane had said seemed to have satisfied the little woman.

When they were finally done, the small troop of cleaners gathered their buckets and full bags of garbage and headed down the elevator. They trudged outside toward the section of the parking lot containing the dumpsters.

Raul's van, its side door open, engine running was parked conveniently between Sylvie and the dumpsters. She and Liliane hung back, letting the others move slightly ahead. As they passed the van, Sylvie handed off the bucket to Liliane, heaved the garbage bag into the back of the van and jumped in after it. Without even bothering to close the door, Sylvie ducked down out of sight while Raul cruised out of the lot.

When they had turned the corner, Sylvie unfolded herself from the floor of the van and shut the door. She opened the garbage bag, removed the blue binder from its wrapper, and held it up triumphantly.

Raul's face blossomed into a full-scale smile. "Score!" he said and high fived her.

She felt like she had won the Oscar.

She reached inside her pocket for the flash drive and considered showing it to Raul, then changed her mind.

Thirty Three

Raul pulled up in front of Sylvie's apartment. "I'd love to hear all about it, but I have to relieve a guy on surveillance. "

Sylvie jumped out and was about to slam the door shut when Raul gestured toward the garbage bag. "What about that?"

Sylvie looked at the garbage bag, then back at Raul. "I'll put it in the bin," she said.

"Don't," Raul said. "What you have there is the golden grail of industrial espionage. Go through it. You might learn something."

Sylvie hauled the bag out of the van and dragged it to the front stoop.

LaVonda was in her usual spot, two doors down. She watched Sylvie drag the bag up the front steps, tearing a hole in the plastic.

"You want that?" LaVonda asked. "Cause if you don't, I'll take it."

"I have to go through it. Sorry."

"I feel ya. You might find some good stuff."

Sylvie wrestled the bag into the front hallway, then sank down onto the steps, not yet ready to face the endless climb with a leaking bag of trash.

When she glanced up, Jack Ramsdale was looking down at her. "Want me to put that outside for you?" he asked.

She shook her head. "I have to take it upstairs."

"It's not garbage?"

"It is, but I have to go through it. I lost an earring."

Jack hoisted the enormous bag onto his shoulder and started up the stairs. Sylvie nearly melted with gratitude, even though she knew she'd have to go back down eventually and clean the liquid that drizzled all the way up the stairs.

He dropped it just inside her door.

She considered offering him a glass of her meager remaining stock of wine, but she remembered the last time they had shared a bottle and thought better of it. Instead, she offered to make tea.

He paused, considering. "Better not."

She shut the door behind him.

***

That evening, Sylvie sat on the couch sipping her favorite cinnamon spiced tea. Shipped directly from Harney and Sons, in western New York, it was another luxury she would miss. As she savored the natural syrupy sweetness, a thumping beat vibrated from the girls' bedroom.

The blue binder lay next to her. She'd paged through it twice and didn't understand a word. Clearly, it was a proposal for a software project, and it definitely addressed cyber security. Beyond that it was far above the limited understanding she had picked up from half-listening to her husband all these years.

She reached into the pocket of her mom jeans and pulled out Lisa Chang's flash drive. It wasn't the usual cheap plastic. Made of heavy metal, it felt substantial in her hand. The cap slid off smoothly and closed cleanly.

Clearly she had stolen something that was of great importance to Lisa Chang, who had taken pains to hide it from her co-workers.

And what would happen when Lisa noticed the flash drive was missing? A sense of regret and fear washed over Sylvie. What if security cameras were all over the T & B offices? If Lisa reported the theft and demanded to see the security footage, she would surely recognize Sylvie, despite the disguise.

Then again, how likely was Lisa to report the missing flash drive to the very people she was hiding it from?

Sylvie paced the tiny apartment, her mind spinning. What had she been thinking, burglarizing Templeton & Brewer? She needed to cover her tracks—throw the damn thing away in a dumpster far from Green Street.

But then she'd never find out what Lisa was hiding.

She sat down at the computer, her stomach in her throat. What if she

139

connected the flash drive and it crashed her computer? Or sent some kind of signal to Lisa's computer? Sylvie wished she knew more about this sort of thing. Before, she would simply ask Mark.

She slid the flash drive into the USB slot and held her breath while the computer whirred and sputtered, deciding whether to recognize the foreign object.

A file folder appeared on the desktop. She'd half expected it to be labeled "Sex tape: Mark and Lisa" but instead it was labeled simply, "New Folder." She hesitated. Whatever it held was important to the woman who had stolen her husband. Did she really want to learn the woman's deepest secrets?

Yes, actually, she did.

She double clicked the folder, revealing a series of folders. One was labeled, "Administrator/priv/repoz1." When she tried to open it, she got an error message, explaining that she did not have the correct software. Another folder was labeled with Chinese characters. When she double clicked it, a document appeared that seemed to be a letter in Chinese, followed by a lengthy document, also in Chinese.

After trolling the Internet for a promising translation website, she copied and pasted a random section of the letter into the box provided. But as was often the case with general translation sites, the English version, with its convoluted language, made no more sense to her than the Chinese.

Sylvie doubled clicked the third file labeled, "Assuranzproposal." Inside were numerous documents in Microsoft Word. She scrolled through them, recognizing much of the same language as the blue binder, starting with a Statement of Work that listed phases, each containing a series of tasks, none of which made sense to her. From what she could tell at first glance, it was probably a digital version of the same proposal.

She went back to the beginning of the digital document, opened the binder beside her and paged through both at the same time, to look for any differences.

After an hour, Sylvie's eyes were bleary and her head ached. The digital copy, with an earlier date, was divided into seven sections, two of which were missing from the blue binder. This had to have been intentional, because the sections in the blue binder had been renumbered to reflect the change.

Sylvie struggled to understand enough to figure out whether the missing sections had been incorporated into the rest of the report or were omitted. It could simply be the normal consequence of editing a document.

Her gut told her that "The Assuranz Project" was somehow key to what she now thought of as "Mark's breakdown." But she would have to find someone who understood software development to tell her whether her gut was right.

She had promised Florence she would return the blue binder the following day, but she had no idea how long it would take to find someone to help her. So she spent the next four hours scanning the blue binder, page by page, into her computer, before falling asleep with her head in her arms, drooling onto her keyboard.

Thirty Four

Sylvie woke at dawn on Friday, stiff and aching from sleeping at her desk. It took her a moment to remember why she was there. Then her emotional memory kicked in and she recalled the fear of getting caught along with a little thrill of pride in her audacity.

She checked her watch. She needed to return the blue binder by this afternoon.

She copied the scanned version of the binder onto Lisa's flash drive, labeled it "blue binder," then deleted the document from her hard drive, ejected the flash drive and replaced its cover. About the size of two AAA batteries, it wouldn't be difficult to hide.

The first place she thought of was the back of her dresser drawer, hidden among her underwear. But every movie she'd ever seen of searched homes showed dresser drawers overturned, their contents spilled everywhere. She considered slitting open a couch cushion and concealing it inside, but that was probably one of the first places someone would think to look. Inside a Kotex in the linen closet? What if Diana accidentally used it? She needed a place where the girls wouldn't happen across it.

She placed the flash drive inside a zip-locked plastic bag, rolled it up and secured it with a rubber band. Then she opened the refrigerator and considered the contents. Her eye fell on the bottle of Grey Poupon mustard she'd brought from the house in Weston. It was probably well over a year old and still nearly full. No one in the family used it except Sylvie.

She unscrewed the top, poured most of the mustard into a small bowl, inserted the wrapped flash drive into the bottle and replaced the rest of the mustard, careful to make sure it wasn't visible from the outside of the bottle. Then she returned the bottle to the refrigerator, placing it behind the capers.

Done and done.

Next, she needed to find someone who could explain the Assuranz Project.

Sylvie returned to the computer and googled "software development at MIT," Marc's *alma mater*. The place was crawling with graduate students at the top of their game. The search revealed a student software design group. According to the website, Sundar Patel, who ran the organization, also taught a number of computer courses with names like "Elements of Software Construction." The web site showed the location of his office in the Computer Science and Artificial Intelligence Lab at the Stata Center, which had opened just after Mark left MIT. Patel's office hours were listed as well. With any luck, he was there now.

She showered and dressed as her old self—wife of a successful software developer—in a flirty dress with a contrasting blazer. She checked in with the girls, who were already dressed and on their way out the door. She walked Sugarbear, then returned and slid the blue binder into her tote bag. She kissed Sugarbear on the nose, told her to be a good girl, and headed out.

***

The Stata Center looked like something out of a Dr. Seuss story, so randomly constructed it appeared to be perpetually about to fall in on itself. Sylvie had read that the design, by noted architect Frank Gehry, was supposed to be a metaphor for freedom. To her, the odd mixture of metals and bricks of varying colors was a hot mess, albeit an intriguing one. But given that MIT nurtured the up and coming leaders of the world, she figured they must know more than she did about a lot of stuff, including architecture.

She crossed the white brick courtyard littered with students lingering in the rare April sunshine, chatting in small, animated groups or cherishing the first bounties of spring in blissful solitude. Here were young people from every imaginable ethnic background, much like the women she had cleaned beside the day before. Like so many others who had immigrated to this country, those people had accepted their positions on the bottom of the social hierarchy so that their children could prosper. Her own great grandparents had done the same when they'd come to America to escape the pogroms in Eastern Europe. They would have counted themselves fortunate to have her cozy little apartment in Central Square.

Inside the Stata Center, the circular lobby was lined with displays depicting MIT's cherished history of pranks. In her search for the elevator, Sylvie passed a display listing the rules for ethical "hacking," defined as "an inventive anonymous prank." A quote from a former MIT president read, "Getting an education at MIT is like taking a drink from a fire hose." Beside the display stood a fire hydrant connected to a fire hose that had been turned into a working drinking fountain.

Past an enormous neon question mark, Sylvie found the elevators. On the seventh floor, the doors opened to reveal a communal area with sofas and chairs dominated by a chessboard painted on the floor, complete with chess pieces the size of toddlers.

She wound her way through a labyrinth of corridors lined with offices until she came to one with an open door labeled *Sundar Patel.*

The young man inside, intent on his computer screen, looked to be in his thirties with a sleek, black ponytail that fell half way down his back. He wore a hot pink shirt and a black retro vest probably purchased at great expense from Bobby from Boston, the local vintage treasure-trove. Enormous earphones covered his ears.

Sylvie cleared her throat.

He didn't respond.

She touched his shoulder. The hunched figure nearly jumped out of his skin. He whipped around, saw her, and his startled expression softened. He pulled the earphones away from one ear.

"May I help you?" he asked.

"I hope so," she said. "I was wondering if you could explain something to me."

The young man shoved his spectacles up onto the ridge of his nose. He gestured toward the only other chair in the tiny office and placed his earphones on the desk.

Sylvie sat and pulled the blue binder from her shoulder bag. "This is a proposal for software my husband wrote. Can you explain what he's working on?"

"Have you asked your husband?"

"My husband is a very smart man. He's tried to explain, but I don't understand and he's starting to treat me like an idiot. I was hoping—"

She sounded lame even to herself. She was about to get up and leave when the young man reached for the binder.

He flipped through it, then turned to the table of contents and studied it. He paged through the entire document again, more slowly this time. Finally, he looked up. "I didn't know Templeton & Brewer was working on cyber security."

Sylvie shrugged.

"Your husband is Mark Wolff?"

"You know him?"

"I know *of* him."

Sylvie smiled her most innocent smile. "So, can you explain Assuranz to me?"

He tapped the page with his finger. "In the simplest terms, this proposes a new approach to intrusion detection and prevention for governments and corporations to protect their intellectual property and their secrets. But this takes prevention to another, much more aggressive level. A sort of reverse RAT."

"RAT?"

"Remote Access Tool. The proposed software would not only detect and prevent access to sensitive information, but it would allow reverse spyware to be installed on the hackers' computers—sort of a Trojan horse—which would allow the targeted corporation to spy on the hackers without detection."

"So this software would allow a company to spy on the spies without getting caught? Could that really work?"

"Theoretically. But I'd have to take a closer look to see if this particular approach is feasible. Lots of companies are jonesing to address industrial espionage and repel hackers. It's the execution that's tricky. The theft of intellectual property by rival corporations and even foreign governments is rampant. And it's costing big business a lot of money."

"So, solving the problem could be worth a lot?" Sylvie asked.

"Yes. But, frankly, nothing I've seen in this proposal would convince me, as a potential investor, that this method has much chance of success. It's long on theory, short on specifics."

Sylvie reached for the binder. But Patel kept one hand on it and made no move to release it.

"However," he continued, "I know Mark Wolff's reputation. I doubt he'd claim to be able to do something if he wasn't convinced he could do it. I'd like more time with this."

"I'm afraid I have to replace it before my husband finds out I took it."

"If I had more time, I could probably tell you whether this might work."

Sylvie shrugged. "Oh, I don't care about that. I simply wanted to make sure he wasn't using his late nights at the office to cover up an affair."

This time when she reached for the binder, Patel reluctantly let her have it.

She slid it into her shoulder bag. "Do you think there could possibly be portions missing from this proposal?" she asked.

"That would explain a lot. But why would someone like Mark Wolff purposely leave out the meat of his proposal? Especially if he's trying to convince someone to invest big bucks in its development?"

Why indeed? She stood. "Thank you so much, Mr. Patel."

He unfolded his lanky form from his chair and stood, towering over her. "If you change your mind—"

"I'll be in touch."

She found her way back along the corridors to the elevator and pushed the button. While she waited for the doors to open, she glanced back over her shoulder.

Sundar Patel stood half way down the corridor, watching her.

The binder in Sylvie's bag weighed heavily on her shoulder and on her mind. Had she made a mistake showing it to a stranger? The sooner she returned it to Florence, the better she would feel.

Thirty Five

Sylvie strode along the waterfront toward the offices of Templeton & Brewer, shielding her eyes from the glare off the water.

She ducked inside the building and checked in with Mitchell, who looked her straight in the eyes this time and greeted her warmly. When the elevator doors opened to the third floor offices of Templeton & Brewer, Florence was waiting. She hustled Sylvie directly into her office.

A large manila file labeled, "COBRA: Wolff" in red block letters lay prominently on Florence's otherwise pristine desk. She gestured for Sylvie to take a seat, then shut the door.

Sylvie sank into the chair, removed the bag from her shoulder and steadied it between her legs, relieved to have the weight off her shoulder. She started to speak but Florence shook her head and held a finger up to her lips. Sylvie heard faint footsteps approaching.

The door opened and Lisa Chang stuck her head in. She registered Sylvie's presence but chose to ignore her, speaking directly to Florence. "I need to speak to you."

Florence's tone was cold. "What's your problem, Ms. Chang?"

"That document I asked you for this morning. I need it now."

"I'll look for it as soon as I have a minute."

"Tell me where you filed it and I'll get it myself."

"If I knew where it had been misfiled, I would have found it by now." Florence took an imperious tone. "This is what happens when we try to save money by hiring temps." She stood. "You remember Mrs. Wolff. She dropped by to discuss health care options for her family, now that Mr. Wolff is no longer employed here. As you know, any discussion of health care is confidential. I'll need you to step outside and please knock next time. We don't want anyone reporting a HIPAA violation."

Florence stood beside the door until Lisa stepped out, then shut it brusquely, nearly smacking Lisa in the process.

Both Sylvie and Florence remained silent until Lisa's footsteps retreated.

"Sorry. She must have seen you come in." Florence handed the large manila folder to Sylvie. "Your COBRA is paid for the next three months with an option to renew. You can let me know what you decide."

Sylvie put the folder into her bag, removed the blue binder and handed it to Florence. "Is this what Lisa was looking for?"

"She asked for it first thing this morning. I've been avoiding her all day." Florence carried the binder to an oversized file cabinet and crammed it inside one of the drawers. "Did you find out what you needed to know?"

"Not yet. But I'm working on it."`

***

Sylvie emerged from the Central Square T station and hurried down Green Street. It was later than she'd hoped. She couldn't help noticing the difference between the pristine expanse of the waterfront and the litter strewn human chaos that was Central Square.

LaVonda was perched in her usual spot, puffing contentedly on a generous cigarette stub. Sylvie waved and smiled but kept walking, eager to get home.

As she passed, LaVonda called out, "Things around here sure got more lively since you got here. But not to worry. Sounds like things have calmed right down."

That's when Sylvie noticed the barking. As she climbed the front steps to her building, then the next three flights, the canine cacophony grew louder.

She opened the door and was nearly knocked off her feet by an enormous, slobbering bullmastiff, who greeted her so enthusiastically she was pushed back into the hallway. The drool pooled in its drooping jowls threatened to spill over onto her.

Behind the enormous beast, a small dog that looked like a cross between a ferret and a dust mop yapped furiously. And next to the barking mop, Sugarbear obligingly joined in the chorus, looking unsure why they were all barking but happy to be part of the pack.

Claire came bounding out of her bedroom. "Guess what, Mom. I got a job." She tugged on the mastiff's collar, pulling him back inside the apartment. When Claire let go, the enormous animal shook itself and slobber flew everywhere.

Once Sylvie determined she was not in immediate danger of being eaten alive, she squeezed her way past the canine welcome committee into the apartment. As soon as the door shut behind her, the barking ceased and all three dogs converged around her, sniffing her from head to toe.

"This is Bigger," Claire said, indicating the mastiff. She pointed at the animated mop. "That's Gus-Gus."

The dogs finished vetting the newcomer and charged off together down the hallway. Bigger tripped over Gus Gus and went sprawling, but miraculously managed not to crush the smaller dogs.

"He doesn't know how big he is. He's only a puppy, " Claire said, nearly dancing with excitement. "I was walking Sugarbear down by the river and two people asked if I was a dog walker. I said 'yes.' Twelve bucks an hour per dog. Fifty for an overnight. Paid in advance."

She dug in her pocket and extracted a crumpled fifty-dollar bill. "Bigger is staying over," she said, and handed the money to her mother.

Sylvie hesitated for only a few seconds before she took the money and kissed the top of Claire's head.

Claire beamed and produced a slimy green tennis ball from her pocket. She whistled. When all three dogs came crashing back down the hallway toward them, Sylvie braced herself against the wall.

Claire opened the door to the landing. "Want to see our new game?" She stepped to the railing and dropped the ball straight down the center of the staircase so that it landed all the way down on the first floor.

All three dogs bounded down the stairs. After a brief tussle over the ball, they bounded back up, arriving only slightly winded. Sugarbear dropped the ball at Claire's feet, then, all three dogs stared up at her, then down at the ball, then back up at Claire.

Claire offered the ball to Sylvie. "Want a turn?"

Sylvie regarded the slime-covered ball and considered cautioning Claire against annoying the neighbors before she remembered that their only neighbor was Jack Ramsdale.

Instead, she headed back inside the apartment. "Thanks, but I think I'll have a cup of tea. How about a snack?"

***

When the storm had abated and Claire and her pack had snacked and were on their way to the park, Sylvie girded herself to confront the garbage bag from Templeton & Brewer. She hoped nothing was rotting in there. Anything that resembled food could be pretty rank by now.

Her cell phone rang and Sylvie grabbed it. It was Fran.

"I've been meaning to call," Fran gushed. "How are you and the girls doing?"

"We're good. It's nice to hear from you." Sylvie resisted the urge to say "finally," preferring to retain what little dignity she had left.

"Do you have a minute?"

"Sure." Sylvie hit the speaker button and placed the phone strategically on the kitchen counter so she could use both hands to clear dishes off the counter while she talked. She spoke with a deliberately cheerful lilt in her voice, grateful that her old tennis buddy couldn't see her face and know how badly her feelings had been hurt when none of her old pals had bothered to check in on her after her fall from grace. "What's up?"

"Remember the other night when I ran into you at the Shubert?"

"I do. How was the show?"

"Dense. But that's not why I'm calling. I looked for you at intermission but I couldn't find you."

"I had to scoot outside to make a quick call. Sorry."

"Yeah, well some creepy guy who smelled like a can of air freshener blew up all over him, cornered me at intermission. He wanted your phone number."

"Did you give it to him?"

"No. He didn't seem like your type."

Relief washed over Sylvie. "Thanks, Fran."

"The thing is—"

"Yes?"

"I think he followed me home."

"Did something happen? Are you all right?"

"I'm fine, so far. But he must have used my address to figure out my name and phone number. He keeps calling and insisting I give him your number and address. I told him you moved out of the neighborhood and I didn't know where you were. Which is sort of true. But I'm afraid if John answers the phone, he might give that creep your phone number to get rid of him. Do you think we should call the police?"

"I don't really know. He's a friend of a friend. I'll call my friend to see if he can convince Big Eddie to leave you alone."

"Big Eddie? Jesus, Sylvie, what's going on with you?"

"Let me get right on this so we don't get the guy any more riled up than he is. I'll call back later and tell you the whole story."

That seemed to appease Fran's growing interest. After empty promises to get together for coffee, they hung up.

That was all she needed—a stalker named Big Eddie. At least she could smell him coming. What if Big Eddie tracked her down and showed up when one or both of the girls were here alone?

Raul didn't answer her calls. Sylvie sent a text requesting he call back, ASAP. Then she headed for her bedroom. There, instead of the neatly tied garbage bag she had climbed over all morning while getting dressed, the plastic had been chewed open and the contents, which included several rotting pieces of fruit now covered with fruit flies, had been strewn everywhere. Sylvie took a moment to marvel at the phenomenon that was fruit flies. Where the hell did they come from, and how could they possibly procreate so quickly?

Besides the rotting fruit were papers scrunched into tight balls, now thickly coated in what she could only hope was Bigger drool. Hadn't those computer geeks heard of recycling?

She searched under the kitchen sink and emerged victorious, with a pair of rubber gloves and an ancient bottle of Manischewitz Concord Grape wine that had been tucked away in the furthest corner of the upper level of the kitchen cabinets, a relic from her kitchen in Weston.

She found a saucer, filled it with the sweet wine mixed with dish soap, and placed it on her night table. Generations of fruit flies would be lured by the sweet fermenting sugar and drown happy.

Pulling on the rubber gloves, she tackled the mound of garbage. At the bottom of the mound she found the smaller wastebasket liner from Lisa's office. It was still intact, save for a couple of small holes. She gathered up the rest of the garbage into a new extra strength bag, then set about going through Lisa's trash more carefully. She untangled each ball of paper, smoothing it out and reading it as best she could. Most of it was junk mail, along with a few generic empty window envelopes, discarded wrappers for office supplies, and one empty scotch tape dispenser. She also found an illegible office memo and an unopened envelope full of generic coupon offers.

The one item of interest was a half filled-out form with questions in both Chinese and English entitled "Supplementary Visa Application Form of the People's Republic of China." Only the very top section of the form was filled out. The section provided boxes requesting a name, passport number and date of birth. The answers to those three questions had been provided in Chinese, but the remainder of the questions had been left blank.

Sylvie smoothed the paper, folded it neatly in half, and slipped it inside her pillowcase.

She dumped the rest of the trash into the new bag and dragged it into the kitchen.

She was about to lug it down the back stairs when she heard Claire returning with the dogs.

While Claire got fresh water for herself and her three charges, Sylvie presented her with the garbage bag. "Take this down the back stairs and put it in the bin, please." She turned to go, then turned back. "And in the future, make sure my door is closed when we have canine visitors."

"Sorry, Mom." Claire took the garbage bag and headed down the back stairs. The dogs crashed along behind her, happy to be running anywhere.

A few moments later, Claire was back in the kitchen. "What's with the pulley thing in the back hall?"

"The dumbwaiter?"

"What's a dumbwaiter?"

"It's like an elevator for stuff," Sylvie explained. "This building was designed in the 1920s, when the people who lived here had to haul firewood and ice all the way up here. When I lived here, I used it for groceries and laundry."

"Can you show me how to use it?"

"Nope. Off limits. The rope is too old and frayed. I don't want any accidents."

"But it's so cool. Can we get it fixed?"

"Maybe Mr. Ramsdale will get around to fixing it," Sylvie said. "He seems like the handy type."

"Great. Cuz I could send Sug down in it, and if we put in a doggie door she could go outside to pee in the mornings all by herself before I get dressed. Can you ask him?"

"We're not asking for any favors."

"Why not? He likes you."

Sylvie spun to face her daughter. "Why would you say that?"

"He looks at you the way guys look at girls."

"That's not true. Really?"

"It would serve Dad right."

"It *would* serve Dad right," Sylvie agreed. "But when Jack Ramsdale looks at me, all he sees is the pathetic lady in the attic."

"Like the crazy wife in Jane Eyre?"

Sylvie crossed her eyes and lurched playfully at Claire, who shrieked and turned to run. That was when Bigger leapt at Sylvie, hurling her to the ground.

She landed hard on her tush and banged the back of her head on the linoleum. From her position, flat on the floor, she looked up to see Bigger glaring down at her. Massive threads of drool hung, suspended, over Sylvie's face.

She froze, wondering if she was about to become Bigger's dinner.

Sugarbear, clearly conflicted, stood behind Sylvie's head and growled low in her throat, a half-hearted warning to her new best friend.

Claire's face materialized behind Bigger's. She wrapped her arms around the dog's neck and pulled him away so Sylvie could climb to her feet.

Claire threw her arms around her mother's waist. "Are you okay? Do I have to give him back?" Her voice quavered. "He didn't understand that we were playing. He was trying to protect me."

Sylvie caressed her daughter's hair with one hand and reached for a dishtowel with the other.

Bigger looked back and forth between the two of them.

When Sylvie sat down, Bigger planted his enormous head in her lap, big brown eyes gazing sorrowfully into hers. She regarded him for a moment, then cupped the huge head with both hands and lifted it, scratching behind his ears.

This enormous beast had placed himself directly between her child and potential danger.

Suddenly she didn't feel quite so alone.

She kissed the wet shiny nose and was heading for her bedroom to change when her cell phone rang. Raul's number appeared on caller ID. He was downstairs, having come straight across the river from Boston University as soon as he read Sylvie's frantic messages.

***

Raul sat at Sylvie's kitchen table, enjoying a cup of her precious cinnamon spice tea while he explained the problem of Big Eddie to his friend, Mike, over the phone. Gus-Gus was a contented ball, curled in his lap, while Bigger lay at his feet, presumably only because he couldn't fit on Raul's lap, too. Sugarbear's head rested on one of Raul's boots.

Sylvie listened anxiously to his end of the conversation, wondering why the dogs exhibited this strange attraction to Raul. Perhaps it was because he smelled like leather and sunshine.

When the call ended, Sylvie did not like the grim look on Raul's face. "So, is he going to take care of it?" she asked.

"He's going to try."

"Try? He can't try. He has to make Big Eddie leave Fran and her family alone."

"Apparently, Big Eddie has the hots for you."

"That's only because he doesn't know me. Tell your friend to tell Big Eddie he doesn't know what he's getting into. I'm neurotic, spoiled and broke."

"That's his type. So, if you're looking for a sugar dad—"

"Thanks. I'll keep that in mind for when I'm slightly more desperate."

Raul inhaled, savoring the sweet aroma wafting from his cup. "Mike said he'd threaten to send a photo of you and Big Eddie to his wife if he doesn't back off."

"Great, a picture of Big Eddie and me out there in cyberspace. With my luck, he'll post it on Facebook."

"If he doesn't back off, we go to Plan B."

"There's a Plan B?"

"Yeah, I call a friend who will shoot him in the head and dump him in the Fens. But that's expensive. Cheaper to chop him up and feed him to this guy." Raul scratched Bigger's head.

Sylvie studied Raul's face. "I can't tell if you're kidding."

He grinned at her. "How about you show me what you found in the garbage?"

Sylvie went into her bedroom and returned with the visa application.

Raul studied it briefly. "Does the Chang chick have family in the People's Republic?"

"Mark never mentioned it. Of course, he also failed to mention that he was sleeping with her."

"She could have family there, business or both. Or simply a yen for travel."

Sylvie smiled as her cell phone trumpeted.

When she answered, Florence Whittaker's voice was tense. "I only have a minute. I'm on my way to the Bean Pot. There's been a crisis at TechnoData and Gertrude needs help."

Sylvie's stomach lurched. "Is anyone hurt?"

"Just the repository."

"What's a repository?"

"I'll explain over coffee," Florence said. "She wants you to come, too."

"Why didn't *she* call?"

"She doesn't want your number showing up on her phone. Just come."

Thirty Six

Sylvie joined Florence and Gertrude, who were deep in conversation at their usual table in the back of the Bean Pot Coffee Shop.

Florence scooted over to make room on the bench as she continued comforting Gertrude. "It's the way people behave when they're panicking. Don't take it personally."

Poor Gertrude was shaking so hard she could barely lift her oversized cup to her lips. "I don't understand why they're treating *me* this way. I'm the office manager. I don't even have access to the repository."

"What the hell is a repository?" Sylvie asked.

Florence glanced up. "It's the definitive version of a program while it's in development— the version that contains the most up-to-date copy of the software program. Programmers working on the program can check out a sub tree, then update the main copy. The repository can only be updated by one person at a time in order to prevent a merge conflict."

"Okay. So, what happened to it?" Sylvie asked.

Gertrude gripped her cup like a life raft. "The repository has been corrupted. Months of work. Gone."

"Can't it be fixed?"

"Sure. But it will cost close to half a million to reconstruct it, and the lost time will devastate the project."

Sylvie's heart sank. Mark's big gamble was their one hope to replace the money he had "borrowed" from their joint accounts. She had simply assumed that because Mark was Mark, he would eventually succeed, as he always did. Then he could replace the girls' college funds and repay her parents. And she could have her house, her life and her tennis club membership back.

Florence stirred her coffee thoughtfully. "Surely there were backups. Mark was always tyrannical when it came to backups."

"The whole program is backed up several times a day. All the backups have vanished," Gertrude said.

Sylvie resisted the urge to panic. Mark didn't make mistakes like this. She was the one who made stupid mistakes, like not backing up the PTA data base and having to beg Mark to help her reconstruct it.

Florence shook her head in disbelief. "But why is Mark blaming *you*?"

Gertrude placed her cup carefully in the saucer, her trembling hands spilling half the contents on the way down. "It isn't Mr. Wolff. It's Lisa Chang. She screamed right in my face that I should have made sure someone double-checked the backup every day. I don't know why that woman hates me."

"She hates everyone," Florence said.

"Except Mark," Sylvie pointed out.

"Besides, that's not your job. You're the office manager, not their mother," Florence insisted.

"Mr. Wolff should have hired seasoned professionals instead of a bunch of arrogant kids moonlighting from their graduate programs because they're young enough to be covered by their parents' health insurance. You get what you pay for," Gertrude said.

"So, how does a repository get corrupted? Did someone do it deliberately?" Sylvie asked.

Gertrude removed her glasses and rubbed her eyes. "Maybe." She turned to Sylvie. "That's why I wanted you to come. I wanted to warn you. Your name came up."

"Me? Why me? I know nothing about computers or software."

Florence frowned. "You happened to be in my office the day I couldn't locate the proposal for Assuranz right away."

"Crap," Sylvie said.

"Relax," Gertrude said, "I could tell from the look on his face that Mr. Wolff doesn't really believe you had anything to do with the missing repository. Ms. Chang's just grasping at straws, lashing out. You have no reason to sabotage your husband's work even if you knew how."

"I would be the last person to sabotage him," Sylvie said. "Every dime we had, not to mention my parents' money, is invested in that business."

"So then, the question is—who *did* want to derail TechnoData?" Florence asked.

"The competition?" suggested Sylvie.

"It's possible that a company working on similar software made one of our young geniuses an offer he couldn't refuse," Gertrude said. "None of us are paid much. We're all working for a piece of TechnoData's future. But that's not going to pay the tuition or rent."

"Young men that age don't always have much regard for the long term," Florence added, "they're bad at long-term planning and they're serious risk takers. You know the old saying, young men make the best soldiers and the worst drivers,"

"But no one outside of TechnoData knows what we're working on," Gertrude said.

The image of Sundar Patel regarding her from his office at MIT flashed across Sylvie's mind. Too late, she noticed Florence and Gertrude staring at her.

Florence peered into her eyes. "Did you show anyone the binder you borrowed?"

Sylvie shook her head and focused on keeping her guilty conscience from showing.

Gertrude intervened. "I'm quite sure Mrs. Wolff had nothing to do with any of this. We're better off trying to figure out who did."

Relieved, Sylvie asked, "How many people work for TechnoData?"

Gertrude counted on her fingers. "There are five programmers, all graduate students recruited by Mark. Then there's Mr. Wolff and me. That's it. The accounting and bookkeeping is done by an outside service. Ms. Chang doesn't work there officially. She's still at Templeton & Brewer, but she drops by on a regular basis. And from the way she throws her weight around, she probably has some sort of financial stake in the company—like providing part of the seed money to get it up and running."

"Or supporting the CEO so he can afford to work there for nothing," Sylvie said. "Isn't that some kind of professional conflict of interest with Templeton & Brewer?"

"That depends," said Florence. "If TechnoData tanks, no one will care. But if it's a success, I would expect some serious investigation into whether Assuranz had its beginnings while Mr. Wolff was under contract to Templeton & Brewer or if he applied for copyrights or patents before he quit. Lisa and Mark both signed contracts agreeing that anything they developed while under salary belongs to Templeton & Brewer."

Gertrude stirred her tea with a trembling hand. "Now that the repository is gone, it's a moot point. Because unless we find a working copy, we're all screwed."

Thirty Seven

As soon as Sylvie turned the corner onto Green Street, she saw the blue flashing lights of a police car in front of her building and a small knot of people gathered in the street.

She broke into a run, her maternal instincts exploding. Too late, she remembered she was wearing dress heels. As she neared the front stoop, the heel of her shoe caught in a manhole cover and snapped. She stumbled and her ankle twisted painfully, pitching her forward toward the concrete.

Before she landed, two arms grabbed her, breaking her fall. Jack Ramsdale's voice spoke softly in her ear. "You know, you don't have to fall to the ground every time you see me. If you want my attention, just ask."

Sylvie noticed a purple lump on Jack Ramsdale's forehead and bloody scrapes on his hands. "What's happened? Where are my girls?"

"Someone tried to break in. Don't worry, no one was hurt," he said. He turned her so she could see Claire and Diana standing on the porch talking to a uniformed policewoman with skin the color of ebony. Claire held Sugarbear in her arms and Diana held Gus Gus. Bigger stood at attention, a massive barrier between the girls and the rest of the world.

Relief flooded Sylvie's soul. She slipped off her broken shoe and tried to step on her foot but her ankle gave way. Again, Ramsdale's grip held her steady.

He walked her to the stoop, helped her sit, then disappeared into the building.

Bigger's enormous head loomed above her. He sniffed her, then sluiced her face with his tongue.

Sylvie saw Diana point her out to the officer who came over and sat down on the stoop beside her. "It appears a couple of kids broke into your building," the officer said, "but your neighbor stopped them before they entered any of the apartments."

Goose bumps formed on Sylvie's arms. First TechnoData, now her home?

Ramsdale reappeared with two bags of frozen corn. He handed one to Sylvie for her ankle and pressed the other against his own forehead. "They got away," he said, "Probably looking for something they could sell."

A red Jaguar barreled down the street and screeched to a stop somewhere in the vicinity of the curb. Mark leapt out and started up the steps, but came to an abrupt halt when Bigger stepped toward him, blocking his way.

"What the hell?" Mark jumped back, nearly falling off the step.

"This is Bigger, Dad. I'm getting paid to take care of him," Claire said.

The officer raised her eyebrows. "Not sure who's taking care of who."

"Sorry, Mom," said Diana. "We called him when you didn't pick up your cell."

Mark turned to Sylvie and demanded, "Where exactly were you when all this was going on?"

None of your goddamned business. "On the subway," Sylvie replied, her voice shaky.

"I told you this neighborhood wasn't safe. I'm taking the girls home with me." He turned to his daughters. "Get in the car."

"I can't, Dad. I have to take care of the dogs," Claire said.

"I said—get in the car. Now."

The officer stepped forward. "There are only two seat belts in your car, sir. Where exactly do you intend for them to sit?"

Mark said nothing. Sylvie knew he was seething inside. Mark did not like to be thwarted.

"I have a date tonight," Diana said. "And we're fine."

"I'll call a cab," Mark said to the officer.

The officer turned to the girls. "Do you want to go with him?"

Both girls shook their heads.

The officer turned to Sylvie. "Does he live here?" she asked, indicating Mark.

Sylvie shook her head.

"Do you want him here?" the officer asked.

Sylvie shook her head again.

The officer turned to Mark. "I suggest you step down off the porch, sir. Everyone appears to be fine. I'm sure these young ladies will be happy to give you a call as soon as I'm finished getting the information I need for my report."

Mark stood his ground. "My daughters are not safe with all these indigents and criminals on the street."

The officer eyed Bigger, then looked back at him. "You sure?"

Bigger growled and Mark backed down off the porch. He walked around to the driver's side of the car and got in.

As he tore off down the street, a soda can bounced off the side of the Jag.

Mark slammed on the brakes and threw the sports car into reverse, then stopped, leaned out and addressed the officer. "Did you see that? Who the hell did that?"

LaVonda leaned against a nearby building, the butt of a cigarette dangling from her lips.

The officer never looked up. "I saw nothing," she muttered.

Mark floored the gas pedal and peeled off.

Thirty Eight

Sylvie sat on an overstuffed armchair in Jack Ramsdale's living room. Her leg rested on a pile of pillows stacked precariously on an ottoman. Her foot was mummified with an ace bandage covered by an ice pack. She had dosed herself with Advil to reduce the swelling in hopes of staving off a costly deductible for emergency room care. Classical guitar music played in the background and Bigger lay spread at her feet, refusing to be lured from his post by the promising aroma of garlic, rosemary and a few other spices she didn't recognize. The girls had been sent down the street to Whole Foods for salad ingredients and pasta. From the sound of their chatter, they were now happily assisting Jack with dinner preparations while Gus Gus and Sugarbear skittered underfoot.

The perfect family scene, Sylvie thought, except this wasn't exactly her family or her home. Still, Jack was good with the girls. He had done a cursory check for obviously broken bones and she'd been impressed with his expertise and gentle touch. Which might have, for a moment—if she wasn't completely delusional—crossed the line from cursory exam to caress. On second thought, she *was* delusional.

Even so, she had to admit, the attention was nice.

She forced herself to remember that, as nice as Jack Ramsdale was being, with his aromatic pasta sauce, and soft, seductive music, he still wanted her booted out of her apartment as much as Mark.

As desperate as they both were to get her out of her apartment, she was just as desperate to stay, even if she had to bump up and down three flights of stairs every day on her butt.

But exactly how desperate *was* Mark? Gertrude had said it would cost half a million to restore the repository, and Mark was already short of the funding he needed to bring his precious software to market.

Did that make him desperate enough to send a couple of punks to break into her home? To convince the girls that they were unsafe? What if the girls had been there alone?

Maybe Mark no longer loved *her*—she was beginning to get used to the idea that he had moved on—but his girls? His babies? Would he really put them in harm's way? She couldn't wrap her mind around the concept.

What if Mark wasn't behind the break-in? What if someone was looking for something they thought she had?

Like a flash drive.

She had taken it from Lisa's office at Templeton & Brewer late on Friday. Over the weekend, TechnoData's repository had been mysteriously corrupted. Today was Monday and someone had tried to break into her apartment. Could it all be connected?

Then there was the letter written in Chinese on the flash drive that she couldn't understand and the visa application for China. She had to find someone who could read Chinese.

Surely MIT had plenty of people who could translate for her. But whom could she trust? Look what had happened when she showed the blue binder, incomplete as it was, to Sundar Patel.

Sundar Patel. She remembered the tall, lanky figure with the long black ponytail standing in the hallway at MIT, watching her as she entered the elevator. How badly did he want to get his hands on that proposal?

She couldn't shake the feeling that she was missing something. The answer tickled at her memory, just out of reach, and she knew she'd never rest until she figured it out.

If all the events of the past few days *were* connected, the answer could be on that stupid flash drive.

She must know someone who could read Chinese—someone she could trust—at least a little.

Monica Jen-Wilcox. Her old tennis buddy. Monica's parents had fled to Hong Kong during the Cultural Revolution where Monica had been born. Years later, when she was accepted at Harvard, the whole family had immigrated to the States and settled in Boston, where Monica had met and married her husband, the orthopedic surgeon.

In Sylvie's other life, back in her tennis club days, she had considered

Monica a friend. Funny what she'd thought of as friendship back then. Back when one didn't overstep one's boundaries by asking for favors because one didn't ever admit to needing help.

But that was then, this was now.

Thirty Nine

Diana and Claire were gone.

Thankfully, it was only for the night. Mark had seduced them with promises of steamers at the Sail Loft and tickets to a Norah Jones concert at the Opera House. They had been enthusiastic about dinner and the concert, less so about spending a Saturday night at the condo "to get to know Lisa better." He would drop them at school the next day.

Initially Claire had declined, worried that her mother's sprained ankle would hinder Sylvie from climbing three flights of stairs to walk the dogs. But Sylvie had encouraged her daughter to go, hoping that if the girls spent enough time with their father, he would think twice about suing for custody. When it came to the reality of meeting their daily demands, his attention span had always been stunted. And she could only imagine Lisa's reaction to their teenage paraphernalia being strewn all over her perfect domain.

Besides, her girls needed to come to terms with their new potential stepmother. No matter what Sylvie's feelings were toward the woman, the girls needed to form their own opinions. Anything Sylvie said about her would be written off as sour grapes.

Gus-Gus had gone home to his family. While the apartment was noticeably quieter without the two small dogs yapping and tumbling over each other, Sylvie found she missed the little guy. Bigger had stayed on, awaiting his owners' return from Italy.

Now the dogs were out with Ahmad, another dog walker Claire had met at the dog park. Ahmad had agreed to walk Bigger and Sugarbear along with his own pack while Claire was gone and Sylvie recovered from her injury.

Sylvie limped around her kitchen, tidying up and waiting for Monica to arrive. Her friend had said she'd come over right after Sunday brunch at the club. Sylvie's ankle was better after two days' rest and lots of ice. Not broken. A little sore, but definitely better.

The doorbell rang and Sylvie buzzed Monica in. It had been awfully nice of her to agree to fight Cambridge traffic and attempt parking in Central Square, where even though you didn't need a permit on Sundays, finding a spot was always a challenge. Back in the days when Sylvie had lived in Weston, it had seemed an overwhelming hassle to brave the narrow streets of the city in her massive SUV.

When Sylvie opened the door to her apartment, expecting to greet Monica on her way up, she was surprised to hear several pairs of footsteps clomping up the stairs. She peered over the railing. First Fran Forsythe, then Monica, then Delia Grafton rounded the turn, panting from the climb.

Even tennis can't compete with the Green Street workout, Sylvie thought.

Fran entered first and handed Sylvie a box from Romano's Bakery. It smelled like her old life—mornings spent around a friend's kitchen table, drinking homemade lattes and chatting about the kids' ballet classes or plans for an upcoming ski trip.

The determined look on Fran's face as she entered the apartment made Sylvie want to retreat to her bedroom and hide under the covers. The others trooped in behind her, the same resolved look on each of their faces. This couldn't be good.

"What a lovely surprise." Sylvie lied, closing the door behind them.

They looked at one another, each waiting for someone else to speak.

Sylvie limped into the kitchen and gestured grandly at her tiny table. As they chose their seats, she turned her back and retrieved a plate from the cupboard to serve the fragrant Romano muffins, careful to keep her weight off her sore ankle. She hoped her face was more composed than she felt and that her little apartment didn't look as shabby as she knew it did.

"Coffee?" she asked.

They all nodded and she focused on grinding the beans and setting up the coffeemaker since she could no longer afford the pods for her beloved Keurig. She turned the machine on, then settled into a chair and waited.

All eyes were on Fran, who shifted uncomfortably in her chair as she glanced at the others, then fixed her gaze on Sylvie. "Honey, we're all worried about you," she said.

The others nodded and tilted their heads to the side, a study in pity mixed with kind concern.

"Thanks, but I'm okay. I mean, I twisted my ankle but it's not broken and I can even walk on it a little today."

Fran shook her head and looked sad. "It's not only your ankle, sweetie. It's the fact that you left your husband and got involved with that lowlife."

"Lowlife?" Who was she calling lowlife? LaVonda? Raul?

"The one who keeps calling me to get your number," Fran explained. "At least I think it's you, except that he keeps calling you Monica."

Monica frowned.

"Big Eddie? I'm not involved with Big Eddie," Sylvie said. "And I didn't leave Mark. He left me."

Their heads tilted to the other side. Their expressions read "poor Sylvie's lost touch with reality."

Sylvie looked at each of them, sitting around the table, staring at her and realization dawned. "Is this some kind of intervention?"

Monica reached for a muffin and tore off a crumb. "Dan ran into Mark at the club. Mark was there as a guest. He told Dan he had to give up his membership because you couldn't stop spending money."

Sylvie's face flushed hot and she stood up to get mugs, cream and sugar because she couldn't trust herself to speak.

So now Mark was contacting her friends, laying the groundwork, convincing people to buy into his version of reality. Her hand shook as she poured the coffee. They all watched her shaking hands, which made them shake even more.

Delia stood, took the pot from her and finished pouring. "We thought, as your friends, we should tell you," she said. "Mark feels you're unstable. He doesn't think you should be taking care of the girls right now. And from what Fran's been telling us, well, frankly, we're worried."

"We've been meaning to come see how you're doing," said Monica. "And then when I got your call that you needed help, well, I thought we'd all better come right away before—"

"Before what?" Sylvie demanded.

Delia patted Sylvie's hand. "Before we agreed to testify for Mark at the emergency custody hearing he requested."

There was a knock on the door. The knob turned and Jack's head poked in. "Sylvie?"

The women all looked up as Jack entered, looking like a model for L.L. Bean in his jeans, flannel shirt and Timberland boots.

"Sorry, I didn't know you had company," he said. "Just wanted to ask if you needed anything at the store and to check on your ankle."

The women looked at Sylvie in amazement.

Sylvie looked at Jack and saw what they saw. A handsome man who wasn't her husband and who had casually entered the apartment before anyone answered his knock. A stud who acted like he owned the place— who hadn't had to be buzzed in. Sylvie couldn't tell if her friends were horrified or jealous.

Fran started toward the door and the others followed. "I think we'd better go," she said. "Please call if you need to talk." She kissed Sylvie on both cheeks.

Delia followed next. "We're here for you, dear."

Before following the others, Monica squeezed Sylvie's hand and asked, "What was it you needed my help for?"

Sylvie shook her head. "Nothing, really. Just checking in. I'm so glad you all stopped by."

Monica raised her hand to her ear, her thumb and pinkie outstretched in a silent "call me" gesture, and followed the others down the stairs.

Jack shut the door behind them. "What was all that about?" he asked, reaching for a muffin.

Forty

Sylvie hobbled around the apartment, attempting to bring some order to the mess. Back in Weston, the house was so big, her family had barely been aware of each other's presence. But here in Cambridge, Sylvie found she had grown used to the constant sound of adolescent drama, whether screams of outrage or shrieks of laughter.

The buzzer sounded. Sylvie hobbled to the intercom and buzzed in Ahmad with the dogs. She opened the door to the apartment, stepped aside and whistled. Bigger and Sugarbear bounded up the stairs and sat nicely for their treat. Sylvie smiled to herself, proud of Claire's entrepreneurial spirit.

The dogs collapsed in the living room, tired from their ramble with Ahmad.

Sylvie wandered into the girls' room. She missed them. She bent over, lifted a crumpled shirt off the floor, and inhaled the smell of Claire— coconut shampoo and eau de Sugarbear. She picked up dirty underwear and socks, tossed them into the basket, then straightened the beds and organized Claire's menagerie of stuffed animals.

Her foot throbbing, she sat down on Diana's bed and curled up on her side, resting her head on the pillow and inhaling the calming scent of lavender. Her eyes pushed closed and she let herself drift off, only for a minute.

In her dream, Sylvie meandered through the oversized Queen Anne Victorian on Garfield Street in North Cambridge that was her childhood home. In this dream home, so familiar yet so different, fireplaces led to tunnels that opened onto secret rooms she had never seen before.

A wet nose in her ear startled her awake.

She peeled one eye open, then the other. Sugarbear gazed down at her, panting puppy breath into her face. Beside her, Bigger's chin rested on the bed, his fleshy jowls inches from her nose, his brown, troubled eyes locked on hers. A low guttural rumble, barely audible, came from his throat.

That's when she heard it. The sound of drawers sliding open in her bedroom, across the hall.

It was probably Diana, searching for a pair of tights or a pair of earrings to borrow.

But both girls were gone.

Fear washed over Sylvie, freezing her in place as her brain raced to parse the danger.

She needed to call 911. Where was her cell phone?

She remembered leaving it on the little Moroccan table next to her favorite chair in the living room. Might as well be on the other side of the planet.

She had to get out of the apartment. No, she had to get out of the apartment *with the dogs.*

She planted her bare feet on the floor, scooped Sugarbear up under one arm and stood, praying her ankle wouldn't give way.

With her free hand, she gripped Bigger's collar. He stood and patiently allowed her to lean on him, his back rigid, reflecting her fear.

Silently, she urged him toward the open door where she peered out. The hallway was empty but, across the hall, the door to her bedroom was shut. *And someone was in there.*

The low growl in Bigger's throat grew slightly louder. Sylvie tugged his collar and he quieted.

She backed them down the hall, through the kitchen to the back door, never taking her eyes from her closed bedroom door.

She released Bigger, so she could pull the door toward her with one hand and turn the dead bolt with the other to escape down the back stairs. But as she reached out to retrieve Bigger's collar, her bedroom door flew open and Bigger tore off toward the intruder, barking ferociously.

A strange man's voice yelled, fueled with fear and rage, "What the fuck!"

Bigger's furious barking morphed into a scream of pain. Sugarbear squealed, struggling in her arms and Sylvie nearly dropped her.

For a split second, she was torn between Bigger's cries and the need to get to safety. But her flight response won out. Sylvie limped out the door to the back stairs. There, she stopped short. There were too many steps between her and the street. With her weakened ankle, she'd never make it.

Her eyes landed on the dumbwaiter. It probably wasn't safe, but it was her only chance.

From inside her apartment, Bigger's screams died to a whimper. She had to get down to the street to get help.

She climbed into the dumbwaiter, grabbed the rope and tugged. The rope creaked and the entire conveyance jerked, then began to move slowly downward.

Sylvie glanced up. A pair of dark eyes that seemed to float in the dim light were leaning over the shaft above her, like an alien from another planet. Then she realized that the alien was a human wearing a ski mask. The eyes, the only feature she could see, looked Asian but she couldn't be certain.

The dumbwaiter gained speed, hurtling past the second floor landing, almost in free fall. If she didn't slow it down, it would crash land in the basement. She wrapped her hands in her sweater and grabbed onto the rope. It slid through her hands, burning the flesh through the sweater. She let go, unaware she was screaming until the cage bumped to an abrupt stop, three feet above the cement floor of the basement.

Holding Sugarbear, she rolled out of the dumbwaiter and landed with a thump on the cold concrete. She scooted across the floor and hid behind a half wall that separated the open basement into storage units.

High above her, a grimy window filtered hazy light from outside. She saw two figures flash by. A deep male voice shouted, "Hey, you!" followed by an impossibly loud crack.

Then quiet. She waited.

A familiar scent mixed with rancid sweat drifted toward her.

The dim fluorescent bulb overhead popped, flashed and struggled to go on. Sylvie tightened her grip on Sugarbear, whose tiny body trembled in her arms. An immense silhouette, a drawn gun held out in front with both hands, cautiously made its way down the stairs.

Big Eddie had found her, and now she was going to die.

Sylvie squeezed her eyes shut, resigned to the inevitable.

"Yo, Monica."

Sylvie opened her eyes to see Big Eddie peering over the half wall at her.

"I was outside. Heard you screamin'." He looked her over in the dim light. "You okay?"

He took her hand and tried to pull her to her feet, but she winced in pain. He turned her palms over so he could see them in the dim light. "What the hell happened?" he asked.

She stood, keeping her weight off her swollen ankle. "You mean you're not going to kill me?"

"Kill you? Why'd I wanna do that?" He tucked his gun into the back of his pants. "Some little twat in a ski mask ran out of here. I mighta nicked him."

She stepped forward on her bad ankle and it gave way under her.

"Jeez, Monica, you're a mess." He placed her arm around his neck and half-carried her on his hip all the way up the stairs. Sugarbear followed close behind, yipping at his heels.

By the time they reached the fourth floor and entered her apartment, Big Eddie was wheezing for air.

Inside, they found Bigger lying in the hallway, whimpering, his paws clawing at his eyes.

Big Eddie sniffed the air. "Pepper spray," he announced.

"What do I do? How do I help him?" Sylvie asked.

Big Eddie left her on the floor beside Bigger and returned with a quart of milk and a dishtowel. "Hold him still," he ordered, pouring milk over Bigger's head and into his frothing jowls.

Bigger stopped whimpering and struggled to open his eyes while Sugarbear ran around him in frantic circles.

"Got any saline solution?" Big Eddie asked.

She pointed toward the bathroom. "Medicine cabinet."

He returned from the bathroom with saline and her first aid kit—Mark's last gift to her, on the occasion of her thirty-fifth birthday. The size of a toolkit, it had come fully loaded.

He directed her to lift Bigger's eyelid so he could flush one eye, then the other with the saline. When he'd used up the bottle, Big Eddie got her and Bigger to their feet and helped them to the kitchen where he sat Sylvie at the table. Bigger lay his head on Sylvie's lap.

Big Eddie filled a bowl with warm water and added a squirt of Dawn. Together they bathed Bigger's face until, finally out of pain, he stretched out on the floor beside Sylvie and covered his head with his paws.

"Poor guy," Sylvie said, blowing on her burning hands and wondering why they suddenly hurt so much worse. "I know how you feel."

"It's the adrenaline," Big Eddie said. "You don't feel the pain 'til the crisis is over. Then it hurts like a motherfucker." He placed a bowl of water and a dishtowel in front of her. "You'd better wash those hands. Don't want an infection."

Sylvie dipped her hands in the water and winced while Big Eddie searched through the first aid kit and extracted bandages, tape, and a can of spray anesthetic. He turned both Sylvie's hands over in his huge paws, assessing them for damage.

Sylvie watched him in amazement. This emergency medical expertise and gentle touch were not what she'd expected. "I don't want you to think I'm not grateful," she said. "But why were you lurking behind my building?"

He looked sheepish. "Getting ready to ring your doorbell."

She waited.

"I gotta tell you somethin'. Face to face. Like a man." He tugged at his collar like it was choking him.

"Okay?"

"I gotta break up with you."

Sylvie plunged her hands back into the soapy water. "You do?"

He nodded, sadly. "I met someone. She's classy like you. And she's crazy about me."

Sylvie bit down hard on her lower lip.

"We didn't mean for it to happen," he said. "Guess it was one of those—fate things." He cleared his throat. "At first she didn't want me around. But I got her to change her mind."

Sylvie flashed on the gun in the back of Big Eddie's waistband. *Was that what persuaded her?*

"I had to come tell you first. I know how you girls are. Didn't want you hearin' it from her." He paused. "Cause she's a friend of yours."

Sylvie stared at him. She had no friends—not one—who would ever, in a million years, consider taking on Big Eddie.

Or did she?

She had to admit—he possessed a certain brute charm. *And a gun.* "A friend? Of mine?" she asked, aghast at the tinge of jealously in her voice.

He looked doubtful. "You won't go after her?"

"I swear." She held up her right hand.

Relief spread across his face. "It's Fran."

"Forsythe?"

"Hey, you're not gonna cry or nothing, are you?" Big Eddie looked panicked. "Cause you'll always have a special place right here." He smacked his heart with his fist.

Fran Forsythe? Who bragged she would never consider fucking a man who couldn't afford a "proper wardrobe." Who, behind their backs, of course, and with great glee, positively decimated any man who dared appear in public wearing cargo shorts or crocs? *Fran Forsythe and Big Eddie?* Perhaps size did make up for a multitude of sins.

She accidently knocked over the bowl and spilled water all over Big Eddie's pants.

He stared down at the wet spot spreading across his crotch and sighed. Then he reached into his pocket and pulled out a damp business card for The Pasta Palace. "You need me, you call me. But don't say nothin' to Fran."

As he stood to leave, they heard Jack's anxious voice calling up the back stairs: "Sylvie, are you all right?" followed by pounding footsteps.

Jack Ramsdale burst into the room, stopping short when he saw Big Eddie, whose eyes narrowed and whose hand slipped behind his back and stayed there.

Jack straightened. His chest expanded.

The whole encounter reminded Sylvie of the mating dance of the blue-footed boobies she'd seen on vacation in the Galapagos Islands.

Jack's eyes went to Big Eddie's wet crotch, then to Sylvie. "Why is there blood all over the side of the house and broken glass in the hallway?" Jack asked.

"Nicked the bastard," Big Eddie announced, a triumphant smile on his face.

"Bigger got pepper sprayed," Sylvie said. "Sugarbear and I had a close encounter with the dumbwaiter. And Mr. Abruzzi here saved the day."

Jack gave Big Eddie a curt nod. "Cops on their way?" he asked.

Big Eddie's arm came from behind his back. It was empty. "I gotta go," he said and started toward the door. He turned back, grabbed the can of anesthetic spray from the table, and motioned for Sylvie to raise her hands.

She obediently held them out for him to spray. In seconds, the burning subsided. "Thanks. For everything," she said and kissed his cheek.

Big Eddie blushed and moved toward the door. "Yeah, well, I got experience. Stuff happens at the Palace." He shouldered Jack out of the way.

"Who the hell was that?" Jack asked when Big Eddie was gone.

Sylvie gave an exaggerated shrug. "Not exactly sure," she said. "But it turns out, he's a handy guy to have around."

She waved her hands in the air to dry them while Jack moved through the apartment. At the doorway to her bedroom, he stopped and gave a low whistle.

Sylvie stood and limped to her bedroom. Between her concern for Bigger's eyes and the pain in her hands, she hadn't thought to worry about what the intruder had done or what he might have taken.

Her bedroom was literally torn apart—mattress and pillows slit open, their liberated feathers drifting everywhere. Clothes littered the floor, pockets turned inside out. Every jar from her bureau had been opened, the contents scooped out and smeared onto delicate lingerie, then tossed aside.

Jack stepped into the room. "Two break-ins in two days. That's got to be some kind of record, even for this neighborhood." He lifted one of the empty jars. "Whatever they're looking for is pretty small. Any jewelry missing?"

Nothing in the kitchen had been disturbed. *Thank goodness, Bigger interrupted the intruder before he got to the Grey Poupon,* Sylvie thought.

Jack glanced at his watch. "You did call the cops, right?"

"I can't. Mark's suing for custody on the grounds that the girls are living in an unsafe environment. Another police report would settle the matter."

"Maybe he's got a point."

Sylvie froze. *But the girls weren't here. They were safe at Mark's. What if that wasn't a lucky coincidence?* She studied Jack's face. "That would suit you, wouldn't it?"

"Excuse me?"

"How do I know you're not in cahoots with Mark? You both want us out of here." Sylvie collapsed on top of the chaos that was her bed and curled up into a fetal position.

Jack sat down on the bed beside her, smelling of grapefruit and alderwood. "Cahoots? I don't do cahoots with anyone who hasn't bought me dinner. You really think your husband and I hired someone to break in here?"

"Well?"

Jack grinned at her. "Think it would work?"

She wanted to give him the finger, but her hands were too sore. She flashed the back of her hand at him, which sort of diluted the point.

"Tell me everything that happened," he said. He was so close that she could see flecks of gold in his green eyes and feel the heat from his body. For the past fifteen years, there had been only Mark. And Mark in bed was much like Mark anywhere else: efficient and goal-oriented.

Sylvie recounted the events of the day, from the time she woke from her nap until Big Eddie found her hiding in the basement. Jack gave her his undivided attention in a way that made her increasingly aware that their bodies were nearly touching. The space between them seemed charged with energy. *If men only knew that all they really needed to do to make themselves irresistible to women was pay attention,* she thought.

"I didn't think the dumbwaiter would hold us," she finished, remembering the oily feel of new rope in her hands. "But the ropes weren't old."

"Yeah, well, you know kids. I replaced them."

Sylvie felt a wave of gratitude. "It fell so fast," she said. "I couldn't make it slow down." She searched his face, but his features were inscrutable. And handsome. And he knew how to fix things. What the hell was wrong with her? After fifteen years of marital fidelity, why was she suddenly thinking about good old-fashioned, mind-bending sex? With a virtual stranger? Who wore a tool belt?

His brows furrowed as if he'd picked up on a subtle shift in energy between them. Or had she said something out loud? *Oh, god, let me not have said something out loud.*

"The mechanism wasn't meant to hold so much weight," he said.

177

"You calling me fat?" she asked, deadpan.

A look of alarm flashed across his face, then relief when he realized she was teasing. "Never," he said. "But I have noticed Sugarbear's chubbing out. And then there's *that* big old thing." He nodded toward her swollen foot.

He stood. "I'm going to fix the back door," he said, and left her alone.

What just happened?

Was it obvious to Jack that she was fantasizing about having mind-bending sex with him? Had she made a complete fool of herself? Did he reject her, or was he oblivious to the pheromones her body was probably shooting out?

She told herself she had dodged a bullet. She'd read somewhere that great sex was ten times more addictive than heroin. The last thing a single mother with two impressionable teenage daughters needed was an addiction to late night booty calls with an attractive downstairs neighbor.

And what made her think it would be great sex?

It was just as well. If Mark got wind of another man hanging around the girls, it would put one more check on his side of the column in a custody battle. With her luck, she'd get one of those buttoned-up, conservative, misogynistic judges who stubbornly clung to the traditional double standard. This was the Commonwealth of Massachusetts, after all. Mark might be living openly with his home-wrecking mistress but that kind of behavior, while understandable for a red-blooded male, was unacceptable for a mother.

It was all moot anyway. Jack Ramsdale wasn't interested. Even her stalker had blown her off. She might as well face the fact that she was never going to have sex again.

Had she misread the tension between them completely? She was utterly, unrecoverably humiliated. Was it possible to simply vaporize into another dimension?

She considered her options. She could throw herself off the Zakim Bridge. Or jump in front of a passing Mercedes on Brattle Street and hope for brain damage, memory loss, and a large settlement, solving all her problems in one fell swoop.

And leave my girls in the care of a woman who killed puppies.

She lifted her head and noticed the blanket lying on the floor—bright white embroidered letters against a royal blue background spelling out *Ghost*

Rider. It was the blanket the nice man with the red beard had given her the day she'd jumped into the harbor to rescue Sugarbear.

Surely, the nice man expected it back. She would simply have to limp down to the waterfront and return it. Right now. It was the only polite thing to do.

And if she happened to catch a glimpse of her daughters while she was there and remember why she shouldn't throw herself onto the third rail of the MBTA, well, so much the better.

Forty One

Sylvie sat in the back of Desiree's taxi, dressed in jeans and a sweatshirt, confiding the details of her close encounter and desperate to hear the comforting words only another woman knew enough to say—that the world wasn't going to end just because you'd made a complete ass out of yourself, which you probably hadn't done at all.

Desiree didn't disappoint. "You're not old and fat," she said. "Hey, if I went that way, I'd do you."

Sylvie dabbed at her eyes with a crumpled tissue. "You would?"

"No question." Desiree glanced into the rearview mirror. "But like I said, don't get your hopes up. I got my hands full in that department."

Sylvie blew her nose.

Desiree adjusted the mirror. "I overheard Raul tell my brother he thinks your skinny white ass is hot."

"You're just saying that to make me feel better."

"Yeah. But that doesn't mean it's not true."

"What *exactly* did he say?"

"Forget it. Raul's nothing but trouble for women. Don't make me regret telling you."

"Raul thinks I'm hot?" Sylvie persisted.

"Yeah, so, this handyman—any chance he's gay?"

"No."

Desiree shook her head. "It ain't natural. You gotta think to yourself, why would a straight guy turn down a shot at getting laid?"

"He's just not that into me?"

"Honey, in my experience, all you gotta do with most men is show up."

"Maybe he doesn't want to screw me because he's already trying to screw me, over my condo."

"If so, that's the first time I heard about a dick with a conscience." Desiree eased the cab into a "No Stopping" zone next to Lisa Chang's building. "I'd wait if I could, but I got a pickup."

"Go. I'm fine." Sylvie handed Desiree some cash, pulled the hood of her windbreaker over her head, eased herself out of the cab and stood, pleasantly surprised to find her ankle holding firm beneath her.

She made her way along the brick path toward the harbor but as soon as she turned the corner, leaving the shelter of the tall buildings, a biting wind off the water blasted her face, forcing her to squint.

She hugged the blanket to her, searching the top windows in Lisa's building for signs of movement. Against the bright sunlight, the opaque white windows revealed nothing.

Down on the open dock, Sylvie felt completely exposed.

The boats, bobbing in their slips, showed no signs of human occupation. She should have anticipated that no one might be on board the *Ghost Rider*, and she should have brought a decent bottle of wine to leave with the blanket. With the spring chill in the air, it was probably too early for any but the hardiest yachtsmen.

Raising one hand to shield her eyes from the sun, she scanned the dock, following it out to the furthest finger, where the *Ghost Rider* appeared deserted like all the others.

She braced herself and leaned into the wind as she walked down the ramp and out to where the *Ghost Rider* thumped against the dock padding. Visitors were supposed to request permission to board, but what was the proper way to announce oneself? Yell, "Ahoy, there!" or some other yachty greeting?

Before she could make a complete ass of herself, the man with the red beard emerged from the *Ghost Rider*'s cabin. She caught his eye and held up the blanket as offering.

He nodded and said something, but his words were swallowed by the wind. He stepped to the railing and offered his hand. She hesitated. *What if he's a wealthy psycho serial killer?* On the bright side, if she got whisked out to sea and dumped overboard in an ice chest, she would never have to face Jack Ramsdale again.

She reached out her hand. He grasped her wrist and with one fluid motion, hauled her on board. She did not pick up any psycho killer vibes, though up close he did bring to mind an eighteenth-century pirate.

Sylvie bent her knees and swayed to absorb the motion of the boat. Redbeard, unaffected by the movement, headed into the cabin.

Sylvie grabbed the handrail and peered inside. A gleaming wooden galley, bright blue cushions the color of the sea and the smell of coffee beckoned.

She stepped inside and he slid the glass door shut behind her, blocking out the noise, the cold and the wind. She held out the blanket. "I wanted to thank you for your help the other day, Mr.—"

"Grady." He poured a mug of steaming black coffee from a pot in the galley and held it out to her.

Before she could take it, the boat rocked and she reeled backward, landing hard on the cushioned bench.

Grady handed her the mug. "Gotta love spring in New England."

She lifted the mug with both hands and drank, enjoying the warmth.

"How's the pup?" he asked.

"Miraculously resilient. Thanks."

He sat down on the bench opposite her. "I'm glad you've come, Sylvie."

Sylvie's hand jerked and coffee splashed onto the table. She didn't remember telling him her name.

Grady grabbed a sponge from the galley and wiped the spill. "It's my job to know who goes in and out of Lisa Chang's apartment," he said, seeming to read her mind.

"You're watching Lisa Chang?"

"I am."

"Are you a cop?"

"I work for the feds."

Sylvie placed her mug carefully onto the table. "You mean like the FBI?"

"I work under contract for FISMA."

"Sorry?"

"Federal Information Security Management Act. It covers cyber security for systems that affect the government. Which is pretty much everything."

"So, why Lisa Chang?" she asked, her apprehension growing.

"What do you know about Ms. Chang?" he countered.

"I know she's shacking up with my husband. Is Mark involved with whatever this is?"

"Frankly, I was hoping you could tell me."

"Because you think my estranged husband confides in me about his mistress?"

"We thought you might be able to tell us about your husband's specific area of interest in cyber security."

"I wish I could," she said.

Redbeard leaned forward.

"All I know is he spent every dime we had…" she let her voice trail off. *Shut up, Sylvie,* she told herself.

"Do you know anything about Lisa Chang?" he asked.

Sylvie shook her head.

"Ms. Chang's father is a high-ranking officer in Chinese military intelligence—the biggest risk to U.S. cyber security."

"I thought it was the Russians."

"Russian cyber hackers are generally criminal networks who operate for profit, not patriotism. That means they can be bought. The Chinese government, on the other hand, has a professional cyber espionage unit with a budget eight times as big as Russia."

"Mark is not a spy for the Chinese government." She paused. "Is he?"

"Your husband left Templeton & Brewer to start his own company at the same time he moved in with Ms. Chang. That made some people very nervous."

"So, you're saying Lisa Chang is a spy?"

"That's what we're trying to determine. Chinese cyber spies target our financial, defense, technology and research institutions. Mark Wolff has a reputation for developing software that redefines not only solutions, but the problems themselves. Now that he's turned his attention to cyber security and has attached himself to Ms. Chang, she's attracted our attention."

"Attached himself? That's what you call it?" She stood. "I need to get my girls. I don't want them involved in any of this."

He placed a hand lightly on her shoulder. "Sit down."

She sat. "Are my girls in danger?"

"Possibly."

Sylvie's stomach shifted and she fought a wave of dizziness. "What the hell is going on?"

"The way the Chinese work is they form partnerships between Chinese civilian companies and American companies to gain access to American technologies. And Chinese state-run firms are buying up American companies that have access to the technology they want."

"I don't understand what that has to do with Mark—or my girls."

"I thought you and I might share an interest in Ms. Chang, since she's the one who ended your marriage."

"My husband ended our marriage."

"I wouldn't be too sure about that."

"What exactly are you saying?"

"Have you ever been in a room that smells rotten, but you can't figure out where the smell is coming from? Well, something about Lisa Chang smells bad."

Sylvie snorted. "Tell me about it."

He smiled. "I'm trying to find that bad smell and put a name on it. The U.S. is deeply in debt to the Chinese government. So, we can't go around kicking people out of sensitive industries simply because they're Chinese. We need hard evidence before we can take action. Would you like to help me find that?"

"Find evidence against Lisa Chang?"

"That's the gist of it."

"Evidence of what?"

"Pretty much anything illegal." He handed her a card with a cell phone number. "I'd like you to call me if you learn anything that might be of interest. And in return, I'll keep an eye on your girls."

***

When Sylvie reached the street, she paused in the shelter of the buildings lining the harbor walk and dug her phone from her bag. She had to get her girls away from Lisa Chang. There could be no sharing of custody now.

She typed, "Where are you?" and sent the message to Claire's phone.

Seconds later her phone pinged. "Aquarium. Dolphin show."

She typed, "With?"

Claire: "D and LC :-P. Supposed to be girl time. LC outside on phone whole time. Hate her."

Sylvie: "Dad?"

Claire: "Work. Help."

Sylvie: "Sneak away?"

Claire: "15 min. Meet where?"

Sylvie: "Marriott lobby?"

Claire: "K."

Sylvie hurried along the waterfront, only slowing down when she got close enough to the Aquarium to scan the faces of the tourists scattered on the plaza. No sign of Lisa Chang anywhere.

Sylvie pulled her hood over her face, hunched her shoulders and walked past the Aquarium and the signs advertising boat tours, to the entrance of the Long Wharf Marriott.

Inside the expansive lobby, chairs and couches were strategically placed to invite intimate conversations in cozy luxury. Various groups, mostly business types, with a few families of tourists with kids, occupied most of the seating.

It was here, in the Waterline restaurant, just off the lobby that she and Mark had celebrated their last anniversary. Sylvie tried to remember Mark's behavior that night. Had he given any indication that he'd left Templeton & Brewer three months earlier? That he hadn't walked the few short blocks from his old office, but instead had driven from his new office in Arlington? Or perhaps walked here, fresh from a tryst at Lisa Chang's waterfront condo? That he was planning to move in permanently with his mistress? That the entire evening celebrating and reminiscing over their fifteen years of marriage had been a farce? Had she missed some vital clue that could have somehow warned her that their lives were about to implode?

Sylvie was so caught up in the questions flying around in her brain that she nearly overlooked Lisa Chang, deep in conversation with two older Chinese gentlemen, all comfortably ensconced in plush armchairs beneath an enormous arched window. Lisa's back was to her, but her face was reflected in the window.

Sylvie walked quickly past, hoping she hadn't been spotted. The last thing she needed was for Lisa Chang to complain to Mark that Sylvie had dragged the girls away from their "girl time." What were the chances he would listen if she tried to explain that to protect their girls, she had to keep them away from Lisa?

Especially with Lisa's voice whispering in his ear that Sylvie was nothing but a hysterical, scorned woman.

That she was either hallucinating or outright lying.

That she would claim anything, make up any outrageous story, to keep her kids.

On the other hand, what if Mark knew that Lisa was involved in shady activity and he was complicit?

Sylvie stole a look back. Lisa and the gentlemen were still deep in conversation, the two men leaning forward, apparently hanging on Lisa's every word. The looks on their faces reminded her of Sundar Patel, whose words resonated in her head. *Mark was proposing to take computer security to another level. A reverse RAT, installing reverse spyware on the hackers' computers, allowing the target to spy on the hackers without detection.*

Sylvie glanced outside and spotted Claire and Diana, giggling conspiratorially as they hurried toward the hotel entrance.

In less than one minute they would step inside.

Sylvie grabbed her phone and quickly texted, "Stop! LC in Marriott lobby. Wait in Legal."

Outside, Claire paused, took her phone from her pocket, then glanced around. The girls did an abrupt about-face and scampered off toward Legal Seafood.

Sylvie's phone pinged. "Starving. Can we get chowder? Dad gave us money."

She texted: "yes" and hoped Lisa Chang and her friends didn't get a sudden craving for steamers.

When the girls were safely out of sight, Sylvie edged closer to the group, moving casually along the periphery of the room until she was close enough to hear Lisa speaking in rapid Chinese. Sylvie couldn't understand a word, but Lisa's tone was confident, knowledgeable.

Sylvie sat with her back to the group, opened the voice memo app on her phone, and hit "record."

Forty Two

Sylvie and her girls sat on the sofa with mugs of warm Burdick's cocoa made with the last of Sylvie's stash.

"Do you think Dad will be pissed we ditched Lisa?" Claire asked.

Diana stretched out her legs, plopping her feet onto Sylvie's lap. "We'll tell him we couldn't find her after the show, so we went home," she said.

"Yeah, let's see if he gets pissed at Lisa for ditching *us*." Claire lifted Sugarbear onto her stomach. "But I don't think we should tell him Mom was there." Claire stole a glance at her mother. "Why *were* you there, Mom?"

"I had a bad feeling," Sylvie said. "Mother's intuition."

Sylvie considered telling them the truth about her conversation with Redbeard. But then she would have to explain about returning the blanket, and about why she had the blanket in the first place. That would lead to a discussion of Lisa as attempted puppy killer. The girls would insist on telling their father that his mistress was a murderess—all based on information provided by Sylvie, the woman scorned. She wasn't ready to go there.

The girls nodded. Sylvie knew their previous experience with her "intuition" made no further explanation necessary. For Sylvie, mother's intuition legitimately covered cases where a little judicious snooping had come into play.

Diana wiggled her toes, her sign for Sylvie to rub her feet.

Sylvie complied, happy and grateful that the girls were safe at home.

Diana's phone dinged. She glanced down. "It's Dad. He wants to know where we are. What do I do?"

"Tell him the truth," Sylvie said.

Diana texted and they waited for another ding.

"The Changster is up to something," Claire said. "I don't trust her."

Sylvie did her best to sound casual. "Why do you say that?"

"For one thing," Claire said, "she has two different phones. One, she answers in front of us. The other never rings. It vibrates and she goes in another room and closes the door to answer it. Even though she talks in Chinese."

"And Dad doesn't even notice," Claire said. "She thinks she's so slick. She's not. Dad's just clueless."

The girls glanced at each other and smirked.

Sylvie recognized that look. "All right, fess up. What did you two do?"

"Promise you won't get mad?" Claire asked.

"I can't make that promise," Sylvie answered. "You know that."

"Fine," said Diana. She crossed her arms and let her eyes drift to the ceiling.

Sylvie looked from one to the other, then raised her arms in a gesture of defeat. "All right. I promise."

Claire grinned. "We got hold of her secret burner phone."

"When she was in the shower," added Diana, her voice dripping with disgust. "With Dad. They were giggling."

Both girls made vomiting gestures.

Sylvie squeezed her eyes shut in a vain attempt to block the image before it was burned into her brain.

Diana nudged her mother with her foot to bring back her attention. "And we installed this cool new app called ListenOut. It lets you let other people listen in on your conversations. So they can give you advice on what to say. Like if you meet a guy in a bar." Diana paused, then said in a rush, "Which, of course, I've never done because I'm only fourteen."

The girls exchanged a look.

Claire said, "We set it up so we can go on the computer and listen to the step monster's phone calls."

"So we know what she's saying about us," Diana said.

"Or about Dad," Claire added. She looked at her mom, then looked away. "Or you. It's rude. Like whispering in front of other people."

"We have the right to know what she's saying about us behind our backs," Diana said.

Sylvie studied her daughters. They must have been paying attention when Mark explained technological stuff, unlike their mother. "But you said she speaks Chinese on that phone," she said.

"Most of the time," Claire said. "But not always."

"How do you know?" asked Sylvie.

"Because we listened," Diana said.

"Besides," Claire said, "even if she does speak Chinese, the phone can translate. Sort of."

"Really?" Sylvie felt a sudden burst of energy. "Can you show me?"

Claire turned on the computer and downloaded a free translation app, then showed her mother how to use it. "Be careful," Claire cautioned, "it's pretty good word for word but it can really screw up a phrase or a sentence. Especially if there's more than one meaning for a word."

It seemed similar to the app Sylvie had used on the Chinese letter, except this one was for verbal conversations.

Claire downloaded the ListenOut app and entered her login. "When Lisa's talking, it'll ding on my phone," she explained. "It's supposed to alert the Chang that someone's listening in, but I found a workaround to disable that function."

The intercom buzzed, followed by a series of short blasts.

Sylvie hit the button to buzz open the door, then stepped out to the landing. Even the perfectly toned Lisa was a little out of breath when she and Mark reached the fourth floor.

Mark rounded on Sylvie. "How dare you snatch them? I'll take out a restraining order." Without waiting to be invited, he stepped inside the apartment.

When Lisa stepped in just behind him, Sugarbear started to bark furiously. Lisa's eyes opened wide at the sight of the angry puppy. Diana had to hold Sugarbear and shush her to get her to stop barking.

Claire looked up innocently. "Hi, Dad."

"Don't you ever disappear like that again," Mark said.

Diana stood up and gave her father a peck on the cheek. "We didn't disappear," she said, waving a dismissive hand toward Lisa Chang. "She did."

Claire edged away from the computer, which dinged and burped in the final stages of shutting down.

"I told them to come home," Sylvie said.

Claire pointed a finger at Lisa. "She left to make a call during the show and never came back. We waited in Legal for her to call, but she never did."

"That's because you entered your phone number wrong on my phone." Lisa offered a view of her phone to Mark.

Claire squinted at the screen. "Oops. I wonder how I did that."

Mark barely glanced at the screen. "Get your jackets. We're going to dinner."

Claire and Diana glanced uncertainly at their mother.

"Would you like to finish your visit with your father?" Sylvie asked.

Claire glared at her father. "Not if you're going to ditch us again."

"I didn't ditch you," Mark said in a tone that suggested even *he* didn't believe it. "I wanted you to get to know Lisa. She's an important part of our lives now."

"Maybe she's important to you, but—" Diana stopped abruptly when Claire gripped her arm in a warning squeeze.

"No ditching," Claire warned her father.

"Chocolate buffet at the Cafe Fleuri?" Diana pushed.

"Fine."

Claire and Diana high-fived each other and raced out the door, followed by their father.

Sylvie called after them, "See you after school tomorrow."

Lisa moved across the room to hover near the computer, whose screen was finally blank. "If you try to use those girls to drive a wedge between Mark and me, it won't work. He'll choose me. And the girls will choose the luxuries we can afford to give them over"—she swept one arm regally across the tiny expanse of the apartment—"this. And you. Because you raised them to be entitled little princesses."

191

With that, Lisa Chang glided out the door.

Sylvie stepped to the stairs and called down, "I'll tell Mark what I saw."

Lisa glanced up. "You mean what you *think* you saw."

Sylvie shut the door behind the cold bitch, leaned her forehead against the wood and closed her eyes. Lisa's words had hit a nerve. Would the girls choose Mark—and Lisa—over her? Because she could no longer afford to take them out to fancy restaurants with chocolate buffets?

She heard footsteps climbing the stairs and a knock on the door.

"Go away, Mark," she told the closed door.

"It's Jack. Can we talk?"

"No."

A pause, then Jack's voice said, "I feel like I gave you the wrong impression earlier."

Sylvie wiped her nose with the back of her sleeve. "Not a problem," she said.

"Can you open the door?"

"No."

"Are you crying?"

"Not over you."

"I didn't—that's not what I meant." Jack sounded so awkward, Sylvie almost felt sorry for him.

"Go away," she said. "This isn't a good time."

"I need to say something to you. Open the door."

She turned the knob and opened it wide enough to peer out with one eye. He looked as miserable as she felt.

Jack pushed the door open, stepped inside, and kissed her.

Forty Three

Sylvie lay in bed the next morning, eyes closed, unable to move. Her mind kept replaying that perfect kiss, which had literally left her weak in the knees. Then, maddeningly, Jack had once again retreated downstairs. She couldn't decide whether she was relieved that he'd left before things continued in the direction they were going, or if she was bitterly disappointed. Most of all, she was surprised at herself for wanting to have hot, passionate sex with a man she barely knew. She barely recognized herself these days.

Lisa's accusations that Sylvie had raised "a couple of little princesses" played over and over in her mind, an endless soundtrack. She threw off the covers and reached for her embroidered silk robe with the cozy terrycloth lining that reminded her of her old life. But instead of nostalgia, she felt annoyed.

First things first, Sylvie thought as she poured coffee into her travel mug while the dogs wolfed down their breakfasts. She attached their leashes and they descended the stairs, then walked down Brookline Street to the dog park at Pacific Street.

As she approached the dog park, her phone vibrated in her pocket. She closed the gate behind her, set the dogs free to meet and greet their friends, then fished for her phone.

"Mom?" Claire's voice sounded furtive.

"What's wrong? Where are you?"

"Dad dropped us at school. Mom, you have to do something."

Dread seeped through Sylvie's limbs. "Tell me what's going on."

A toilet flushed in the background and she could picture Claire huddled in a stall in the ladies' room, terrified that if she was caught using her phone during school hours it would be confiscated.

"Dad's filing for emergency custody," Claire whispered.

Sylvie took a deep breath and forced herself to ask the question that terrified her. "Do you *want* to live with your father?"

Claire made a sputtering noise. "Hell, no. I hate The Chang. She ignores us, and Dad gets all gooey and disgusting around her."

There was a long pause, while Sylvie remembered to breathe.

"Mom? Say something. Say you'll fix it."

"I'll fix it," she said. "Go back to class before you get in trouble."

***

The attorney sitting across from Sylvie looked like she could eat porcupine sandwiches for lunch, then use the quills to pick her teeth. According to legend, Harriet Cadmire of Lukeman, Berg and Cadmire was a bitch on wheels. Just the gal Sylvie wanted in her corner when she went up against Mark for custody.

Attorney Cadmire removed her glasses and placed them on top of a new yellow legal pad on which she had recorded Sylvie's name, address and phone number. "Let me be frank with you, Mrs. Wolff," she said, leaning forward. "At the moment, neither you nor your husband have enough liquid assets to sustain a lengthy legal battle. Though to be fair, I've seen more than one tech startup bust out on the Nasdaq or get bought up by IBM and turn into millions overnight. Which means any settlement we work out will have to provide for that possible eventuality. But for now, we need to focus on the custody battle. They never go smoothly. And are, therefore, expensive."

She sat back in her chair. "As an alternative, you could try mediation, even binding arbitration, but you may not like the results. If you want to engage this law firm, I'm going to need a ten-thousand-dollar retainer."

"Now?" Sylvie had no idea how to get her hands on that much cash. "I could sell my apartment. Someone's offered to buy it."

Cadmire nodded and jotted something down.

"But if I sell it, we'll have no place to live. The girls would have to live with Mark. And that would defeat the whole point of fighting for custody."

"Tell you what," Cadmire said. "Come up with five now and another five in one week."

Sylvie stepped outside the building and into bustling downtown Boston. She dug in her pocket for Grady's card.

Forty Four

Sylvie had balked at the idea of meeting on the *Ghost Rider*, so Grady had suggested the carousel at the Waterfront Park, across from Faneuil Hall. She sat beside Grady, who looked like set dressing on the stationary pirate ship. Just in front of them, a little boy clung to a grinning whale while his mother rode a lobster, both rising and falling to "Sweet Home Alabama," as the Greenway Carousel circled at a surprisingly rapid speed.

"Let me get this straight," Grady said. "You want me to pay you five thousand dollars—for what, exactly?"

"Information about Lisa Chang. Information you asked me to provide."

"We didn't discuss a fee."

"I figured it was an oversight."

"And you believe you already have information worth five thousand dollars?"

"I'm sure of it," Sylvie lied. She withdrew her phone from her purse, attached a pair of earphones, handed them to him and hit "play."

"It sounds like Chinese," Grady said. He reached for the phone, but Sylvie tossed it back into her purse and snapped the purse shut.

He paused, then said, "Fine. It's a deal."

***

Harvard's Fairbank Center for Chinese Studies was located next door to Cambridge Rindge and Latin High School. Before entering with Grady, Sylvie called Nancy at Cambridge Trust to confirm that five thousand dollars had been transferred into her account, and instructed Nancy to transfer the entire amount to Lukeman, Berg and Cadmire.

Sylvie and Grady followed Pe Chu, a thirty-something graduate student,

195

into a tiny cubicle where they watched him peel open a new flash drive and plug it into the side of his computer. He held out his hand for Sylvie's phone.

Grady watched Chu adjust his headset and hit "play." He adjusted the levels and filters on his computer and frowned. "Background noise, hang on."

They waited in silence while Chu listened, his concentration deepening. When Sylvie shifted on her stool, he held up one finger for quiet.

Grady's body was so rigid Sylvie was afraid if she touched him, he might shatter.

Chu listened to the recording a second time without speaking before he removed his headset and set it on the desk. "It's difficult to hear," he said. "She has something she wants to sell them? The men don't think it's happening fast enough. She assures them that the person who owns the asset is growing desperate for money due to several financial setbacks." Chu paused. "I can provide a line by line translation if you prefer."

"Later," Redbeard said. "For now, only the broad strokes. Did they discuss the specific terms of the deal?"

"The sticking point isn't the price, but the owner's willingness to take on a foreign partner," Chu explained. "She replies that the owner will have no choice. The gentlemen pressure her to complete the deal quickly."

"How quickly?"

"The offer is only on the table for twenty-four hours."

Grady stood up, in a hurry to leave.

"There's something else," said Peter Chu.

Grady turned back.

"It's the way the men speak to the woman—the tone of voice and the choice of words. Frankly, it sounds like a threat—should she fail to deliver what she promises."

"What kind of a threat?" asked Redbeard.

"Nothing specific. The men are always polite, well mannered. But they refer to her responsibilities. Her family."

"Are the men threatening to harm her family?" Sylvie asked.

"I believe the gentlemen want her to believe that, yes." Chu unplugged the flash drive and the phone and handed them both to Grady, who pocketed the flash drive and deleted the recording from Sylvie's phone before she could stop him.

***

Grady and Sylvie stepped outside into the bright afternoon sunlight. She glanced at her watch. It was later than she'd realized. In two minutes, the doors of the sprawling high school would open and thousands of teenagers would spill out onto the grounds, the street, and the adjacent campus of Harvard University. A half hour later, due to the staggered schedule, Claire's school day would end. She wanted to check in with them about their weekend with their father.

"Did you get what you wanted?" she asked Grady.

"No complaints," he said and headed back toward Harvard Square.

More than a little pleased with herself, Sylvie stood on the edge of the campus to get her bearings as a tsunami of denim-clad teens surged through all six exits, swamping the grounds. She sent a quick text to Diana, asking to meet her and received a text back: "Outside Fitzgerald Theater."

Sylvie found Diana waiting just outside the theater entrance. "Didn't you get my text?" Diana asked breathlessly. "I'm on the crew for the drama competition. Everyone's staying late to work. We're getting pizza."

"But I thought you didn't—" Sylvie started.

"The shop teacher's helping me. I gotta go back in. We've got to practice building the entire set in five minutes. We get timed." She waved at her mother as she dashed back to the building.

Sylvie watched Diana haul open the heavy door to the auditorium and skip inside. She couldn't remember the last time she'd seen Diana this excited about anything besides Bobby Wise.

Forty Five

Sylvie texted Claire on the way to the upper school. A return text from Claire read, "Left school early. Cramps. Home."

Sylvie cut down Prospect Street and headed for home. She opened the door to find Claire curled on the couch with Sugarbear.

"Your note," Sylvie said. "When did you get…"

"My period? I didn't. It's just what all the girls say when they want to go home. Bigger's mom is coming to get him, and I wanted time to say good-bye."

The front doorbell buzzed a few minutes later. Claire jumped up and pushed the button. "Yes?" she said.

A woman's voice answered, "It's Anne-Marie, Bigger's mom."

"I'll bring him down." Claire attached Bigger's leash and led him down the stairs. Sylvie was torn between feeling that she should go with her daughter and feeling so exhausted she could barely move. She compromised by watching from the window. Bigger leaving made her unaccountably sad.

She saw Claire step outside to greet Anne-Marie, and she saw them hug. Claire handed the leash to Anne-Marie. Sylvie heard Claire bound back up the stairs. Claire tossed the day's mail onto the table next to Sylvie's computer and took Sugarbear into her room.

Sylvie needed a lot of cash, and fast. Harriet Cadmire wanted five thousand dollars more in only one week. If she took a low-paying job at Starbucks or Whole Foods, she'd never make enough to feed a family of three, let alone support an expensive custody battle. She needed something she could sell.

She considered the mountain of boxes cluttering her room. She had both a storage problem and a money problem. Maybe it was time to solve them both, check the internet for high-end consignment shops in the ritzier suburbs like Newton and Lincoln. Not Weston, though. She couldn't bear the thought of her friends recognizing the dresses from parties and charity events she'd attended when she'd belonged in their lives.

Not that my friends would consider patronizing a store that sold second-hand clothes.

Sylvie remembered her collection of designer bags and shoes at the storage facility. She headed back to the computer to find the name of a high-end consignment store when she saw the pile of mail. Sylvie sorted through it, praying she'd won some kind of national lottery she hadn't even entered.

She had an oversized packet half open before she realized it wasn't hers. The envelope was from National Insurance and addressed to Mr. John Ramsdale. It must have been placed in her box by mistake. Judging from the thick envelope, it probably had something to do with a new or renewing policy—probably important. She considered going back down the stairs to deliver it, but going down three flights would mean coming back up, and she wasn't ready to face another climb. It was *his* package. Let him come up and get it.

She dialed his number. While it rang, she stared at the torn envelope. She put the phone on speaker and placed it on the desk, then lifted the envelope to the light. Nothing showed through. But the first page was already partly visible. It was indeed a new policy— *for a four-family apartment building.*

But Mr. John Ramsdale didn't own a four-family building. He owned three units in a four-family building. Sylvie owned the fourth.

Jack answered the phone, and Sylvie suggested he come up to retrieve his mail. While she waited, she peered inside the envelope once more. Jack had probably changed the policy weeks ago, when he thought he'd closed the deal with Mark. The date of the new policy wasn't quite visible, but as she considered tearing the envelope a little more, there was a rap at her door.

"It's open," she called.

Jack entered and she held out the packet to him. "This ended up in my box by mistake. Sorry, I almost opened it."

He took it from her. "I've been waiting for this."

"Insurance?" she asked. "I've been meaning to update the policy here. Do you like National?"

"Don't really know yet. This is new. They have a pretty good reputation. After all the recent break-ins, I thought I'd better upgrade my policy."

Sylvie's phone rang. Cambridge Trust. It couldn't be good news, not the way her life was going. She steeled herself and hit the talk button.

It was her old friend, Nancy, the bank manager, with a heads-up. Her property taxes were due and the automatic payment was about to overdraw her account, triggering overdraft fees.

"Luckily, I had a watch on your account because of the issues with your husband. I managed to stop the automatic payment, but I wanted to let you know that the city is going to want their pound of flesh," Nancy said.

Sylvie closed her eyes. "How much?" When she heard the amount, she nearly gagged. "For a one bedroom? In Central Square?" *When did the taxes in this neighborhood go into the stratosphere?*

"It's crazy, I know, but since Google and all the biotechs moved into Kendall Square, this neighborhood has gone nuts. It's now considered 'shabby chic.'"

"Bad news?" Jack asked when she'd hung up.

"You were clever to buy up these apartments. I guess I've been in the suburbs so long I didn't realize this area had become so desirable."

He shrugged. "It sort of happened around me."

Jack was still watching her, and she could only imagine what he could see in her face. Surely he had picked up on the gist of the last phone conversation, and could smell her desperation. Were those dollar signs glistening in his eyes?

Besides, Mark would probably end up with custody no matter what she did. He would eventually wear her down with expensive legal maneuvers. Lisa seemed to have an endless stream of income, and Mark had endless access to it. But without any money of his own, he had no obligation to support his children, much less his discarded wife.

She might as well sell the apartment, pay off her debts and rent something nearby. At least she'd be able to manage for a while.

She looked up at Jack. "Make me an offer," she said, nearly choking on the words.

Forty Six

The following Sunday, Sylvie woke to find an envelope that had been shoved under her door. Inside was a Purchase and Sale agreement for her apartment.

She made herself a cup of coffee and studied the contract in front of her. The price was fair, even generous. She had checked every recent sale in the neighborhood on Zillow and every other real estate site she could find for comparables. By selling directly to Jack, she would save the agent's fee. The final amount would pay her attorney's fees and probably her rent for a few years, if she was careful. She would find a job so she could help support the girls and go to school at night to increase her earning capacity. She'd manage somehow.

While she was distracted, the girls left with Sugarbear, whispering conspiratorially. Sylvie thought they'd said something about a walk along the river, though Sylvie had been so thrilled that they were getting along so well that she hadn't asked too many questions.

She signed on the bottom line and placed the paper in an envelope, on the front table ready to give to Jack the next time she saw him. He'd be thrilled. She planned to negotiate for a generous deposit, but it would take weeks for the closing and she needed money now.

She looked around at her little apartment, which had begun to feel like home.

It was time to sell her designer bags and shoes. She sat down at her computer and searched for high-end resale stores, weighing their Yelp reviews against their accessibility to public transportation. After numerous phone calls, she found that while they were eager to do business with her, they all wanted to control the pricing and keep sixty percent of the profits.

When Sylvie studied the listings on eBay, she realized that she could widen her market and control the price point herself. It was time for a trip to Cambridge Self Storage. She called Desiree and offered to barter cab rides for first choice of any of her bags.

Desiree was on her way.

Before leaving the house, Sylvie did her usual check—purse, phone, keys, wallet— and headed down the stairs to wait for Desiree. She checked one more time to make sure her phone ringer was on and the volume was as high as it would go, in case the girls needed to reach her.

When she got down to the front stoop, LaVonda was squatting on the top step, smoking the tiniest cigarette butt Sylvie had ever seen. It was so short that LaVonda's fingers appeared to be blackened from the flame. But she seemed oblivious to any pain. Sylvie inhaled and realized it didn't smell like tobacco. She inhaled again, and memories of college days came flooding back.

Sylvie sat down beside her and LaVonda offered her a hit. Sylvie shook her head.

LaVonda glanced at Sylvie and said softly, "Girl, you got bad times. I know."

Sylvie nodded, staring into the distance, trying to catch a glimpse of her future or Desiree's yellow cab. Neither appeared.

LaVonda sucked on the flickering stub and inhaled deeply. "It's gonna be fine. There's a path for you. Don't be afraid to take it."

A taxi glided by, but it wasn't Desiree.

LaVonda patted Sylvie's knee. "I see the light shining on you, girl. Yellow. Like sunshine."

"Is that good?"

"It's hopeful," LaVonda whispered. "You gotta have hope."

Sylvie placed her hand over LaVonda's. "Thank you. But let me know if you see a lot of cash. Or power. I could sure use a little power."

They sat together until Desiree pulled up. When Sylvie stood to leave, she waved to LaVonda, who ignored her, focusing instead on keeping the light alive on her diminishing stub.

Sylvie stuck her head into the front passenger window of the cab. "Can I sit up here with you?"

Desiree patted the seat next to her. "Were you talking to LaVonda?"

Sylvie nodded. "You know her?"

"Sure. She's been sitting on stoops here forever."

"Who is she?"

"Who knows? She knows stuff. That's for sure."

Before she could ask another question, Sylvie's phone rang. "Diana" lit up the screen.

"Mom?" Diana's voice was soft, but Sylvie could hear an edge of excitement.

"Where are you?"

"I'm in a closet at Dad's. We were walking on the waterfront and ended up here. Don't be mad. I can't talk any louder. Can you hear me?"

"Barely. Is something wrong?"

"I don't know. I've gotta tell you something."

Sylvie pressed the phone closer to her ear and stuck her finger in her other ear to block the noise from Desiree's radio and the outside traffic. "I'm listening."

"Dad and Lisa are fighting about some business deal."

So, all was not well in Harborview heaven. Sylvie felt a smile tug at her mouth.

"Lisa says Dad could be rich but he's too stubborn, so he's going to end up losing everything. And Dad said it was all Lisa's fault because she lost something. I can't remember the word. Suppository or something. Hold on."

More silence.

"Do you want me to come get you and bring you home?" Sylvie asked, trying to keep the pleading out of her voice.

"Not yet. Claire and I aren't done finding things out."

"Are you sure you feel safe there?"

"Oh, yeah. I don't think she'd do anything to us. Dad would be too angry. And even though they're fighting, you can tell she's still sucking up to him." There was a long pause, then, "But maybe..." Diana's voice trailed off.

"What is it, honey?"

"Maybe you should come pick up Sugarbear. I don't like the way Lisa looks at her."

"I'm on my way." Sylvie hung up and turned to Desiree. "Change of plans."

***

When Sylvie arrived at the waterfront condo, Claire was waiting in the lobby, holding Sugarbear. Lisa Chang stood stiffly beside the elevator, arms crossed. Something was different about her. She was somehow less cool, less elegant than before.

As soon as Sylvie entered the lobby, Claire rushed to her, threw her arms around her and kissed her loudly on the cheek—a PDA unusual even for Claire, who handed Sugarbear to her mother and glanced over at Lisa.

"When are you planning to come home?" Sylvie asked.

"We thought we'd stay a little longer. If you can watch Sugarbear for me."

Lisa did not seem pleased.

"Are you sure it's okay?" Sylvie asked.

"Dad wants us to stay."

Lisa remained mute.

Sylvie kissed her daughter's cheek but when she turned to go, Claire blurted, "Dad's going to sell his company for a lot of money, so maybe he can help us and you won't have to worry so much."

Sylvie turned to address Lisa. "Congratulations to you both," she managed. "Sounds like quite a windfall."

Lisa's expression hardened and she fixed Claire in her gaze. "If I were caught listening at doorways, my father would have beaten me senseless."

"I didn't know it was a secret," Claire protested. "You guys were yelling pretty loud."

Lisa ignored Sylvie and continued to glare at Claire. "I was taught to close my ears if adults spoke behind a closed door."

She turned to Sylvie. "Don't think you'll be sharing any of the proceeds from our work. You have no right to anything. It is for us and *our* family." Lisa touched her stomach.

Could the Ice Queen be pregnant? It seemed almost unnatural.

"But *we're* Dad's family," Claire said. "What about *us*?"

"If you behave yourself, your father will look after your needs. But your mother is merely a part of your father's history. He owes her nothing."

Lisa turned on Sylvie. "I know you were at Templeton & Brewer. I saw the security footage. You stole something from me, and I want it back. Unless you'd prefer to spend the next ten years of your life in jail."

Sylvie felt her knees go weak.

The elevator doors opened. Lisa stepped inside and held the door open. "Are you coming?" she asked Claire.

"In a minute," Claire said.

"The elevator doors closed behind Lisa.

Only when Sugarbear squirmed in her arms did Sylvie realize she had been holding the little dog too tightly. She hastened out the door, followed by Claire. Sylvie paused outside the lobby long enough to let Sugarbear relieve herself on the small patch of perfect lawn, in full view of the doorman.

"Mom," said Claire, "I need to show you something. Can we go somewhere?"

Sylvie opened the back door of the cab and gestured for Claire to get in. Then she climbed in next to Claire, who gently peeled the dog from Sylvie's arms.

Desiree looked skeptical. "That dog better not pee in my cab," she said as she lowered the window next to Claire so Sugarbear could hang her head out.

"Claire, this is my friend Desiree," Sylvie said.

"Cool," Claire said. "Can you drive us around the block, please?"

Desiree flashed a smile and nodded.

"Diana wants you to hear this," Claire said. She handed her earphones to Sylvie, tapped the voice memo app on her iPhone and hit "play."

Forty Seven

Sylvie heard two voices on Claire's recording, both muffled, as if they were on the other side of a closed door.

"I said 'no." It's off the table." That was Mark, and Sylvie recognized that tone. When Mark used it, she seldom bothered to argue. It was pointless.

Not so for Lisa, who remained resolute, if slightly restrained. *"That was before the repository disappeared. I could understand your preference for an American company over a Chinese if the offers were similar. But that's all changed now."*

Mark: *"It makes no sense. McCauley only reduced his offer to cover the cost of rebuilding the repository. Why didn't Chu do the same?"*

Lisa: *"I'm not going to second-guess their thinking."*

Mark: *"We live here, not in China."*

Lisa: *"Stop being so sentimental. This is business. No one is stopping McCauley from raising his bid."*

Mark: *"McCauley's bid is more than enough. We were hoping for five million. They've offered ten."*

Lisa: *"Chu Industries offered fourteen."*

Mark: *"And what if the missing repository shows up?"*

Lisa: *"No one can complete the program but you, Mark. It's not worth anything to anyone but us and whoever buys us."*

Mark: *"Like the Chinese."*

Lisa: *"You think they destroyed the repository? Why would they do that? It undermines their own investment. It makes no sense."*

Mark's tone had become cold. *"It makes their original offer look a whole lot better than what the competition can afford."*

Lisa: *"But they would have had no way to know what the competition offered."*

Mark: *"Unless someone told them."*

There was a pause. Sylvie glanced at Claire, who held up one finger. Then…

Mark: *"Set up a meeting. Next couple of days. Let both parties pitch their offer. Tell them to bring their contracts and checkbooks. Let's get this done."*

Claire clicked off her phone and looked up at her mother. "Do you know what he's talking about?"

"No idea," Sylvie said. "Wow. Fourteen million dollars."

"I know, right? And you stay up at night worrying about money to buy eggs and bread."

"How do you know I'm up at night?"

"Newsflash, Mom. It's a really small apartment. We can hear you walking around."

"I never told you I was worried about money."

"And we're not stupid."

Sylvie shrugged. "You heard Lisa. The only way I'd get any of that money would be by paying an expensive lawyer, which I can't do because I don't have any money."

"That's so wrong."

"I know, honey." Sylvie kissed her daughter's cheek. "It's awful being poor."

From the front seat, Desiree gave an unsubtle "Hmmmph."

Claire grinned. "Does that mean I should suck up to the Chang?"

Sylvie considered. "Depends on what you can stomach."

Desiree rounded the corner and pulled up once again in front of the Harborview.

Claire kissed Sugarbear and handed her to her mother. "See you after school tomorrow," she said, then hopped out and disappeared inside.

Desiree reached over and scratched Sugarbear's ears. She glanced at

Sylvie. "You okay?"

"I need to talk to Raul," Sylvie said.

***

The Student Union on Commonwealth Avenue was swarming with students when Raul opened the back door of the cab and climbed in beside Sylvie. "I've got five minutes before my class. What's the emergency?"

"Lisa Chang has a security tape that shows me dressed as a cleaning lady snooping around Templeton & Brewer." Sylvie sniffed. "She's threatening to have me arrested for corporate espionage."

Raul looked at Desiree, who shrugged and handed Sylvie a tissue.

"What, exactly, did she say?" Raul asked.

"She said I stole something and if I give it back, she won't send me to jail."

"The garbage bag?"

"No. A flash drive."

"She saw you steal a flash drive?"

Sylvie thought for a moment. "No, not exactly. She saw security footage of me at Templeton & Brewer the night it went missing. "

"And *did* you take the flash drive?"

Sylvie hung her head. "Yes," she said. "It was hidden, taped to the leg of her desk chair."

"Why would she have a flash drive taped to her chair?"

Sylvie dabbed at her eyes with the tissue. "That's why I took it. To find out what she was hiding."

"And did you find out?"

"No. The files are in Chinese. I was going to have a Chinese friend take a look, but that didn't work out so well."

"What did you say when Lisa Chang asked if you took it?"

"She didn't *ask* if I took it, she *told* me I took it."

"And what did you say?"

"Nothing."

"So why hasn't Lisa gone to the police and demanded they get the flash drive back from you?"

Desiree turned to face them. "Because she doesn't want anyone to know about it."

"Exactly," Raul said. "She's bluffing."

Sylvie sniffed. "Are you sure? How do you know?"

"Think about it. If she were going to turn you in, she would have done it already. And I doubt she's absolutely sure you're the one who took it. She's fishing. Lucky you didn't spill your guts. Lots of women like you would have."

"Women like me?"

"Women like you who grew up not having to worry that one wrong word could land them in jail."

Sylvie's first instinct was to protest but she bit the words back. Deep inside, she knew he had a point.

"Gotta go to class," said Raul. "You know anyone who can translate this for you?"

Sylvie thought about Peter Chu at Harvard. The problem was, she couldn't be sure what the relationship was between Peter Chu and Grady. She couldn't risk it.

"The guy that teaches my class in computer forensics is from China," Raul said in response to Sylvie's silence. "Owes me a favor. His sister had a problem with a guy who didn't know how to take 'no' for an answer. So, me and some friends explained it to him. Go get the flash and meet me back here in ninety minutes." He scooted out of the cab and dashed across Commonwealth Avenue, beating the oncoming traffic by a nanosecond.

Desiree checked her watch. "Ninety minutes. Plenty of time to check out those designer bags."

***

At the Cambridge Self Storage facility, Desiree parked the cab among the numerous construction vehicles that facilitated the city's never-ending attempts to repair each winter's damage. With Sugarbear on her leash, Sylvie punched in her code for Bay 2 and the garage door jolted into action. They entered a labyrinth of hallways lined with rows of padlocked doors and adorned with random art, probably rescued from abandoned lockers. They stopped at 238 B and Sylvie checked her phone, where she'd recorded the combination for the lock.

Inside the locker, the rows of boxes reached almost to the ceiling. She couldn't remember many of the items carefully recorded on the labels of the boxes, but she was grateful she had labeled them so meticulously. Thanks to Kevin and Connor, the boxes were neatly stacked with their labels facing out.

Locating the large box labeled "Shoes and Bags" was easier than Sylvie had feared. Accessing it was another matter entirely. It lay below three other large boxes, but Sylvie and a highly motivated Desiree managed to slide the carton out from under the others.

The next challenge was the thick layer of interwoven packing tape the boys had enthusiastically applied to keep the boxes from falling open. Sylvie had neglected to bring anything sharp enough to cut through all the layers. She pulled out her house key and began sawing through the tape, one layer at a time.

Desiree rolled her eyes and muttered a disparaging, "White girls," under her breath. She produced a switchblade from her pocket and flipped it open. It looked like it could do some serious damage. "Meet my little friend," she grinned.

"Wow," said Sylvie. "Careful with that thing."

Desiree brandished the blade. She turned to address the carton. "Don't nothing stand between me and my new bag. Or I cut you three ways. Long, deep, and frequent." With that, she proceeded to slash through the packing tape.

Inside, shoeboxes depicting high-heeled designer shoes that Sylvie could barely remember wearing alternated with layers of tissue-wrapped purses.

There was no room in the locker to sort through it all, so Sylvie went back to the bay entrance and grabbed a hand truck. Together, she and Desiree wrestled the carton out of the locker and into the trunk of Desiree's cab. Since it was too large to allow the trunk to close, Desiree secured the lid with a bungee cord.

***

Back at Green Street, they unloaded the carton and dragged it to the back of the building, where they loaded it into the dumbwaiter. They took turns pulling the rope until the container reached the end of the line on the fourth floor.

Finally, entrenched in the living room, Sylvie watched while Desiree lovingly removed each parcel and carefully unwrapped it, revealing Sylvie's abandoned treasures. She stroked the buttery leather, the snakeskin, the silken linings, opening and admiring each one with suitable reverence.

All Sylvie could see were dollar signs.

When Desiree unwrapped the python leather Brunello Cucinelli, Sylvie remembered that terrible day when she'd last used it—the day her life had fallen apart.

Unlike the others, the Brunello looked bloated, and Sylvie realized she had forgotten to empty it before packing it away. That was unlike her, because everyone knew that a good bag would last forever if you took proper care of it. That meant emptying the bag before storing it. But really, who could blame her for her lapse? It had truly been an awful day.

She reached for the bag and Desiree reluctantly handed it over. Inside were the contents of the safety deposit box she had discovered at the Bank of Weston. She removed the original mortgage document for their house, along with Mark's heirloom jewelry, and slipped it all into her purse to be dealt with later. There would be a certain irony if she sold it all to help pay her legal fees.

Desiree checked her watch. "We'd better get back to BU to pick up Raul. Don't forget that flash drive."

Sylvie went into the kitchen and opened the refrigerator. She didn't see the mustard jar, and had a moment of dizziness. But after moving aside a large bottle of blue Gatorade, she found the jar of capers and behind that, the Grey Poupon mustard, where she'd left it. She stuffed it into her purse.

"So, what about the bag?" asked Desiree.

"You choose. That was the deal."

Desiree pointed to the Cucinelli. "Honey, I'd drive you to Mexico for this one."

"Take it," said Sylvie.

As they headed out the door, Sylvie noticed the envelope addressed to Jack, the one with the Purchase and Sale agreement, still sitting on her front table. She'd have to remember to give it to him as soon as she got back.

***

By the time they arrived back on Commonwealth Avenue, Sunday's adult classes at Boston University had ended and parking was easy. Desiree locked the cab. Together they walked the few blocks to the computer lab, where Raul was waiting for them with a young Asian man wearing suspenders and red sneakers.

"This is Hai," Raul announced. "He teaches my internet research class.

His expertise is computer forensics."

Sylvie was about to say, "Hi," but stopped herself.

"Don't worry about it," Hai said. "It happens all the time." He held out his hand.

Sylvie reached into her purse and retrieved the mustard jar, then realized that, as usual, she hadn't thought this through. She opened the jar, dipped two fingers in, and after a feeling around, gingerly retrieved the plastic bag, now covered in mustard.

Hai was staring at the yellowed bag with distaste. "There's a ladies' room down the hall," he said, pointing the way. Sylvie took the bag to the ladies' room, where she rinsed it off along with her mustard-covered fingers. She blotted the bag carefully with a paper towel, opened it and retrieved the flash drive.

She returned to the computer lab and handed the flash drive to Hai, who inserted it into a USB plug on one of the computers. Sylvie held her breath until the icon appeared. Then she took the mouse and worked her way through the folders until she came to the document she wanted translated. "This is it," she said.

Hai reached into his shirt pocket and retrieved a pair of glasses. Everyone waited while he perused the entire document, then started over at the beginning.

"Well?" Sylvie pressed. "Can you tell what it is?"

"There's a formal greeting to what appears to be an esteemed client or customer—Chinese names, some with military titles," Hai explained. "Do you want me to pronounce them for you?"

Sylvie shook her head. "So, it's a letter?"

Hai peered at the screen. "A formal business letter, recommending the purchase of a substantial interest in a start-up software company."

Sylvie leaned over Hai and took the mouse. She opened the document labeled, "Administrator/priv/repoz1." This time, instead of an error message, a series of folders appeared. "Do you know what this is?"

Hai took the mouse from Sylvie's hand and scrolled through the folders, uncovering folders within folders, until he opened one with an odd looking combination of 1's and 0's that seemed to go on forever. "It's a software program."

Forty Eight

On the way back to Cambridge, Raul sat in the front of the cab next to Desiree, while Sylvie rode in the back, barely able to stay in her seat. "It looks like Lisa copied the repository, then destroyed TechnoData's copy."

"Are you going to tell Mark?" Desiree asked.

"Nothing would please me more," Sylvie answered. "But he would never believe me. He'd twist it around and convince himself that I framed her."

"How would you even know how to do that?" Raul asked.

"I wouldn't," Sylvie said. "But it seems I'm responsible for everything that's gone wrong in his life. And I think Lisa Chang might be pregnant."

They pulled up in front of Sylvie's building and she got out.

Raul stuck his head out the window. "Put that somewhere safe," he said. "As long as you have it, you've got 'em by the balls."

Sylvie nodded and waved them off. *What I wouldn't do to have Mark's actual balls in my grip.* She felt the flash drive in her pocket and smiled.

As she passed Jack Ramsdale's door, she could hear Charlie Parker's sweet and somber tones. She thought about knocking on the door, letting him invite her in for a glass of wine and seeing where the evening took them. She thought about how good it would feel to ask his opinion on what to do about Mark. Jack knew Mark, at least a little. And he was a guy. He might have some great advice about how to tell Mark that the woman he loved was forcing him into a business deal he didn't want.

Sylvie raised her hand to knock, then thought better of it. The fewer people who knew about the repository and its value, the better. And what made her think she could trust Jack Ramsdale? Hadn't he plotted with Mark to get her out of her apartment?

She started up the stairs. It was Jack's apartment now. At least it would be soon—as soon as she remembered to hand him the signed Purchase & Sale Agreement. Jack had gotten what he'd wanted after all.

When she reached the top, her phone vibrated in her pocket.

"It's me, Desiree. I'm downstairs. I have something for you."

Sylvie hit the button to unlock the front door and waited while Desiree made the climb and entered the apartment.

When she'd caught her breath, Desiree reached into the Cucinelli bag on her shoulder and retrieved a thick document, folded in thirds, which she handed to Sylvie. "After I dropped Raul in the Square, I was waiting at the cab stand and switching my stuff over from my other bag when I found this stuck inside the lining."

Sylvie unfolded the document. She blinked, trying to parse what she read.

She sank into the nearest chair, clutching the sheaf of papers in both hands.

"You look like you seen a ghost," Desiree said, reaching for it. "I didn't know even white girls could turn *that* white." She took the papers from Sylvie and flipped through the pages. "What does it mean?"

"Mark registered *his* company in *my* name. Actually, it's registered in my maiden name, Sylvia Schofield."

"And that means?"

"That I am listed as the owner of TechnoData—the company that Lisa and Mark are about to sell for a boatload of money."

"But why would your ex put his company in your name?"

Sylvie shook her head, her mind spinning. "Beats me. Wait." She flipped back to the first page. "It's dated two years ago, when Mark and Lisa were both working for Templeton. Anything either of them developed then would belong to Templeton & Brewer. By using my maiden name, no one would be likely to make the connection to Mark."

Sylvie turned to the last page of the document. It had been signed "Sylvia Schofield" in what looked an awful lot like Sylvie's handwriting. Could she have signed it when Mark told her to, without even looking at it? No, Mark had never asked her to sign her maiden name to a document. She would remember that.

Sylvie started to pace. Sugarbear followed, dancing around her feet. "This is what Mark was looking for when he tore my bedroom apart that time he

214

came to get the girls. He must have gone back to the safety deposit box to retrieve it and found the box empty. Then he must have found out that I'd been issued a key after he disappeared."

Sylvie scooped Sugarbear into her arms. "And that Asian man who broke into the apartment and attacked Bigger must have been sent by Lisa when Mark couldn't find it. But why not ask me for it? Why not offer me a deal in exchange for it?"

Desiree opened her mouth to speak, but Sylvie interrupted. "Because Mark knows me. He knows I wouldn't have paid attention to some random document. Back then. But by God I'm paying attention now. That son of a bitch."

Desiree walked to Sylvie's kitchen cupboard, found a couple of juice glasses, then filled them with wine from an open bottle on the counter. She handed one to Sylvie.

When Desiree had downed half the glass, she said, "Holy shit. You do know what's happened here, don't you?"

Sylvie drank the wine and poured them each another glass. "I have the documents that give me ownership of TechnoData." She reached her hand into her pocket and felt for the flash drive. "And I have the only copy of the repository, not to mention an electronic copy of Mark's full proposal."

"Which means…"

"Which means a few minutes ago I merely had Mark by the balls. Now I'm holding the full package."

Desiree grinned, then sobered and set down her glass. "I have to go. I'm late for my shift. But you keep your little white ass safe, girlfriend."

Sylvie locked the door behind her friend and felt again for the flash drive in her pocket. The feel of it made her uneasy. What was to stop Lisa from sending someone over to search her apartment again? Her bargaining chip would be lost. She had to find a good hiding place. Like a safety deposit box. But the banks were closed now. She thought about leaving it until the morning, but her gut told her not to wait. She walked back through the apartment to the back stairs and out to the landing. She shut the door behind her, leaving Sugarbear inside the apartment where she'd be safe.

Sylvie glanced around, searching for an appropriate hiding place. There was only the dumbwaiter and the stairs leading to the roof—nothing that wouldn't be obvious to anyone searching. She walked up the stairs to the door to the roof and felt above the doorframe for the key, which was still in its old hiding place.

Outside, the rubber membrane that covered the flat surface of the roof was still warm from the heat of the sun that had set hours ago. Tentatively, Sylvie walked toward the rear of the building, where only a few feet separated her building from the dance studio behind it. From here, she could hear the enticing Latin beat and see couples salsa dancing through the windows, so close she could almost reach out and touch them. The bright light from the studio provided the only light besides the glow from the city below. For a moment, she imagined herself moving to the music, in the arms of a handsome attentive stranger. It looked like fun. And it had been such a long time since Sylvie'd had fun.

She stopped some distance from the edge. She'd never liked heights, and this roof had no ledge. It simply dropped off with no warning, and it was too dark to see where, exactly, the roof ended.

She dropped to her knees and crawled to the edge on all fours, feeling her way along. She'd never been brave up here, even when she was young. The wine coursed through her veins, making her slightly tipsy. When she got to the edge, she felt around the flashing that held the rubber membrane to the roof.

In the corner, she found a slit in the edge of the membrane. Her finger probed and discovered a flat cavity invisible to the eye. She folded the document into the plastic bag that already held the flash drive and slid the bag into the space between the flashing and the membrane.

She backed carefully away from the edge and headed back down the stairs to Sugarbear and her well-lit apartment, where she curled up on the sofa and fell asleep.

Forty Nine

The next thing she knew, she was waking to the sound of Sugarbear's insistent barking.

Sugarbear was standing on her chest, alternately barking and licking her face.

Something was very wrong. Sugarbear's face, only inches from her own, seemed hazy, unclear. She rubbed her eyes. Then she smelled it—thick and acrid.

Smoke.

Instantly, she was wide awake. She sat up. Sugarbear jumped to the floor and continued to bark.

Had she left a pot burning on the stove? Sylvie ran to the kitchen. Nothing had been left on.

Where are the girls? Were they still at Mark's? Or could they have returned while she was asleep? She ran through the smoky apartment, calling their names. No one answered. No one else was there.

She rushed to the front of the apartment. The smoke was thicker here. When she opened the door to peer down over the staircase, a wall of smoke pushed her back inside.

She shut the door, grabbed her purse from its hook, and pulled the strap over one shoulder and across her body. She lifted Sugarbear, popped her inside, and zipped the bag almost closed.

"I got this," she said with as much conviction as she could muster, as much to reassure herself as the pup.

The little dog threw her an "it's about freaking time" look, pulled her head inside the bag and fell quiet.

Out, she thought. *I have to get us out of here.* The smoke was hijacking her lungs, making her cough. She was terrified she would run out of air before she reached the back door. She dropped to her hands and knees and crawled the length of the apartment, then stood and eased the back door open slowly, in case there were flames on the other side. She prayed she could make her way down the back stairs to safety.

When she saw the thick smoke here as well, she knew the back staircase offered no refuge. But if she held her breath and moved quickly, she might be able to get to the roof, where she could at least get some cool air into her lungs and wait for the firemen. Surely a neighbor had seen the smoke and called 911 by this time. She listened, straining to hear the sirens, but heard nothing.

The key. Where did I leave the key to the roof door? She couldn't remember whether she had returned it to its usual hiding place or left it somewhere in the apartment. There was no time for a general search, so she exhaled, took a deep breath, and stepped out onto the landing, praying fervently that it was back where it belonged.

Her lungs screamed for release. She fought off the urge to breathe, climbed the flight of stairs to the roof door, and felt along the top of the frame until her frantic fingers made contact. The glorious key. The key to safety.

She slipped it inside the lock. The key turned and the door swung open.

Sylvie stepped out onto the roof, where she gratefully sucked in clean air. Sugarbear shifted inside the bag against her belly. Sylvie patted the bag and for the first time, thought of Jack Ramsdale. Was he lying on his floor downstairs, overcome by smoke? Or was he standing outside, watching the building burn so he could collect on his brand new insurance policy?

Where were the sirens?

Up here, there was no fire escape. Unless she did something, no one was coming to save her.

She felt inside the outer pocket of her purse for her phone. It wasn't there. She patted her pockets and found it, tapped it to bring it to life, but in the dark, it didn't recognize her face. Instead, it demanded she enter her security code.

She tried, but it refused to acknowledge her touch.

She wiped her damp hands on her jeans and tried to punch in her code, but her shaking fingers kept tapping the same number two or three times, forcing her to start again.

There was a way— she knew there was a way — to dial 911 without unlocking the phone. She stared at the screen. *She couldn't remember.* She tapped frantically and yelled, "Siri, help me."

"How can I help you?" answered the automated voice.

Sylvie shrieked into the phone, "Call 911. Now."

Calmly, Siri responded, "Calling 911."

She heard the sirens almost immediately after she hung up. The nearest fire station was only a block away, on the corner of Mass Ave and Sidney Street, in Lafayette Square. But the fire truck would have to thread its way down narrow Green Street, which was often blocked by cars double parked or parked halfway onto the sidewalk on the illegal side. Locating the owners and having the vehicles moved could take serious time.

Sylvie crawled cautiously along the roof toward the front of the building. The closer she got to the street, the hotter the rubber felt under her hands.

The fire must have started here in the front. That meant her best chance of surviving was in the rear of the building, where there was no hope at all for a fire truck to access the alleyway between her building and the dance studio.

The sirens had approached the front of her building, but she didn't dare go back. Had the 911 lady asked her where she was? Had she explained that she was on the roof? Her brain felt full of concrete. Why couldn't she remember?

Sylvie stared into the lighted windows of the dance studio. People were inside, but they were moving rapidly toward the exit. She waved her arms and shouted.

The lights in the dance studio went out and Sylvie knew she had to act fast.

She reached into her purse and felt around Sugarbear's trembling body until she came up with a lipstick, a comb and a handful of wrapped Ricola lozenges. She pelted the window first with the lipstick, then the comb. No response.

She flung the entire handful of lozenges at the window. A man's shadow appeared. She jumped up and down, waving her arms and yelling, "Help me," at the top of her lungs.

The window opened and a head emerged. She couldn't make out a face, but the person waved at her.

Relief washed over her.

Then the head disappeared.

"No, no, no. Shit, shit, shit," she wailed.

Two figures appeared, struggling with an aluminum ladder. They shoved it out the open window, straight across the five-story chasm toward her. Miraculously, it bridged the gap between the two buildings. She grabbed the end and anchored it at the edge of the roof.

On the other side of the ladder was safety. But to reach it, she would have to crawl along the ladder, across the abyss. Even if a fireman appeared, willing to fling her over his shoulder, and carry her back, it was unlikely the ladder would support them both. She was going to have to do this by herself. *Crawl or die.*

Voices yelled from the window, but her addled brain refused to decipher the words.

She unbuttoned her shirt, then rebuttoned it around her purse to secure Sugarbear to her chest. She knelt, steeling herself, and placed her hands on the first rung.

Then she remembered. The flash drive. The documents. She couldn't leave them here to burn.

She was so close to the corner where they were hidden. She let go of the ladder and felt along the flashing, searching for the chip in the rubber membrane.

The men holding the ladder shouted at her to hurry.

She was about to give up when she felt the bump and, under that, the cavity. She reached inside and grasped the plastic bag between her fingernails, but it slid from her grip. She tried again. This time, she held on and managed to coax it from its nest. She shoved it inside her purse, crowding Sugarbear, who had gone frighteningly still.

Her heart pushed up into her throat. Had she hesitated too long? Allowed the poor little thing to be overcome with fear and smoke?

She checked the zipper, making sure the precious contents were secure, and buttoned her shirt around the purse to bind it close to her body.

Then she crawled onto the ladder.

Pain shot through her knees as the rungs dug into them. She shifted more weight onto her hands and forced herself to crawl forward, out past the ledge.

The alleyway below was a black hole. Sylvie tried not to look down or think about the ground five stories below. She inched ahead, then froze. Unable to move forward, she clung to the ladder—the only thing between her and certain death.

She couldn't stay here. She had to keep moving. But her hands refused to release their grip so she could reach for the next rung. She and Sugarbear were going to fry up here. Alone.

Her arms and legs began to shake.

Then, from the other side of the chasm, she heard a familiar voice say, "You can do this. I'm right here."

She focused on her right hand, willing her fingers to obey. But they wouldn't budge.

"I can't," she said.

"One rung at a time," Jack Ramsdale said. "I won't let you fall."

Finally, her muscles responded. Her fingers relaxed and let go.

"You're doing great, now the next," he said.

She reached for the next rung, gripped it, then focused on her left hand until it, too, obeyed. Then the right knee, then the left.

"Almost there," he said.

One rung at a time, she made her way across, never looking down or thinking about anything but Jack's voice until she felt his hands grip her forearms and pull her inside to safety.

She tried to stand, but her knees buckled beneath her and she crumpled to her knees, her body wrapped protectively around her purse as heavy footsteps pounded up the stairs of the studio. Four Cambridge firefighters in full regalia burst through the door.

A layer of soot coated her mouth. She tried to explain that Sugarbear was inside her purse, but no sound came out.

She closed her burning eyes, unbuttoned her shirt and unzipped her purse, allowing Sugarbear's head to show.

Then she shut her eyes.

When she opened them, she was being hoisted into the air on a stretcher. She felt her purse, but Sugarbear was no longer inside.

Someone was trying to put a mask on her, but she swerved her head from side to side, searching frantically, until she saw the puppy in the arms of a fireman who held a tiny, puppy-sized mask over the little face.

Only then did Sylvie hold still long enough to allow a mask to be placed over her own nose and mouth.

Then she was floating down around the bends in the staircase, out onto the street, and into the back of an ambulance. The door slammed shut and the siren wailed.

Fifty

When Sylvie woke up in the hospital, daylight lit the room. Her throat hurt, her knees and hands felt bruised and tender, and she was shivering all over.

She glanced under the blanket and saw that she was wearing a thin hospital gown. From the feel of the rough sheets on her bare bottom, it was open in the back.

Her bladder ached and she realized she would have to get out of bed. Luckily, she could see a bathroom only a few feet away.

She hesitated, her teeth chattering, dreading removing the thin blanket until she had no choice.

She rolled over to get out of bed, but a side rail blocked her escape. She jiggled it, but it didn't move. Now she really had to pee. She tried lifting the rail, but it didn't budge. Her bladder was about to burst.

She was searching for a button to call the nurse when she spotted Jack Ramsdale, sound asleep on the reclining chair across the room. His face was unshaven, his jeans and flannel shirt were dark with soot. But his rumpled hair was kind of sexy in a hero-who-saved-her-life kind of way.

What is he doing here?

First things first. She jiggled the railing again. When that failed, she smacked it in frustration.

Jack's eyes popped open. "You're awake," he said.

She nodded toward the bathroom. "Can you get this down? I really need…" Her voice came out in a strange rasp, as if she'd smoked a carton of cigarettes.

He stood slowly, unkinking himself from the chair, and pushed a button. The railing lowered.

Sylvie swung her legs over the side and beelined to the bathroom, remembering halfway there that her ass was hanging out. She made a feeble attempt to clutch the ends together behind her. Looking back, she saw Jack quickly turn his gaze toward the window.

When she returned, he was rinsing his mouth in the sink. His eyes were red and he looked like he was suffering from a bad hangover.

"How are you feeling?" he asked.

"My knees.... my throat..." she whispered.

"The doctor doesn't think you have any lung damage from the fire," he said.

Sylvie's mind flashed back to the little puppy face, so still beneath the oxygen mask. "Sugarbear?"

"Stayed overnight at Angell Memorial. I called a few hours ago. She's fine. We can pick her up this afternoon."

"Was anyone hurt?"

"No. Thank God." He sank into the chair and rubbed his hand across his forehead. "I thought you were dead."

"About that," she said. "If you hadn't—"

"Forget it."

"Not very likely." She sat on the edge of the bed and pulled the thin blanket around her shoulders, hoping for some degree of modesty. "How did you know where to find me?" she asked.

"When the smoke alarms went off, I tried to get up the stairs to make sure you got out. When I couldn't get up either staircase, I figured you couldn't have gotten down either. That left the roof."

"And you knew to go to the dance studio?"

"I may have taken a salsa class or two." He looked slightly sheepish. "And I remembered looking out their fifth floor windows onto our roof and thinking how great a green roof would be—for the environment. You know, global warming and all that."

"Not to mention adding a significant amount to the resale value of the top floor."

"That too."

"What you did up there. How do I thank you?"

"Forget it. I mean it."

"But the way you—" She stopped when she realized how terribly uncomfortable he looked.

"You're alive," he said. "That's enough."

Were his eyes watering from smoke damage, or was Jack Ramsdale tearing up?

"The building?" she asked.

"Not good. The fire damage is mostly in the stairwells. But there's smoke damage, water damage from the fire hoses, and broken windows from fighting the fire. Turns out firemen don't tiptoe around. I called my insurance company. They had a cleanup crew board everything up. But we can't go back in until their inspectors figure out what started it."

"Do you think it was one of those old boilers in the basement?"

He shook his head. "The fire didn't start in the basement."

"It had to be the basement. Both staircases were…"

"We'll have to wait for the investigation and the official report. But…."

Sylvie felt the blood drain from her face. "But what?"

"Everything's pointing to arson." His eyebrows furrowed. "Someone started a fire in both staircases. There wasn't supposed to be a way out."

"Someone really wanted me dead?" She knew that Mark thought of her as an obstacle to his new life, but trying to burn her alive? Had Lisa progressed from killing puppies to humans? "What do I do now? Where do we go?" she asked.

"Start with your insurance company."

Insurance? Mark had always dealt with things like insurance. *Until he stopped dealing with all of it months ago.* But perhaps he had paid this one bill, because the apartment was their one remaining asset. And what kind of an idiot would burn his own asset if it *wasn't* insured?

"I need to call Mark." Sylvie found her purse on the bedside table, dug out her phone and turned it on, though she couldn't remember turning it off. She waited for a service connection and saw that her girls had each tried to reach her several times. Each text message was increasingly frantic. She wrote a group text back quickly: "I'm fine. At Mt. Auburn Hospital. Long story. Will call asap."

Then she punched in Mark's number. It rang, but he didn't pick up. Coward.

She clicked off without leaving a message and texted him: "Need to know where our property insurance is for Green Street."

Moments later, the alert sounded and the text came back: "Insurance lapsed."

No home. No insurance. No money. She climbed back into the bed and pulled the covers over her head. "Jack," she said from under the covers, "can you please ask the nurse if she has any really good, powerful drugs. I'm going to need an intravenous."

Jack tugged the covers from her head and handed her a wad of Kleenex.

She blew her nose and mopped her face. "I need a grownup," she said.

"I hate to tell you, but—"

"No," she said, "I'm not. Grownups make sure they have insurance." She fell back onto the pillow. "I'm sure Lisa Chang has insurance."

Lisa Chang.

Sylvie sprang to her feet, opened the closet door, and found the filthy clothes she'd worn the night before—probably all that was left of her wardrobe. She turned her head to address Jack and realized that, once again, he had an unobstructed view of her ass. She quickly turned her back to the wall. "Please leave now," she said. "I need to get dressed."

Jack lifted a Gap shopping bag from next to the recliner and handed it to her. "I bought you these." He moved toward the door. "I'll wait outside."

"That's okay. I'm sure you have better things to do."

"I'll wait outside," he repeated. "We need to talk."

Fifty One

Sylvie rang for the nurse, eager to check out of the hospital. She opened the Gap bag and found yoga pants, a white shirt, sports bra and underwear. She was surprised at how well Jack had guessed her size. She also found socks and a pair of sneakers. The sneakers were a little large, but manageable. Better than too small.

She wondered at Jack's solicitude. He was being almost too kind, too considerate. It gave her an odd feeling. Yes, she was attracted to him. There was no denying it. And perhaps he was attracted to her as well. But Sylvie knew when a man was nice to her because he was courting her, and this felt different.

The more she turned over the events of the night before, the more something nagged at her subconscious—something that didn't fit.

She was stuffing her old clothes into the shopping bag, when Jack knocked and came back in.

That was when Sylvie realized what was bothering her. "You said you heard the fire alarm go off. That's what made you try to come upstairs to check on me."

Jack nodded.

"Why didn't *I* hear the alarm? Shouldn't *my* smoke detector have gone off?"

He took a deep breath and let it out, looking like he'd suddenly aged ten years. "I took them out— the day before you showed up and told me the sale wasn't going to go through. They were old and outdated, and I intended to replace them. Then everything fell apart, and I forgot all about them."

He'd removed the fire alarms. Why hadn't she noticed?

"I'm sorry," he said.

Her stomach turned to liquid. "I could have died. The girls could have died." Sylvie wished she knew whose side Jack was on— hers or Mark's? Or maybe simply Jack Ramsdale's?

She starred at him, her mind whirling. She'd signed the Purchase and Sale Agreement, but she'd never gotten around to handing it to him. It was probably still sitting on her front table, covered in soot. He hadn't known he'd won, that she had agreed to sell him the apartment.

"Don't look at me like that," he said.

"I wasn't thinking what you think I was thinking," she lied.

"Yeah, you were. But why would I burn down my own building?"

"To get me out?" She smiled, hoping he'd think she was joking.

"Do you really think I'd kill you for an apartment?"

She shrugged.

"Jesus, Sylvie."

"Maybe just smoke me out?" She laughed, but it sounded false even to her.

The nurse popped her head in the door. "We're working on your discharge papers, waiting for the doc to sign off and write up some aftercare instructions." She popped back out.

"About the insurance—" he began.

"What about it?"

"There's still a way to get your losses covered."

"I doubt it. It's probably been way too long since Mark paid the premium."

"There's another way. But you're not going to like it."

She sat down. This did not sound good. But she was desperate. And Jack Ramsdale knew it. "I'm listening," she said.

"Remember that insurance document you opened by mistake? I applied for insurance on the entire building when I thought the sale was on. If we go through with the sale, that policy will cover the entire building." Jack ran his fingers through his hair until it stood straight up. "I know this looks bad."

"You took out insurance on the entire building before you even owned it?"

"I had to. To get a mortgage."

She remembered clinging to a ladder five stories above the ground. She had been certain she would die up there. Without Jack Ramsdale, she would probably still be on that roof. But had he saved her out of guilt? Had he set the fire, knowing he had removed the fire alarms, then chickened out when he was afraid she might die in the inferno?

The nurse showed up with discharge papers. Sylvie gathered her things and headed toward the door.

"Where are you going?" Jack asked.

"Home."

"You can't," he said. "It's a mess."

"I can't help that," she said. "I have nowhere else to go."

"That's what I need to talk to you about."

She headed to the elevator with Jack Ramsdale so close behind that when her phone rang and she stopped to answer it, they collided. The caller ID read Desiree.

"I heard about the fire over the radio," Desiree said. "I drove over but when I got there, you were being loaded into an ambulance. Are you okay?"

"I'm fine. I got discharged."

"I'm here in the lobby with Raul. We came by to check on you. And LaVonda."

"LaVonda?"

"The firemen found her passed out behind your building."

Fifty Two

Sylvie, Jack, Desiree, and Raul surrounded LaVonda's bed, watching the machine inhale and exhale for her. It sounded like a giant breathing. Technically none of them had any business being here because they weren't "family," but this was Cambridge, where the definition of family was up for grabs.

LaVonda lay in the bed, a tiny brown body surrounded by white.

"What happened to her?" Sylvie asked.

"Don't know," Desiree replied. "Raul's looking into it."

Raul glanced up at her and frowned.

"Is it a secret?" Desiree asked him.

"Not with you around."

The nurse came to take LaVonda's vital signs and kicked them out.

Desiree announced, "I'm going to the cafeteria for coffee. Anyone else?" She stared pointedly at Sylvie, who realized her caffeine headache was about to kick in.

"I'll come," she said.

When the elevator closed behind them and they were alone, Desiree said, "Last night, on my way over, I thought I saw that Chang woman on Mass. Ave., about a block away from Green Street, walking toward the subway station."

"Are you sure it was her?"

"No. I only saw her for a second. She had a hat on, but I recognized that long black hair and that way she walks."

"But you're not sure?"

"I guess I couldn't swear to it."

"Was she walking toward you or away?" Sylvie asked.

"Toward me, away from your street, down Mass. Ave. I passed her. She was moving fast."

"How sure are you that it was Lisa? Scale of one to ten?"

"At the time, I would have said eight. But now— I don't know. There are so many Asians around MIT."

They headed back, each carrying a large coffee cup filled to the brim. At the ICU, Jack and Raul were deep in conversation. They stopped talking abruptly when Sylvie and Desiree arrived, which made Sylvie uneasy. She had to stop seeing conspiracies everywhere she looked, or it would drive her crazy.

Her phone vibrated.

"Where are you?" Diana's voice demanded.

"I told you. Mt. Auburn."

"No, you're not. We're in your room, but it's empty. They said you were in a fire. They stripped the bed. We thought you died."

"I'm not dead. I'm in the ICU."

"ICU?"

"Intensive Care Unit." Sylvie regretted it the moment she said it.

"What?!" She could hear Claire's wail on the other end of the phone.

"I'm fine. I've been discharged. I was looking in on a friend. I'll meet you in the lobby."

***

The moment Sylvie left the elevator, both girls ambushed her, nearly knocking her over. She hugged them as hard as she could, feeling the wet tears on their cheeks. She didn't know whether to laugh or cry as the questions poured out of them.

She herded them to a lounge area where they could sit and catch their breath. Yes, there was a fire, no, she wasn't dead, not even badly hurt, and Sugarbear was fine.

When they'd calmed down, Sylvie asked, "How did you hear about the fire?"

"Lisa told us when she dropped us off at school. We wanted her to drop us at home so we could ditch our stuff, and she said there was no home to go to." Claire's eyes were red from crying.

"That's not true," Sylvie said. "Whenever the three of us are together, we're home." She paused as fresh sobs broke out all around. Finally, she asked, "How did Lisa know about the fire?"

"She said it was on the local news feed," Diana said.

"Does she know you're here?" Sylvie asked.

They glanced at each other and shrugged.

Claire said, "We told her, but she wasn't listening."

"She was busy getting ready for some important meeting with Dad," Diana said.

An alarm went off in Sylvie's head. "Did they say what kind of meeting?"

Diana thought for a minute. "No, but it sounded like a really big deal. The Chang spent the whole morning yelling at that poor lady who works for Dad about what kind of food she should have and where to get it. Some big deal special Chinese restaurant."

"Oh, sh....shoot," Sylvie said. She opened her purse to make sure the documents and flash drive were still inside.

Both girls rolled their eyes. "Honestly, Mom," Diana said, "we've heard you say 'shit' before."

The elevator doors opened. When Desiree, Jack and Raul emerged, Sylvie ran to Desiree and grabbed her arm. "I need a ride," she said.

"Mom?" Claire said.

For the first time, Sylvie noticed that the girls each had a backpack with them. They looked at her expectantly.

Jack cleared his throat. "I have a great idea," he said, "but I haven't had a chance to run it past your mom." He turned to Sylvie. "I've booked two suites at the Cambridge Inn right near the high school. They serve a great breakfast in their garden."

Sylvie stared at him, puzzled.

"For all of us," he explained. "Least I could do. I can take the girls there now. Get them settled."

Sylvie looked at the girls. "Aren't you supposed to be at school?"

"I'll call and tell them about the fire. I'll tell them the girls will have a written note tomorrow," Jack said.

Both girls nodded vigorously.

"Okay," Sylvie said. "I'll be back as soon as I can."

"Take your time," Jack said. "After we settle in, we're walking to the Border Cafe for lunch. And Lizzy's Ice Cream for dessert. Then it will be time to pick up Sugarbear."

Sylvie watched the three of them walk out to the street together, laughing and jostling each other, as Jack took the girls' backpacks and loaded one onto each of his broad shoulders.

Raul followed them outside, heading for Green Street to find out what the neighbors knew about the fire and LaVonda. When they were all out of sight, and Sylvie was alone with Desiree, Sylvie called the hospital for news of LaVonda and was told her condition was "stable." Then she dialed the office of TechnoData, thankful when Gertrude answered.

In response to Sylvie's questions, Gertrude's answers were perfunctory, as if she was trying to mask the fact that she was speaking to her boss's soon-to-be ex-wife. Despite the terse replies, Sylvie managed to learn the location and time of the upcoming meeting. TechnoData had rented a conference room at the Boston Harbor Hotel on Rowe's Wharf, only a short walk from Templeton & Brewer.

There, in less than an hour, TechnoData would be accepting sealed bids for their acquisition from two competing companies, one American and one Chinese. The American team would present first. The Chinese team, pitching second, had been given the end-game advantage.

Sylvie took a deep breath and explained her plan to Gertrude.

"Yes, I'm quite sure I can manage that," Gertrude said and rang off.

Fifty Three

Sylvie's next call was to Raul, who promised to meet them at the hotel. Yes, he had things to report, but that would have to wait until he saw her.

Sylvie and Desiree made a pit stop at the consignment store, where Sylvie traded Mark's grandfather's cufflinks for two dressed-for-success outfits. When they emerged from the store they looked formidable, Sylvie in a Chanel knock-off with a cream colored jacket and pencil skirt, and Desiree in a fitted navy blue pantsuit and man's tie. Both wore heels and carried faux, but convincing, leather briefcases with their old clothes stuffed inside.

Sylvie checked her watch. They had less than half an hour to get downtown. Back in the cab, they raced straight down Broadway. Traffic wasn't terrible, and it looked like they would arrive in time. But when they approached the Longfellow Bridge, connecting Cambridge to downtown Boston, it was undergoing construction and "closed to vehicular traffic." Only the bike lane and pedestrian walkways remained open.

They circled Kendall Square, finally abandoning the cab in a semi-legal spot near MIT, then hurried back to the bicycle sharing station next to the canal. That was when Sylvie remembered her credit cards were no longer functioning. So Desiree stepped up to the kiosk, pushed the "Rent a Bike" button, inserted her credit card and rented two bikes. They each lifted a bike by the seat and pulled it from its dock.

Sylvie hiked her tight skirt up to her thighs. Desiree led the way, pedaling across the bridge, past Mass General Hospital and up the hill on Cambridge Street, dodging traffic as they rode and getting a healthy share of catcalls along the way. They pedaled hard down State Street to the Aquarium, turned right onto Atlantic Avenue, and arrived at Rowe's Wharf at twenty past one. If all went according to plan, they should make it in time.

They inserted the bikes into the dock at the drop-off station, patting down their hair and straightening their clothing as they hustled into the hotel.

They nearly missed Raul in the lobby. His hair was slicked back and he wore an expensive dark blue jacket that covered his numerous tattoos. His sky blue shirt was the exact color of his eyes. The open neck hinted at an intriguing patch of chest hair, making him look slightly dangerous—exactly the image Sylvie wanted.

She glanced over as the elevator doors opened, revealing a familiar face, though she couldn't quite place it. She looked closer and blinked. Gone were the beard and the yachting clothes, replaced by expensive tailored pinstripes. Grady, sans red beard, was engaged in an intense conversation with a no-nonsense looking woman in her fifties and a large man in a tight suit.

Why would a government employee be here? Sylvie wondered. She turned away, hoping he hadn't noticed her. She retrieved her cell and managed to surreptitiously take a photo as they passed.

Adrenaline pumping, Sylvie waited with Raul and Desiree for the text from Gertrude calling them upstairs. She checked her watch. It could come at any minute. Still the others hadn't arrived.

What could possibly be keeping them?

When her text alert finally dinged, she glanced down and nodded. "Show time," she said and stood, along with Desiree and Raul. They filed onto the elevator.

Just as the doors were closing behind them, a man's foot shot inside and stopped the doors from closing. They reopened reluctantly. Richard Templeton, Charles Brewer, and Florence stepped inside. Florence caught Sylvie's eye and nodded. Sylvie smiled back with relief. *Not a moment to spare,* she thought.

On the third floor, all six of them followed the signs toward the John Adams Conference Room. They headed down the corridor toward an open reception area, where Gertrude was disposing of what looked like the remains of an elaborate Chinese feast. Just beyond the reception area, the door labeled "conference room" opened as they approached. The two elderly Chinese gentlemen who had spoken to Lisa in the lobby of the Long Wharf Marriott emerged, followed by Mark and Lisa Chang. The two gentlemen wore an air of triumph, and Lisa's eyes gleamed.

"We'll be in touch," Mark said, shaking their hands. Lisa bowed her head respectfully. When the two men turned and headed down the corridor, Lisa and Mark gave each other a silent but exuberant high five.

235

Then Lisa spotted Florence leading the charge toward her. Her elation morphed into a look of horror. Seeing Lisa's face, Mark spun around and turned a sickly shade of green, as if he might be in danger of revisiting his lunch.

Gertrude tossed the last of the leftovers into the trash. "The third team is here," she announced. "I felt sure you'd want to hear them out before you made your final decision."

She opened the conference room door and held it while Richard Templeton stepped inside. He claimed the seat at the head of the table, where Charles Brewer joined him on one side and Florence on the other. Sylvie, Desiree and Raul took seats on one side of the table, while a reluctant Mark and Lisa placed themselves opposite.

As Florence opened her laptop, Mr. Templeton folded his hands on the table and directed his attention to Lisa. "Ms. Chang, you can imagine my surprise at seeing you here. I'm sure I don't need to remind you of the non-compete clause in your contract. Perhaps you'd like to wait outside so we don't muddy the waters any further. Florence will let you know when you may return."

Lisa glared at Mark, who wore a puzzled expression, before she stood and stalked from the room.

Sylvie turned to address the Templeton & Brewer team. "Thank you so much for agreeing to come on such short notice."

Richard Templeton said, "We're grateful to be included, although we were not notified in time to prepare anything in writing. Hopefully, we can sort things out first and work on the numbers later." Without waiting for Sylvie to continue, he turned to Mark. "Let's put aside *your* non-compete contract for the moment. We'll let our attorneys address that issue if it becomes necessary." He placed a hand on Mark's arm. "You know you've always been like a son to me. When you left so suddenly, we were all shocked. Frankly, I was worried about your mental health. I understand now why you felt compelled to leave. Unfortunately, the reasons you left were instigated by a miscommunication."

Templeton nodded to Florence, who placed a blue binder in front of Mark.

Templeton continued, "This is a copy of the Assuranz Software Proposal submitted to me, which I rejected for lack of development. If you glance through it, I believe you'll understand why."

Mark flipped through the pages. He looked up, puzzled. "There are two sections missing."

"Exactly."

Mark turned accusingly to Gertrude. "I don't understand."

Florence peered at him over her glasses. "That's an exact printout of the proposal submitted to the executive committee at Templeton & Brewer," she said. "By the chair of the Research and Development Team—Lisa Chang."

"So, I'm sure you can understand," Mr. Templeton continued, "why I delayed financing your proposal. You would have done the same."

Mark sat in stunned silence.

Florence withdrew a thicker, red binder. "But this is a copy of the proposal you gave Gertrude to submit to Lisa Chang for her review. As you can see, it's complete."

"And rather impressive," added Templeton. "Had I seen the complete proposal, I would have happily allocated generous funding for your project. Someone deleted those crucial sections from your proposal after you submitted it and before I reviewed it. At this time, we can't be sure if it was a mistake or a deliberate attempt to sabotage the project. But let's leave that issue for the moment and move on."

For the first time, Mr. Brewer spoke up. "The fact is, we'd like you back, along with your project."

Mark's expression morphed from confusion to wariness. "I'm happy to consider your offer," he said.

"I'm afraid it's a bit more complicated than that," Mr. Templeton said. "Should you choose to try to sell the Assuranz software to another entity, legal ownership could get rather murky. Or if it were to be discovered that either you or Ms. Chang committed fraud—"

Mark looked at Sylvie, then back to Mr. Brewer. "Fraud?"

"Falsifying documents is a felony. Punishable by significant fines and prison."

Sylvie placed a copy of the document she'd retrieved from Desiree's bag in front of Mark.

His face drained of color. He looked like he might pass out.

"It appears you are not the legal owner of TechnoData," Mr. Templeton explained.

"Naturally, we are not currently in a position to match what I'm sure are rather generous offers from our competitors," Mr. Brewer added, "but, then again, we already own the software, since it was developed while you were under exclusive contract to Templeton & Brewer."

Mark glared at Sylvie.

"Of course," Brewer continued, "we'll provide full funding to complete the project and a generous bonus for you and your team when it goes to market. We will also agree not to prosecute either you or Ms. Chang."

Mark's face drained of color. "Are you threatening me with jail?"

Mr. Templeton nodded sadly. "Up to ten years. But, of course," he added, "I doubt Mrs. Wolff wants to send the father of her children to jail. In any case, no one can complete the project without you. Which is why it's in everyone's best interests to reach an agreement today. And nine months from now, when the project comes to market, we'll all share in the profits."

Mark ran his hand through his hair. "No way I can finish that soon."

"Why not?" asked Mr. Brewer.

"The repository has been corrupted, and the backup is missing. It'll take at least that long to replicate what we've already done."

Charles Brewer turned to Gertrude. "Perhaps this would be a good time for Ms. Chang to join us."

Gertrude went to the door and opened it, nearly smacking it into Lisa who was standing directly on the other side. Sylvie wondered how much she'd heard. Gertrude swept her arm in an exaggerated invitation for Lisa to join them. Lisa entered, her glance shifting from Templeton, to Brewer, to Mark. She never once looked at Sylvie.

When Lisa had been seated, Mr. Templeton turned to Sylvie. "Is there something you'd like to share?"

Sylvie produced the flash drive from her bag. She handed it to Florence, who inserted it into her laptop and slid the laptop to Mark. He searched through the file, then rounded on Sylvie and demanded, "Where did you get this?"

"It was taped to the bottom of Ms. Chang's desk at Templeton & Brewer," Sylvie said.

Mark turned to face Lisa. The look of betrayal on his face made Sylvie almost feel sorry for him. Almost.

Lisa pushed her chair away and stood, shaking with rage aimed directly at Sylvie. "What the hell were you doing?"

Raul rose to his feet and placed himself between Lisa and Sylvie. He seemed to grow larger somehow, inflating like a puffer fish. From his stance, Sylvie wasn't at all sure that he wasn't packing a gun inside his jacket.

"She had my permission to be on the premises," Florence interrupted.

"That was *my* office. You had no right," Lisa raged.

"She's the office manager. She has every right," Brewer said.

"You're nothing but a thief," Lisa spat at Sylvie.

Sylvie rose to her feet, then eased Raul aside so she could face Lisa directly.

"Actually," Sylvie said calmly, "according to this document"—she tapped the paper with her fingernail—"*you're* the one who stole from *me*."

The rage in Lisa's eyes seemed to take on a life of its own and crawl up Sylvie's spine, turning every inch of Sylvie's body into gooseflesh.

Sylvie placed her hands on the table to steady herself. "And while Templeton & Brewer may agree not to prosecute you for the theft of intellectual property, please note that they are not authorized to speak for *me*."

No one breathed.

Lisa looked from Raul to Mr. Brewer.

"Given the circumstances," Mr. Templeton said, "I'm afraid Ms. Chang can no longer remain at Templeton & Brewer." He turned to face her. "Your office is currently being cleared, and the contents will be delivered to your home address."

He held out his hand. Lisa looked confused, then lifted her hand as if to shake his. But Templeton said abruptly, "Your company ID?"

Slowly, as if in a daze, Lisa opened her purse, retrieved her ID and placed it in Mr. Templeton's hand. Gertrude, standing sentry by the door, held it open for Lisa Chang to step out.

Mark stood, as if to follow.

"Please sit," Mr. Brewer said. "We have more to discuss."

"I'm done here," Mark said. He turned and barked at Gertrude, "Get my lawyer on the phone."

"That's no longer my job," Gertrude said. "I'm returning to Templeton & Brewer as liaison for the Assuranz project."

"Liaison?" Mark seemed confused. "What does that mean?"

Florence stood. "It means that I've been promoted to project manager, and Gertrude will be your project's representative. She will be reporting to me, and you will be reporting to her."

Mark shook his head in disbelief and left the conference room.

Fifty Four

Sylvie stood. "I'll be right back," she said.

She followed Mark toward the elevator, but before she rounded the last corner, she heard Lisa say, "It's what you wanted. But you didn't have the nerve to do it. So I helped you. Because I believe in you."

Sylvie peeked around the corner. Lisa stood outside the elevator, one arm holding the door open while she argued with Mark.

He said, "I lost my family because of you."

Lisa let go of the elevator door, letting it move on without her, and turned to face Mark. "You have a new family now. I'm pregnant with your son."

Sylvie's stomach lurched. Lisa Chang was pregnant with the son she and Mark never had together.

Mark sounded petulant. "If I'd known the truth, I never would have left. Sylvie would have—"

"Sylvie doesn't care about your work. If I hadn't stepped in, you'd have always wondered, 'what if I'd had the balls to go out on my own?'"

"Well, thanks to you, I'm back working for Templeton & Brewer, right where I started. Except I'm broke."

"You don't have to go back there," Lisa argued. "We can fight this."

"No, we can't. We'd spend a fortune in legal fees and they'd win in the end. Our only hope was to sell before Templeton & Brewer found out I developed it. If a different company brought it to market, there was a chance they'd never find out. Or at least never be able to prove it. That ship has sailed. If I'm lucky, they haven't given away my old office and I don't end up working from the supply closet."

Lisa stabbed the elevator button. The doors opened, she stepped inside and the doors closed behind her.

Sylvie scurried back to join Raul and Desiree outside the conference room just before Mark passed them and entered the room to join Florence and Mr. Templeton. The door closed behind him.

Sylvie grasped first Raul's hand, then Desiree's. "Thank you," she said.

"We didn't do much," Desiree said.

"Yeah, you did. I wouldn't have had the nerve to go through with this if you didn't have my back. I think it's going to be okay now." She turned to Raul. "You had something to tell me about LaVonda."

"The firemen found her out cold behind your building," Raul said. "She either fell or was pushed, but she has a nasty concussion. The doctors are waiting for the swelling in her brain to go down before they discuss a prognosis."

"Do you think someone did this to her deliberately?" Sylvie asked.

Raul shrugged. "Maybe she saw something. Or someone thought she saw something. We won't know until she regains consciousness."

"Did you talk to any of the neighbors?" Desiree asked.

"A few. Not many were home." He turned to Sylvie. "I'll head back now if you don't need me here."

"I got this," Desiree said.

Sylvie and Desiree watched Raul walk toward the elevators. "Is there anyone we should call for LaVonda?" Sylvie asked.

"Not that anyone knows of," Desiree said. "Raul's been asking the regulars on the street but so far, no luck. When we're done here, I'm heading back to the hospital to talk to her, even if she can't hear me. They say it can help."

The door to the conference room opened and a much-dejected Mark stepped outside and walked past them without saying a word.

Sylvie watched his slumped form disappear around the corner of the hallway.

Florence stepped outside the conference room and beckoned to Sylvie, who turned to Desiree. "I'll sort things out here and meet you at the hospital as soon as I can get there."

***

Sylvie returned to the conference room. Richard Templeton sat hunched over Florence's laptop, which now had a portable printer attached.

Templeton stood to greet her. "I want you to know that we're thrilled that Mark has agreed to return to Templeton & Brewer along with his project. And we're grateful to you for figuring the whole mess out."

"How grateful?" Sylvie asked. "Because I'm pretty strapped for cash right now."

Florence pushed a button and the printer spit out a three-page document. She handed it to Templeton, who presented it to Sylvie.

"We'll need you to sign this," he said. "It simply restates what transpired earlier." He handed her a pen.

Sylvie took the pen and placed it on the table. Then she took a pair of reading glasses from her purse and read through the pages carefully. It stated that Sylvie agreed she had no legal claim to the Assuranz software, and that Templeton & Brewer were the legal owners. There was a place for Sylvie to sign at the bottom of the last page. She removed her glasses and looked up at him. "What do I get in return for signing this?"

Templeton shifted in his chair. "As soon as the software comes to market, Mark will receive a considerable bonus. I'm sure your lawyer can legitimately claim a portion of that."

"That's great," Sylvie said. "But what I really need is a chunk of cash now. I need a place to live and money to live on." She placed the document on the table and pushed it, unsigned, toward Richard Templeton.

Templeton pushed the document back to Sylvie. "As you know, both Mark and Lisa were under contract to Templeton & Brewer when the software was developed."

Sylvie ignored the paper and folded her arms.

Templeton cleared his throat. "Of course, you're entitled to go after Mark legally, even criminally. But, you have to ask yourself, does a drawn-out, expensive lawsuit serve any real purpose? Isn't it better to let Mark focus on finishing his work?"

"Better for me or for Templeton & Brewer?"

"I believe we're all on the same team."

"Are we?" Sylvie asked. "Because I agree it would be in *your* best interest to move forward without having me around to 'muddy the waters.' Me, not so much." She stood. "Why don't you discuss an offer among yourselves and get back to me."

Before Sylvie turned to leave, she was pretty sure she saw Florence wink at her behind Templeton's back.

Fifty Five

Sylvie stepped into the elevator and felt dizzy, as if she had gotten off of a roller coaster and couldn't quite get her bearings. No matter how deeply she breathed, she couldn't quite fill her lungs.

She needed some air.

She stepped through the revolving doors into the crisp spring air. As she walked along the waterfront toward the Aquarium T Stop, she texted Desiree and asked about LaVonda. Desiree texted back that LaVonda was conscious and coherent, but couldn't remember what happened just before she lost consciousness. The doctors thought she might never remember.

Even if she did remember who hurt her, thought Sylvie, would a jury convict someone based solely on the word of a homeless woman?

Sylvie rode the T to Harvard Square, then walked down Massachusetts Avenue toward the Cambridge Inn to check in on the girls and grab a quick shower before heading to the hospital.

When she arrived at the Inn, she found Jack Ramsdale reading the paper in the cozy Victorian parlor. He handed her the key to her room.

"Are the girls upstairs?" she asked.

"I set them loose in the Square with my credit card to buy a few things."

She glanced at him in alarm but he grinned. "I'm not worried. They're good kids."

"You're right," Sylvie said. "They're the best."

***

Sylvie showered and was putting on the same Gap clothing Jack had brought to the hospital when she received a text from Mark. He was on his way to Cambridge and wanted to meet with her privately—it was important. She texted back that she could meet him at Darwin's, a café on Mt. Auburn Street, on her way to Mt. Auburn Hospital.

On her way through Harvard Square, Sylvie stopped to pick up a few things for LaVonda. When she arrived at Darwin's, Mark was waiting at an outside table. There was a cappuccino with a leaf design in the foamed milk topping and a chocolate croissant waiting for her. Her favorite. Just like old times.

Mark slid the peace offering toward her. "Florence said that it was up to me to figure things out with you. Find out what it will take for you to agree to let Templeton & Brewer proceed with Assuranz." He leaned back and gripped his arms across his chest. "Well, Sylvie, it appears you're in the driver's seat. What is it you want from me?"

Sylvie paused, trying to savor the moment. It didn't feel as good as she'd hoped. "I want you to drop the custody suit," she said.

"They're my girls, too. I miss them."

"Do you?" Sylvie asked. "Or the idea of them? Face it, Mark, you have no clue what goes on in your daughters' lives on a day-to-day basis. You only wanted custody because once the girls were out of my apartment, you could force me to sell. Well, now that the apartment's gone up in smoke and you've got your funding, you can give it a rest."

"Smoke? What are you talking about?"

"You mean your girlfriend didn't tell you? Someone started a fire in my building, while I was asleep upstairs. Lisa knows all about it."

"You can't possibly believe—"

"That she started it or had someone start it? Gee, I don't know, Mark. She sabotaged your career, copied your repository then erased it so her chosen buyers would have the distinct financial advantage, tried to drown your children's pet—"

"That's insane."

"Is it? I had to jump into Boston Harbor to save the poor puppy. There were witnesses. Like this man." Sylvie showed Mark the picture she'd taken at the hotel. "Except he had a red beard and was living on a boat right outside your apartment."

"McCauley?"

"Grady. He'll tell you what he saw."

"Grady McCauley would say or do anything to get his hands on TechnoData."

Sylvie stared Mark in disbelief. "That's not true. He works for the government."

"Jesus, Sylvie. Why are you mucking around in things you can't possibly understand? Grady doesn't work for the government. He works for a company that would love to be able to sell Assuranz to the government. So the government can adapt my software for their own purposes."

"Why can't *you* sell it to the government?"

"We can." Mark rubbed his temples, a sure sign he wasn't getting any sleep. For the first time, Sylvie noticed the black circles around his eyes. He spoke slowly, as if he was addressing someone who wasn't very bright. "Or rather Templeton & Brewer can, now that they've hijacked it, thanks to you. But that means McCauley's people are cut out of the middle, and they don't like that." Mark placed his face in both his hands. "Templeton & Brewer won this round. I hope they don't live to regret it." He drew a sealed envelope from his jacket pocket and handed it to Sylvie. She took it from him, but didn't open it. For the first time since she'd known Mark, he seemed defeated.

Gone were the arrogance and self-confidence that had made her feel secure all those years. This was a different Mark. "I'm assuming it's an offer from Templeton & Brewer. Aren't you going to open it?" he asked.

Sylvie slit the top open and unfolded the document. She read through it. It offered a generous signing bonus along with a paid ongoing position on the advisory board for Assuranz. The position came with full health and dental coverage, and a small share in the profits in Sylvie's own name, not through Mark. But Sylvie had to agree not to bring charges against either Mark or Lisa Chang.

Mark raised his head, regarding Sylvie with red eyes, brimming with pain. Sylvie realized that in all their years together, she had never seen him cry.

She placed her hand on his arm. "I'm sorry, Mark."

"So I assume you'll use the cash to pay off the mortgage and move back to Weston?"

Weston? It hadn't occurred to Sylvie that now she might actually be able to return to her old life. Maybe even buy her house back from the bank. She tried to imagine herself there. In her perfect house, with her perfect garden.

247

"I don't think so," Sylvie heard herself say. "The girls like living in the city. They're much more independent here, and Diana's on the crew for the drama festival. I don't want to uproot them again."

"I was hoping—" he hesitated, then placed both hands on the table. "I have no place to live."

"Wait. You mean, you want me to move back to Weston so you'll have a place to live?"

"I can't go back to Lisa's. Not after everything that's happened." He cleared his throat. "I miss our family. The way we used to be together. Anyway, Lisa won't be able to afford the rent now that she's lost her job. And my money's all tied up in TechnoData."

"You mean *our* money's tied up in TechnoData. So any agreement we come to will have to include a schedule to pay me back as well as my parents, and replenishing the girls' college funds." Sylvie paused. "And it looks like you and Lisa will be starting a new college fund."

Mark crossed his arms in front of him and looked away. Classic Mark. "This has nothing to do with Lisa," he said. "I've left her."

"Her, too, Mark? When she's expecting your baby? You can't just keep walking out on your children. You two are in it for the long haul, so you'd better get busy working things out." She stood up. "I'll have my attorney draw something up. She'll be in touch."

Mark stood and placed his hand on her shoulder to stop her. "Didn't you hear me? I'm willing to come back and try again."

Sylvie shook her head, incredulous that she had never understood just how self-centered and clueless Mark could be. But then, that was the life of a genius. Coddled by the rest of the world out of deference and the hope of sharing in the spoils. God help the woman who bargained for security with nothing to offer but youth and beauty. Both came with expiration dates. If a woman wanted security in this world, she had best step up to the plate and hit the ball herself.

"We're not getting back together, Mark. That train has left the station." It wasn't until the words were out of her mouth that Sylvie realized it was true. At that moment, an enormous weight lifted from her shoulders.

***

In her hospital room, LaVonda, her eyes open, sat propped up on a mountain of pillows. Desiree sat by her side. A tray of mystery food in covered containers lay untouched beside the bed.

LaVonda smiled when Sylvie entered.

Sylvie placed her offering of chocolate mice from Burdick's and a package of Nicorette gum on the table beside the bed. She pulled up a metal chair and sat down.

LaVonda patted her hand. "You found yourself a path," she said. "I can see it in your eyes."

***

It was late when Sylvie returned to the inn. Raul was waiting for her in the parlor, enjoying the evening's offering of red wine and chocolate chip cookies. She excused herself to check on the girls and found them sprawled on the bed with Sugarbear, surrounded by shopping bags, watching a movie.

She returned to join Raul, poured herself a glass of wine, and settled on the sofa beside him.

"I think I know who hurt LaVonda," he said.

"Was it Lisa Chang?"

"I don't think so. She wouldn't have risked destroying the repository if she thought you had it. She needed it to clinch her deal with the Chinese company. Besides, several neighbors saw a black Lincoln Continental in the area just before the fire started. I checked out the plate."

Sylvie waited for his words to sink in. Then she shook her head sadly. "Jack Ramsdale," she said.

"Not Jack," Raul said. "But because of Jack. He owed the wrong people money. They got tired of waiting. Maybe they figured they'd collect when the insurance came through. But I'm pretty sure Jack was not in on the plan."

"How can you possibly be sure?"

"I know these people," Raul said. "I know how they work. I know how they think. Jack's a poor schmuck who borrowed from the wrong people because he was desperate."

"Do the police think he was involved?"

"I don't know. And I'm not going to help them figure it out. Because if the insurance company even suspects he's involved, neither one of you will see a dime. Ramsdale had much more to gain by renovating the apartments. He could have raised the capital easily if he could have shown the bank he owned the whole building."

Jack Ramsdale entered the parlor. Raul stood to leave.

Sylvie thought back to the Purchase and Sale agreement, still lying on her hall table.

Fifty Six

Jack spotted Sylvie, grabbed a cookie, and ate it on his way to join her on the sofa. He settled in beside her. For a few moments, neither spoke.

"I signed the P & S," Sylvie said finally. "It was sitting on the front table, ready to give to you. Then the fire happened."

She saw a thousand emotions cross his face in only a few seconds. Then he reached into his jacket pocket and retrieved a plastic zip bag. Inside, covered in black soot, was an envelope with Jack's name scrawled across the front in Sylvie's handwriting.

"The fire inspector let me go upstairs with him," Jack said. "I found this on the table. If you want it back, you can have it." He held it out to her.

She pushed his hand back. "There's no point. Without the insurance, I couldn't possibly afford to rebuild."

"I'm sorry. I would have never—"

"I know."

He placed his hand on Sylvie's. It felt warm and solid.

"I'll make this right," he said.

She laid her other hand on top of his. "I believe you."

He looked into her eyes. "I think we need a do-over."

"Where do we start?"

"First we rebuild. I'm good at that."

251

ABOUT THE AUTHOR

JJ Shelley (a nom de plume) is a filmmaker and the author of several screenplays who lives in Boston, Massachusetts. She is the recipient of an Academy Award nomination, the Edgar Dale Screenwriting Award and a New England Women in Film Screenwriting Award.

She holds a certificate in Professional Investigation from Boston University.

"Hot Water" is her first novel. She is currently writing the second Sylvie Wolff novel based on the true story of a ship that disappeared without a trace.

www.jjshelley.com